THE TALKING OF HANDS

THE TALKING
OF HANDS

UNPUBLISHED WRITING BY
NEW RIVERS PRESS AUTHORS

New Rivers Press
1998

First Edition
Printed in the United States of America
Library of Congress Catalog Card Number: 97-69844
ISBN: 0-89823-190-6, 0-89823-199-X(pbk.)
Copyedited by James J. Cihlar
Book design and typesetting by Percolator

New Rivers Press is a nonprofit literary press dedicated to publishing the very best emerging writers in our region, nation, and world.

The publication of *The Talking of Hands* has been made possible by generous grants from the Beim Foundation; the General Mills Foundation; the Bush Foundation; the McKnight Foundation; the Star Tribune Foundation; and the contributing members of New Rivers Press.

New Rivers Press
420 North Fifth Street, Suite 910
Minneapolis, MN 55401

www.mtn.org/newrivpr

The Talking of Hands

You are in love for the first time. You are twelve.
Next to you is a deaf girl, maybe ten years old.
The two of you are on a train
easing its way through
the Cascade Mountains of Oregon.
You are so sure of this girl
you tell her everything. How
your voice is changing its shape.
How you are becoming something
remarkable. She smiles at you,
touches your arm. Later on,
in a darkening of trees she sleeps
on your shoulder. Gives to you
the soft whispers of her breath.
When she wakes up, you realize
you are over thirty years old.
This young girl says words to you that seem
out of shape, far away. Then
she starts talking to you with her hands.
You begin to understand the makings
of her language—where rain becomes
a drizzle of fingers and where, soon,
it will be a heavy enough rain
that she will show you how to make rivers
with your hands, your thumbs anchors
against the long, wild rush of water.

John Reinhard, *Burning the Prairie,* New Rivers Press, 1988

Contents

ROBERT ALEXANDER / MARK VINZ

....

Editors' Note

Several years ago, we realized at New Rivers Press that our thirtieth anniversary was fast approaching, and that if we wanted to celebrate the event appropriately—given the time lag endemic to small press publishing—we would have to begin arranging for it with all due haste. What to do? We mulled over the question, thinking first of an anthology drawn from the many books New Rivers has published over the years—but, to be honest, the task of going through all these publications, and choosing material to fit within three hundred pages (our self-imposed limit, the weight of a good-sized book on one's lap), was too daunting to face.

And, on the other hand, the notion of putting out a call for manuscripts, without any constraint save a sense of celebration, was too daunting as well, since from past experience we were familiar with the massive number of submissions that would likely land on our doorstep. So we figured that we could, to set a manageable limit, approach only people who had published a book with New Rivers, and ask each of them for a submission. Furthermore, we determined that we would be asking these writers for previously unpublished work, thereby stressing the "new" in our name: nothing warmed-over in this collection.

As a result of this solicitation, we received prose and poetry from over a hundred authors. It's a testament to Publisher Truesdale's good taste over the years that we had an inordinately hard time rationing our acceptances to what would fit into three hundred pages. Even given our preselection process—book-length authors only need apply—we editors fought each other tooth and claw over what we could include, what we had to leave out. However, the cost and weight of paper was something that we, like Atlas, had to balance on our shoulders, and at the end of the day we were left with the collection you now hold in your hands.

We hope that you find as much to enjoy here as we did.

....

Introduction

By their nature, introductions to anniversary anthologies favor the tendentious, especially when such books appear under the extraordinary circumstances as the one you hold in your hands now. I cannot imagine a better time to exalt the exploits of any publisher than the one that occasions the arrival of this book.

Thirty years ago Bill Truesdale founded New Rivers Press. The telling of the true tale of what went down way back when I will leave to the capable pen of Mr. Truesdale himself, but, for posterity, I imagine rustic isolated barns, resurrected ancient letterpresses, tie-dyes and the sweet, swirling scents of the old hippie times. Kennedy and King died and Paris and Los Angeles burned and my fifth grade teacher, whom I loved dearly, regularly employed the world's largest and most aerodynamically sound paddle on the backsides of the naughty white boys in my class. Ah, for the good old days!

Thirty years is a long time for any venture, but in publishing it is nothing short of phenomenal. The average longevity of most ventures in the arts hovers somewhere around an hour and a half, just long enough for the parking meters of those who were suckered into coming to the planning meeting to expire. Those organizations that survive past the initial bickering and lack of purpose tend to peter out within the first year or so. Even a list of local ventures that have passed on to that great arts festival in the sky would surely fill the first dozen pages of this book. That Bill has managed to sustain and nurture New Rivers Press for three decades, through the fits and fads of literature, through the ups and downs of the funding circus, sometimes with just himself and his trusty typewriter and the good faith and credit of the odd printer who shared his vision, all the while maintaining the highest literary standards, is a cause for celebration and the reason we are publishing *The Talking of Hands*.

But, let's get back to the tendentious part.

I want to tell you about the biggest fight I ever had with Bill Truesdale.

Bill had assigned himself to be the editor of my book, *Heathens*. (You'll note I didn't say my "novel" *Heathens*. Bill and I disagreed about this categorization, as well, but I'll save the details of that fight for the sixtieth anniversary anthology.) Doris, in her monologue "One of Them Daughter-In-Law Things," refers to her son's girlfriend . . . well, she refers to her as a lot of things, to be frank, but among the descriptions she uses is "merhinny." In a generally harmonious editing process, I came across an editor's query of my use of the word. So I, of course, called up the editor to find out what his problem was.

"I've never heard the word *merhinny*," Bill replied.

"It's a word," I said.

"Since when?"

"Since I said so."

"Prove it."

"All right, I will."

And, okay, so the conversation may not have gone exactly as I reported it here. It *was* heated. (As heated as it comes with Bill, which is generally not very.) I got the message and set about my quest to prove that my word was a real word. I'll spare you the list of places I called and libraries I visited and experts I consulted, though I can't resist reporting that the estimable Schomberg Center for Research in Black Culture provided me with a sentence that I've found useful in dealing with editors henceforth: "Tell him to turn the page and read on."

He did. We survived. And I salute him.

I salute an editor who cares enough about each of his books to read them with a weather eye and to care about all the pieces: the ideas and the language and the way it's made on the page. I salute an editor who loves language to the point that when he comes across a new word, it jumps up at him, demanding his attention. This love of words is manifest in the hundreds of titles (more than 250) to issue from New Rivers over these past thirty years.

How many of those books might never have seen print were it not for the courage of New Rivers to take a chance on the unknown writer and the unfashionable idea and the tentative voice from the sideline? Projects such as Minnesota Voices and Many Minnesotas have introduced readers to dozens of writers, myself included, who owe their careers to the willingness of Bill and the many dozens of volunteers and very few paid staff members to look beyond the obvious sources in order to find a wide range of new voices and to do everything in their power to see that their books find an audience.

For this anthology New Rivers has invited its many alumni to submit writing that represents their current work. Each piece appears here for the first time. Some might imagine this collection as the inviting scent of fresh baked bread, beckoning them into their favorite trattoria for a sumptuous meal, that meal being the rich archive of poetry and prose that stands behind what you read here. Me, I'm more of a tease. I see our anniversary edition as much like the dazzling couple straggling out of a party at dawn, passing you on the sidewalk headed to work as they announce, "You'll never believe what you've missed." Maybe not, though what you must believe is that, thanks largely to the single-minded dedication of one man, there exist in libraries all around the world thousands and thousands of wonderful books. That is all the reason we need to celebrate. And the good news: there's more to come. Years more, and, Bill, on behalf of all the writers you've queried over words that really are real words whether you thought so or not, and over the line breaks and the images and everything else that keeps the heart of a true editor humming, I say congratulations and thank you, thank you, thank you.

Now, turn the page and read on.

....

New Rivers Press: A History (1968-98)

Those of us who began publishing in the small press literary field in the sixties were likely to be naive, sometimes idealistic, often governed by vanity, and full of illusions about what we were setting out to accomplish.

New Rivers Press was no exception. Even though I was nearly forty years old when I started it in Nyack, New York, in February 1968, it was a wholly new and exhilarating experience for me. I had, by then, been a full-time college professor for more than thirteen years, had a Ph.D. in English and Comparative Literature (which I received from the University of Washington in Seattle in 1956), was married and had three children, and had three books of my own poetry published (the first in Mexico City, the second in Denver, and the third in New York City). The only previous experience I'd had with any small press was with El Corno Emplumado, run by Margaret Randall and Sergio Mondragón in Mexico City (my first publishers). The fact that I was by then a very active and committed poet made me much like almost all of my compatriots in the small press field. And like most of them, too, I was strongly opposed to the Vietnam War (though my older brother John served there as a major in the Green Berets in 1965-66). Also like most of them I had no idea what I was getting myself into. I didn't even know in the beginning that there were hundreds of other small presses and literary magazines being thrown together all over America at that time—that, indeed, a kind of Renaissance was taking place in this country, a literary explosion that lasted well into the seventies.

Unlike many small press publishers in the sixties, I did not start my own press for any political reason, even though most of the books I was to publish over the next dozen or so years had a strong political basis. Primarily, I was motivated by two things: 1) My background was in the centuries-long practice of great literature in England (as a teacher my specialty had been, of all unlikely things, medieval literature—Chaucer, Langland, the Pearl Poet, and the medieval romance—but I

was well-acquainted with other major periods and authors as well).
2) I'd had one hell of a time getting my own first book published. I was
thirty-seven years old when my first book came out, and I wanted to
make it just a little bit easier for other first book authors to get their
poetry published, a motivation that still characterizes the mission of
New Rivers Press.

Starting New Rivers was not something I set out deliberately to do.
Ever since I'd been in Mexico two years before and had observed El
Corno Emplumado, I had, to be sure, dreamed of starting a similar,
though less political, press in the United States. After I left full-time
teaching in the spring of 1967, I did talk a lot about something like that,
but I didn't do anything about it—not until my late ex-brother-in-law
Bill Chaffee (an architect who worked for I. M. Pei in New York City)
bought a farm near Southfield, Massachusetts, in late 1967. Bill told me
there was an old letterpress sitting in a shed near his new old house and
that I could certainly have it if I really wanted to put my feet where my
mouth had been for so long. Otherwise, he was just going to have to get
rid of it. At that time, I knew nothing about printing, had never heard of
letterpresses or offset lithography, and had certainly never even thought
about actually getting involved in printing.

But being my father's son I swallowed that particular hook. I went
up to Southfield to look over the situation and what I saw was an old-
fashioned Chandler & Price letterpress that had not been used for years.
George, the son of the previous owners of the place (from whom he had
inherited the farm as well as this old monster of a machine), told me all
about what it had been used for. The shed where it was located had been
a Christmas card factory of sorts. The cards themselves had been silk-
screened and the press had been used to print Christmas sentiments
inside the folded-over cards.

The press itself was something of a mess. The basic mechanism—a
huge flywheel that closed the two gigantic maws like a clamshell—was
intact, there were a couple of chases (for holding the handset type in
place), but the inking mechanism had been disconnected and scattered
all over the place, and the suction cups that lifted the paper were in
pathetic shape. But George said I would find it a breeze to print. He
showed me the instruction book that came with the press, and it seemed
reasonable and simple enough that I could master printing in no time
flat. I left Massachusetts a little drunk (from exhilaration, yes, and also

from bourbon) and resolved to go up there in a month or two and start the actual printing of what became the first three New Rivers books. I knew myself well enough, however, to figure out that I had no intention of setting type by hand.

I soon found a printer in West Nyack (about ten miles from where I lived) who had an old linotype machine and—more importantly—a guy named Jim who knew how to use it. He was fairly young for a profession that was rapidly disappearing. I had him set the first two books on that machine and bought what I hoped would be enough paper to start printing. All of which—the lead slugs, which must have weighed a thousand pounds, for two small books, as well as the boxes of very expensive and rather elegant stock, and the clothes and other stuff I would need—I loaded up in my Volvo.

When I got to Southfield and found my way back to the farm, not only George but that Chandler & Price instruction manual had disappeared. I really knew nothing at all about printing and was thus faced with what I can only call a truly existential experience. The nearest help was miles and miles away, and, besides, I was just too crazy with pride to admit I needed help.

February in Massachusetts is not like February in Minnesota but it was certainly cold enough. Cold enough for snowmobiles (a relatively new invention at that time) to roar past on those country and very much unplowed roads. The house, which Bill and Connie Chaffee had completely remodeled, was certainly warm enough, but that shed was heated by a small, inefficient oil heater. It took an hour or more to heat up the place—and the printing ink, which I rapidly discovered had an aversion to cold weather.

Heat—or the lack of it—turned out to be the least of my problems. I found out almost immediately that there was no way I could get the automatic inking device on the press to work (I couldn't even figure out how to put it together). This meant I had to hand ink the press, which, in turn, meant that every page I managed to print came out different from all the others, so that the inking throughout both of those two books, especially the first one, was inconsistent and, frankly, a total mess. Since the press was too small to print more than two pages at a time, this inconsistency became very noticeable.

Furthermore, I could never get the feeding device to work properly and had to hand feed each sheet of stock, which meant sticking my right hand between those two great maws before they could close and mangle it. It also took me a long time to figure out how to make each lead slug in the chase come out clearly. After trial and error, I discovered that using little strips of paper underneath some of the slugs did the job well enough. What this meant was that I had to spend at least fifteen or twenty minutes preparing every two pages in the whole book. This wasn't a problem with the first two books because they were no more than twenty-five pages in length. But it became a real hassle with the third book (Al Greenberg's *The Metaphysical Giraffe*), because it was somewhere around seventy pages in length.

That third New Rivers book presented yet another problem. Lead printing slugs are about four inches wide. Al's lines were often no more than an inch to an inch and a half in width. When I tried to print this book, I found that the ends of each slug marked the page with blobs of ink. The only way I could correct this problem was to trim down the ends of each slug with a power saw (which, fortunately, that shed possessed). This certainly corrected the problem of the blobs, but it also meant, since it was now very warm in the shed, that I sprayed my left arm with lead pellets and knicked it constantly. It's a wonder I didn't come down with a bad case of lead-poisoning! It took me most of the summer just to print that third book.

The Metaphysical Giraffe was the very last book I printed in Massachusetts. Not only was I spending an enormous amount of time up there, but I also found that it was costing me far more than I had imagined, even just for the stock alone. I was spending at least three times as much for that paper as an ordinary printer would because such a printer buys it in huge quantities and hence gets a large discount. It would be much cheaper to have New Rivers books printed by offset lithography even if I hadn't been spending an inordinate amount of precious time doing the actual printing. I could spend far less time and money bringing out more and more books each year, and I could do the things like editing and writing that I had much more talent for.

Still, I did learn a great deal about printing—the hard way—a knowledge that makes me appreciate printing technology all that much more. Besides, I have a real respect for people doing physical things with their hands. I've never liked having people do things for me—perhaps that's kind of a reverse snobbism on my part. Even in my first marriage (when we had plenty of money), I did most of the things on our farm (near

Lexington, Virginia) that had to be done—brushhogging the pastures, putting in fields of alfalfa, doing most of the carpentry work on the ancient barn, and even, when necessary, shoeing our horses.

....

One of the things I did learn in Southfield during the six months or so I did my own printing there was that I had no particular interest in the art of fine printing itself. I've always loved beautiful books as objects but I knew only too well that such objects were, for most people who bought them at very high prices, simply objects that were seldom if ever actually read. My own interest lay in the book itself and what it had to say or what it actually created.

What really concerned me from the beginning was the character of the writing, something that, for better or worse, reflected my own taste and judgment as a writer and as a publisher. Thus, though I started New Rivers in the midst of the darkest days of the Vietnam War and was under considerable pressure to publish anti-war books, I always resisted that impulse. From the first, I wanted to publish the very best books by new writers I could find, regardless of their political and social correctness. Although almost all of the writers I published shared my own antagonism toward that war, that wasn't the reason I published them, any more than, nowadays, I am driven to make editorial judgments by multiculturalism or any other current fashion. What interested me then and still very much does is the quality and originality of individual writing voices. For instance, I knew very well from my own background in reading and writing that English and American authors had produced very little in the way of effective poetry with strong political convictions. In all the many centuries of English literature I knew of only a handful of really first-rate political poems. This is probably not true of other cultures—like those of the countries that used to be dominated by the then-Soviet Union, or some of the formerly colonial territories once dominated by the imperial powers. Most of the political manuscripts that came to me in the early years of New Rivers were strident, impersonal, and likely to be manifesto-type utterances.

To say, however, that I was not interested in manuscripts that, at least sometimes, were politically oriented would be misleading. I knew very well that really good writing sometimes reflected strong political engagement and was a way for writers to cope with the social and political issues of the day, and that some of the very best writing came about because the writer was deeply disturbed or even traumatized by such crises as the Vietnam War, or by the prevailing conservatism of the American public, or by the growing violence in our urban centers. Often enough, these writers saw that deep social issues were reflected in their personal lives. I could not myself write directly about the Vietnam War until my brother went over there as a Green Beret.

In that sense, then, many of the writers I was to publish in the first decade of New Rivers' history were very much politically engaged. Not all of them were activists by any means and none of them, so far as I knew, wrote anything like a political manifesto. Few, if any, had anything like final answers. What interested me in them as writers was the character and individuality of their responses and their take on the country they had been brought up in.

Similarly, these days—when the Vietnam War has long been over—I don't pay much mind to the renewed interest in formalist poetry. It runs very much against the grain of what I consider the best American poetry of the twentieth century, much of which derives from free verse techniques first introduced by Walt Whitman, who remains an abiding influence on our poetry. That formalism has always been much more at home in England I certainly appreciate. In fact, one of the very best poets in English in this century is, to me, William Butler Yeats, and he regularly used distinct forms and rhyme. I am not philosophically adverse to formalism per se. I just don't happen to believe that it usually works in American poetry—with rare exceptions. (I have even published a few American formalists simply because that way of writing is best for them. The work of Charles Molesworth, whose *Common Elegies* I published many years ago, immediately comes to mind.)

Because my interest in new writing and highly individual voices has always been paramount to me, and insofar as New Rivers has always reflected my own taste and judgment, this press has never been associated with any particular school of writing—Black Mountain, New York, L.A.N.G.U.A.G.E., Ethno- or Mytho-Poetic, or, today, Hyper-Text— even though I have occasionally published writers who have been affiliated with one group or another. For this reason, New Rivers has often been called "eclectic." Eclecticism is not a negative term as far as I am concerned—so long as that word does not imply absence of taste or slackness of editorial judgment. In my view, every book that New Rivers brings out is like no other book ever published—the last thing in the world I would like New Rivers Press to be seen as doing is publishing clones of my own work as a writer. Really first-rate writing is always unique to the author, never standard.

....

When I think of New Rivers in general terms, as I am doing here, I think of the many, many different voices we have published in individual books and anthologies over the years, and of the enormous variety of subjects that these authors—including those who live in this immediate area and have been published in our Minnesota Voices Project—give unique voice to, and of what American literature would be like without them. Our culture would be very much diminished, I fear, because I know very well how hard it is to get books published these days, particularly those by new authors (whatever their age might be). Many of these authors would probably have given up on the idea of ever being published at all, if New Rivers had not been around to help them gain recognition.

When I think of all of these authors—and of many we simply could not publish—I am just amazed at the depth and variety of writing, and I am very proud that New Rivers has been able to publish as much as we have.

I wrote an essay called "Aire and Angells: Poems About Writing Poetry" that was published in *The North Dakota Quarterly* in the Spring of 1988. Poems written about poetry don't usually interest me in the least (they strike me as being claustrophobic or self-indulgent) but there have been some very great exceptions in English and American literature—poems by John Donne, George Herbert, John Keats, and William Butler Yeats, among others. In that essay, I talked a great deal about editing and my relationship with authors, one of whom, Catherine Stearns, I used as an example of someone who had written an extraordinarily fine poem about writing poetry.

Among other things, I said, "More often than not I don't know these writers or know them only casually. But, because of the way the manuscripts are selected and because of my involvement in the process, I already know them very well on a level which counts very much to me—their work. I make it a practice to conduct meetings as casually as possible because there is a lot of potential fear and awe there, particularly for new writers, as most of them are. It's important for me to get to know them on a friendly, non-intimidating basis, because I want them to concentrate on their work and not on the ultimate fact of publication. Awe can be amusing enough, especially when it is coupled with the rather large egomania that often accompanies the acceptance of a first book, but it is not at all a creative emotion. Shaping a book requires tough, intelligent, objective work on the part of both author and editor. It is important for me to earn the respect of the authors I deal so often with, to establish a confidence in them that I can be of help or service to them. I want them to know that I have their best interests as writers at heart and that I can bring a good deal of experience and critical intelligence to this work.

"I enjoy doing this very much, and basically love working with writers on a creative basis—even if it is sometimes exhausting and very time-consuming. My life has become a complex series of dramatic encounters with some of the most interesting persons in the world. These take place in a structured way and on more basic levels than in ordinary associations, as in therapy, but there the resemblance ends. My role is more or less fixed, but the resulting play of minds and dance of spirits is anything but fixed. And it is rewarding too—both for the author who is likely to get a stronger book out of this process, and for me because stronger books make me look better as a publisher and because it's nice to have the power to be able to influence someone else in positive ways."

What I said of Stearns's poem at the end of that essay applies, I think, to just about any first-rate writer I have ever published: "In writing beautifully about a simple, very private experience, she gives her own voice and substance mythic dimensions, which is what all true poetry does. In doing this, she gives us a rare glimpse into a process that is at once real and tangible but also visionary and transcendent—familiar and ordinary as a doorway, strange and mysterious as a threshold."

THE TALKING OF HANDS

STEPHEN AJAY

....

Eating Persimmons

On the roof in late afternoon the Himal is
gray behind the other hills. I look down into
two tall, almost barren persimmon trees
their fruits hanging in clusters at the top.
I look toward Kathmandu and wait. There are
pink and red swirling clouds. From the Pokhara
side, an eagle flies straight to the mountains:
a few beats . . . gliding, gliding, gliding, and I
wait now for the dark.

It is a hodgepodge from up here: tile roofs,
TV aerials, Western style pants hanging
from the lines, a bonfire in the yard next
door, children holding out their palms to
the flames, smoke spiraling in the sky above
me, tractors moving down the narrow, dirt
street. I see their headlights and the
buildings in the valley coming out slowly
like stars. Many people are on their roofs. I
climb to the very top level where a dozen
pale green gourds are drying.

The moon is three-quarters, directly over
the trees and I wonder if they are leaving
their perches by the Royal Palace now. How
long will it take them to fly this distance?
All the red swirl has turned into ash under-
neath the moon and the first star. 5:31, still
no sign. The Himal is getting dimmer and

dimmer, looking more like a cloud than a
mountain range. I smell human flesh, a
cremation; Pashupati is one half kilometer
to the east. Colors come back into the sky;
it is getting darker but the rose and peach
come back, the grays have faded. The Himal is
almost gone and the persimmons are floating
back into the dark, dead foliage of the trees.

At exactly six o'clock the first one arrives
fluttering like an eyelash, the first giant
fruit bat. As he circles he looks right at
me as if to ask, "What are you doing here?" be-
fore he attaches to the taller tree above the
persimmons, hangs for a moment, then flutters
again and sidles down toward the fruit. Suddenly
there are two more hanging in silhouette off
the dead tree that cantilevers out over the
persimmons. Now five or six have slipped into
position to eat; several are eating and the
same number are just hanging. I can hear one
climb through the tree making noises,
leaping, falling, and landing. Here comes a
larger one and another is crawling down a
long branch, chattering. Others are approach-
ing softly. They bite open the tops of the
fruits, their faces fill with persimmon flesh
while the sounds of forks, water sloshing
in metal buckets, and voices rise.

It is now dark but in the beam of the flash-
light, I see one right in front of me, walking
very carefully he makes his way along a branch.
Quickly three late-comers crisscross before the
moon; their landings are audible as they grasp the
branches, try to stabilize themselves. In the moon-
light they are as bright as charcoal against the

snow. Now three sets of eyes flash the color of
the fruit . . . silence, then a branch shakes and I
see there are many more sets of eyes waving,
picking up the beam as they walk through the
branches. Their shawled hands peel the persimmons,
the persimmon juice falls on their light brown
fur, their warm chests. Now it is so dark it is
hard to distinguish leaving from coming; they float
then settle, then float again, eyes a reddish
phosphorescence; their small tongues wear away the
ripe fruit while planes from the airport flash red
and white, red and white; the red is constant,
white, white, white: steep, steep . . . going up very
steeply; the lights on the tips of their wings pass
right over the tree as I leave the roof, see one
more set of bright eyes bound through the branches. He
squeals like a tiny man with a lantern, "What a
bonanza, what a persimmon bonanza!"

....

Calhoun's Monument

We go to Charleston for our honeymoon, that city of old brick and ethereal black ironwork—and more beautiful women than I've ever seen in one place before. If Richmond was the Capital of the Confederacy, Charleston was its Heart. Calhoun the Nullifier . . . and a long line of fire-eaters later, Edmund Ruffin lit off the first cannon before the Federal resupply ships could reach the beleaguered garrison at Fort Sumter. (Four years later, just days after Lee's surrender at Appomattox, Edmund Ruffin shot himself—becoming, like Abe Lincoln and so many others, one more casualty of the war.)

Late Sunday morning I drive out to see Fort Moultrie—past azalea and wisteria in bloom, past Krispy Kreme, America's Favorite Doughnuts—where one soft April morning like this in the last century thousands of shots were fired "to reduce" Fort Sumter, as they used to say in those days. It's a slightly rainy day and I look over the parapet toward Fort Sumter, a low-lying man-made island in the middle of the channel. At dawn, with rose-gold light gracing the clouds and the sand, peace and quiet erupted into hell . . . that would last four interminable years.

It's vacation, so I've lost track of the date, but in fact this rainy Sunday is the anniversary of the opening bombardment, and there's an encampment of Confederate reenactors set up beside the Fort. I have a brief but vivid fantasy of white men and Asians sitting around a similar scene, years hence, hooches and concertina wire, reenacting the war in Vietnam. On this drizzling morning the reenactors are sitting around straw-covered dirt, underneath the kitchen tarp, talking low and slow—much as they probably would have done a lot of rainy time during the war: ". . . and not a dang thing anyone can do about it anyhow" drifts by me in a Southern cadence that I find soporific— while the mourning doves' lament breaks the hot stillness of the day.

It seems like a long drive back to Charleston and the high-ceilinged ante-bellum room with full-length windows—shutters closed, already in April, against the heat of the day—and a floor of wide pine planks worn smooth by centuries of bare feet. . . .

....

Later that afternoon, after the rain has stopped and the sun has come out, we go to see Calhoun's grave, down by the marketplace. But it's Sunday and the cemetery is chained and locked, so all we can do is look through the gate at the large tombstone with CALHOUN written on it, obscured by a huge magnolia and an equally huge live oak bending low over the grave.

We drive to the Calhoun monument near the center of town where there are decaying buildings and, close by, the College of Charleston with its well-scrubbed white kids. Calhoun on his pillar, one arm akimbo, looks out over the roofs of lower Charleston toward Battery Park and the Bay. In Marion Park—worn grass and dirt—people down on their luck sit on the benches far beneath Calhoun. Across the street the Knights of Columbus and the Soft Rock Cafe. On the pedestal below Calhoun's pillar is written

TRUTH JUSTICE
and the
CONSTITUTION

I've been reading Whitman's *Specimen Days,* and all day long his sentences have been going through my head:

> I have seen Calhoun's monument. . . . It is the desolated, ruin'd south; nearly the whole generation of young men between seventeen and thirty destroy'd or maim'd; all the old families used up— the rich impoverish'd, the plantations cover'd with weeds . . . all that is Calhoun's real monument.

At an antique store downtown we find an antebellum print of Calhoun, a silhouette of the man looking out over a Palmettoed landscape from a window with venetian blinds, at the height of his power and prestige, the peak of his self-confidence or arrogance (it depended, no doubt, on your point of view). I tell the aging couple who own the store—they live in the small apartment upstairs, they inform us, third generation in the antique trade—that it captures the essence of the man. "A few years back they used to talk about pulling him down off his monument and putting up Martin Luther King there," the woman says. "Would've been another war."

....

The next day at breakfast, we read in the morning paper how a homeowner shot and killed a man running away from an attempted break-in. Elsewhere, this might be considered murder. But the County Sheriff is quoted as saying, "I don't anticipate the Sheriff's Department will make charges." On the back page where the rest of the story is buried, I read that the man killed was black, the shooter white. A City Councilman says, "It's open season on black men."

PATRICIA BARONE

Ending with Open Hands

Five bluebirds come to the feeder
Grandpa's no longer able
to replenish, but these are plump
and seem to need no more.

They stay. No contentious grackles
chase the blue birds from nothing or,
making their own drab luck,
scrounge hulls the squirrels spit out.

And still these five, much bluer
than cerulean crayons,
than a grandchild's painting!
Grandpa has only to gaze

out the window. They are
alighting. They stay.

PATRICIA BARONE

....

Dividing the Dark into Parcels

The ones who stay awake all night—
dividing the dark into parcels
                    assigning each
to parts of the body,
to input and output—
write the measurable
truth: The eschar of the wound
in diameter—3.5 centimeters.
The patient is afebrile.

Won't you help me?
Won't you tell me what
to deny. I know
they're keeping me
against my will, so won't you
tell me what isn't.

The night is divided into ever
smaller and smaller pieces, each second
has its task. Each breath
dry or moist, its sibilance.

Won't you turn me, won't you
show me the way
home from here, how far—
I am so tired.

Each tick of dark drops through
the pharmacist's counter, each
time release capsule dissolves
in the acid of the stomach on its own
appointed time.

Won't someone help me,
come help me, no
no one will help me,
guess not.

Room after room, each resident
is lifted, gently or roughly from
wet bed pads, each sheet is whisked
and rolled from under
withered cheeks.

Want my mother
won't my mother
come.

SIGRID BERGIE

Carnival Street

I have met a Rio man
whose emeralds
sparkled in his hand
as he invited me
to his Midtown hotel room.
Instead we played chess
in the 4:00 A.M. rain
in Washington Square Park.

I have met a dying
famous blues harpist
on Bleeker Street
who invited me
to a Greek restaurant
for brandy and sadness.

I have met a young woman
in high heels
whose eyes cut like black onyx
as she invited me
to ride in her limo
to the Cat Club.
I looked at her orange claws
and said "No."

I have met a man
in the Lion's Head
on Christopher Street
whom I loved like my child,
who invited me to shatter
and become
the surgeon of my heart.

I have met many strangers
in the cool wind
of freaky side streets—
each inviting me
to a part of me—
each stranger no stranger
to the lovely hot
carnival of my soul.

JAMES BERTOLINO

....

Sun Worship

Looking like Muslims at prayer, they gather
in rows over the silk
and twig-ridges
of their tents. When the sun
commands, they do a synchronized dance—
weaving side-to-side with a snap
that quickens.

Wearing saffron yellow and
millennial black, they are
the tent caterpillars, and in their millions
an unsavory prey.

Today, we see one march the length
of a bleached log, searching
for the single sacred place where cocooning
feels right. When it pauses, and curls like something soft
you'd want to touch, my companion explains
if you see a chalky spot that glows
against the dark of the forehead, it means
this supplicant has been chosen

by a wasp who's laid an egg.

Later, inside the cocoon, that humid
rebirthing chamber, it will hatch
and feed greedily on the sacrificial host.
Swollen then with such rich nourishment, such
spiritual fat, the young wasp will poke
a portal through

and, like a moth driven ecstatic
by light, ascend.

....

My Parents' Tombstone

My mother photocopied the picture in the catalog
and sent it to me. With white-out, she covered over
whoever's name was on the showroom model,
writing in their own names with the careful hand
she used to print the alphabet for six year olds
along with the dates of their births and two blanks after that,
the hyphen representing their unfinished lives.

This alarmed me, you understand, to open up a letter
and unfold the stone. I guess she wanted me to see
the marker they purchased. It was something my brother
and sister and I wouldn't have to worry about
when that day came round, it was their gift to us,
and so I should have maybe thanked her, but how
do you thank someone for a gift like that?

It's a good stone, but, oh, I would have picked a different location.
Their grave will be in the yard of a church that's moved to town,
leaving its graveyard stranded in the country. It's a graveyard
filled by my father's people. (And my mother made him mad
when she told him she wanted to keep her maiden name
after they are buried.) There are good people there, for sure.
But not enough trees. And on my parent's side, no trees at all.

It leaves their grave open to the encroachment of greedy farmers
edging in to plant another row of corn. And what I like
least about the place is the pig farm across the road.
You can hear the clank of pig-feeders all times of the day
and half the night. You can hear the pigs grunt
with satisfaction at their constant supply of grub
and watch them roll in the mud, not to mention the smell.

These pigs are pampered, kingly even, as they romp in the sun,
they are smart enough to know the time of day that they'll be fed.
They wait by the fence. They grow angry if their food is late.
But they are too stupid to know they are raised for the knife.
This alone is bad enough, this arrogant stupidity, not to mention
the day they'll disturb my grief, squealing and biting at each other
as they line up at the trough.

RON BLOCK

....

The Snow Queen

By Hans Christian Andersen

For Joseph

Ever since she discovered the mirror
didn't love her, she's been looking for you.
Ever since that glass fell and shattered
into smithereens, you've seen ice flowers
gathering in your window.

Some say she's sewn herself into her own
grave with pin-pricks of snow,
a seamstress who mends
the earth and sky into a whole.
Others say a broken mirror's an open door.

They point to her tattered grave-gown
shimmering in the northern lights.
They tell you that's her loneliness
where the grains of the mirror are drifting.
But this is what they never tell you:

If one of these shards ever enters your eye,
then nothing will ever look right again,
and if a piece of the mirror ever enters your brain—
far worse. Soon you will forget the pain
and go on living as before.

MADELYN CAMRUD

Nordland

For Rolleif

This winter I've lost the feeling
of being anywhere near the center
of the continent, loving how far north
we seem to be. Mornings
I walk the edge of the street.
The snow keeps falling, taking me over,
white on white, then white again,
and blowing. Rolleif,

my great-uncle from Norway, left the valley
below Meraker. *Went north,*
relatives said, *came home once for a visit,*
brought ice cream; they didn't know it
would melt set on the stove. He sent poems
to grandmother—wrote about snow,
about roses, how he plucked one, placed it on
their mother's grave, heard her
call for her daughter in Dakota. This winter
I want the feeling of having come
as far north as I can. In my dream,

last night, I held a pewter vessel,
gripped it with my hands, amazed
at its size—its emptiness. All around it
were pictures, carved in relief,
each of them complete; I wish I knew

43

their meaning. This morning, I am remembering
those cousins below Meraker, how they told me
that, in summer, they stop their work
to gaze at reindeer, trekking through snow,
crossing the mountain. This morning, as if entering
the Arctic Circle, I lean my shoulder
into the wind, and glimpse those reindeer
in that space, so empty and so clean.

MADELYN CAMRUD

Flying Home

Just past Fargo, it is night.
There is land far below me,
flat as flat to the edge,
I know this, without seeing,
the way I know, if blind
from birth, I would see pictures
in my head. I have no sense

of the wing, only this flashing
bit of red at the tip. We have started
our descent, will soon be landing,
coming down, the way we've flown
there and back at God's mercy,
not so different from the farms,
up and down the horizon, like stars,
                    disappearing.

The Monkey's Children

Here is a story for you.
The monkey had two children.
She loved the fair one
and cuddled it close to her breast.
She hated the dark one,
who persistently clung to her back.
When the hunters came
and she escaped up a tree,
the fair one fell to the ground,
while the dark brat held on.

I don't know what you do
with the monkey on your back.
I talk to mine when the fair one sleeps.
I pass him coriander seeds and fruit.
I have come to like his tug at my back.
Even when the fair one's awake,
a sweet weight in my arms,
I slip my hand around my waist for a pat.
The other day when the hunters came,
and I scurried to the highest branch,

the fair one slipped out of my grasp.
The dark one flung out a bare-knuckled fist
and caught my love in the air.

....

The Animal Man

I had been working for the welfare department in Glens Falls for years and had handled plenty of odd cases. So when the animal man had to be brought in, everyone looked to me to do it. And I requested Pedersen. They liked two of us to go together, in case the old ones were difficult. Sally Pedersen, remember her? She was no more than five foot even and a bit of a tub, but quick on her feet. And there was something in her voice that made the old ones listen.

For about twenty years the old man had been living in that shack up by Little Kill with a bunch of animals. We knew he was there, but nobody had tried to interfere; he wasn't hurting anybody. But when people began saying that he probably spent his whole check on seeds and feed of some sort, and that he might be getting too weak to keep the stove going, and that the County should do something, then we had to step in. You can't let the old people live like that and die alone.

As Sally and I drove down the access road, we saw a dozen deer, and when we stopped the car, a doe stood up right beside it, not the least bit afraid. But the most amazing thing was the noise. You should have heard it! Like five o'clock in the morning, just after the migrants have returned. All that chatter and singing. And when we got out of the car, we were almost attacked by a screaming blue jay that kept swooping down at us from a nearby pine.

Sally gave the bird a why-don't-you-behave look, slammed the car door, and took in the scene with a glance. Green asbestos shingles and tar paper were peeling off the walls, exposing the original logs, and the porch looked like it was going to topple into the brook any second. She made a sucking noise in disgust and proceeded past piles of unstacked wood, a stove pipe, and a car seat blooming with springs.

I knew the spot well. There was a great swimming hole in a bend of Little Kill, just below the camp, and I had spent many a summer day there, as a kid. Even back then, the camp was pretty dilapidated. It had been built for some of those better-off folks from down state, who come up to the North Country for a few days of hunting and fishing. Guess the place stood empty until the animal man moved in—which, they say, was when his kids sold the farm and moved, tired, like everybody I guess, of the perpetual unemployment in the Adirondacks.

Just as Sally was making her way around a rusty harrow, she suddenly stopped dead in her tracks. I could see why. A family of skunks took its time running Indian file across the path and in under the porch. She almost refused to go on. But a job is a job.

In the middle of the rickety steps, she screamed out loud, though, and stepped back. It's lucky she didn't fall and break her neck. You see, the screen door had opened, all by itself. At least that's what it looked like. Then we heard a hiss and saw a teeny black hand inch around the edge of the door. A little, black nose stuck out, then a pair of eyes in white fur sockets. A raccoon!

Sally took a deep breath and in her most effective oh-isn't-this-nice voice, she called out, "Anybody home?" Answered only by a ruffling of feathers and a scurrying of paws, she raised her voice. "Yoo-hoo! Yoo-hoo!"

The raccoon disappeared, a squirrel ran down the steps, birds flew in and out of the holes in the screening. The animals were obviously at home. Sally rolled her eyes and opened the screen door.

Not only was the porch full of broken-down refrigerators and rusted tools, tarpaulins and boxes—that's what people think porches are for, in this part of the country—but twenty years of barn swallows had left their mark. There wasn't an edge or a beam or a nook that didn't have a construction of mud and saliva. The floor had a covering of droppings so thick you couldn't even see the planks. It was a disgrace!

I stepped up and knocked on the cabin door. There was no answer, not even after I knocked a second time. So I put my hand on the door handle to check if the door was locked.

And it swung open.

Have you ever seen one of those pictures in which children are supposed to find the hidden animals? That's how it was. A rabbit lay in a bread basket on the table. A chipmunk peeked out of a boot on the floor. A beaver was slapping its tail behind the rocking chair. A litter of baby mice were climbing over each other in a red bandanna tucked into a sugar bowl on the windowsill. In the fireplace opening stood a fawn with two legs in splints. And in a rocking chair next to that fireplace, the old man was sitting with a black bird on his shoulder. As if in greeting, the bird cawed.

"Is this what you tried to tell me?" asked the old man as he stroked the bird's back. "Don't worry, little brother. Don't worry."

The animal man must have sat in that very spot for years, because his feet had worn holes through a linoleum patch put down to cover the worn-through linoleum beneath it.

As in most cases, the old man did not want to leave. The old ones never do, no matter what is promised—prepared meals, clean rooms, bingo, free medical treatment, companionship, TV. But many of the old ones could be coaxed into coming, if told they could bring some favorite possession: a fishing pole, a clock, a rocker, photographs, or the "good" china. It was as if they believed the things they loved kept them alive. So Sally asked the animal man if he wanted to bring something.

You could see him perk up. "Yes," he said. "I want to bring the animals."

"Except animals," said Pedersen. "You can't bring animals to the Home. Pets aren't allowed. Health reasons. We mean things like furniture. Do you want to bring your rocker?"

"I got to be with the animals."

Sal and I had handled tougher situations. The animal man was not senile; he could follow our reasoning. We pointed out that it was getting colder by the day. He even admitted having trouble keeping the fire going—and getting himself something to eat. But he kept repeating that he couldn't leave, because the birds and the animals depended on him. He pointed out which critter had come to him for help with a broken wing, a paw caught in a trap, a bullet wound. But Sally was no dummy. She told him we would have a veterinarian look in on the animals.

Although there is something sad about bringing in the old people, I usually feel good about it. Sure, our coming means that their lives are over in some way, but at least they get the care they need. This time, though, I felt like walking off the case.

The old man went from box to bin, from makeshift nest to makeshift lair, saying good-bye and apologizing for leaving. And the funny thing was, the animals talked back. There was no question that they understood him, and he them. I heard the old man tell the raven, "Now, you tell the others to go somewhere else for help." The fawn spoke just as clearly. "Don't worry about me. I'm fine. We will take care of each other. You take care of yourself."

I am not the kind to believe in any funny stuff. My wife died when the kids were small, and having to be both father and mother in this here world sure is a lesson in reality. But I didn't know what to make of what I was seeing. When we finally got the old man into the car, the animals took turns coming up to the car door, to say good-bye. You should have heard the noise. The deer actually followed us up to the highway, and the birds flew along for miles!

There was no rule against bird feeders at the Home, so it wasn't long before staff and residents were saving crumbs for the animal man's birds. More often than not, four, five wheelchairs were rolled up to his window. Chickadees and cardinals, robins and blue jays, pine siskins, mourning doves, and gold finches can be just as entertaining as soap operas. If the animal man was rocking, his visitors felt free to move around and talk about what they saw, but if the animal man was still, or if he stood by the window, talking to some little creature, the visitors knew to keep quiet. Nobody wanted to scare away a martin or a hummingbird, or some other nameless thing that was daring to befriend a human.

Almost a year to the day the animal man was brought in, he was missing. A waitress who was coming to work at six in the morning said she had seen him walking down the street with the animals that lived on the block: a three-legged cat, a dog with a scratched-out eye, and the mutts that hung around that little park where the old folks went on their walks. And a bus driver whose route took him past the Home said he had seen an old man walking down the road with a bunch of animals. He said he had taken notice, because there was a deer among them. Even in the Adirondacks, a deer is no common sight in town.

The old people at the Home didn't seem surprised at the animal man's disappearance. Guess they all dreamed of leaving. A few of them insisted he had been planning on it, for a long time. They claimed to have heard him tell the raven he would be coming, soon.

I couldn't help feeling responsible. Although I was sure he couldn't have walked all the way to the cabin, I decided to go and check it out, anyway.

The access road wasn't usually plowed, so I left the Oldsmobile up on the highway and walked in. To my surprise, there were tire tracks in the new snow. I figured some hunter or lumberjack had been there with one of those four-wheel drive vehicles. But I didn't expect to see a Blazer parked in front of the cabin.

I felt uneasy. It took me a while to realize why. There was not a peep in the air or a sound anywhere, even though the snow was covered with tracks. It was quiet even when I walked up the steps and through the leaning porch. It was quiet when I opened the door.

The afternoon sun was low but bright, so it took a while for my eyes to get used to the darkness inside the cabin. That's probably why I jumped when I heard a voice. "I've been thinking of making a fire."

Then I saw her. Sally. Sally Pedersen. She was standing by the fireplace with a couple of logs in her arms.

The cabin was cold, as cold as only a place that is supposed to be warm can be. I looked around. Chickadee, robin, blue jay, mourning dove. Weasel, rabbit, three-legged cat, and half-blind mutt. Pigeon, porcupine, deer. They were all there but not making a sound. And leaning back in the old rocker was the animal man. A raven on his shoulder, a mouse in a hand, a beaver in his lap, a raccoon by his feet. His eyes were closed, his skin was bluish, the chair did not rock. Everything was absolutely still. Yet the animals all seemed to be talking at once, all saying the same thing.

"Let me give you a hand," I said, knowing I would leave the ending out, if I ever tried to tell the story about the animal man. No living thing should die alone.

51

SHARON CHMIELARZ

....

Driving to Work with Franz Josef Haydn

5:45. Pitch dark and winter-morning cold. Mine was just one in the string of one-driver-no-passenger vehicles heading south on 169. It was December 6, the day after the big commemoration—the two hundredth anniversary of the death of Haydn's friend. "That's weird!" the kids had said yesterday in my classroom. "You remember the dude on his death date?"

What can you expect from humans so close to their birth dates?

Out loud I said, "Remember, thousands of years from now we'll receive today's light from ancient stars."

"No way!" was all they said.

Into this present, my backseat, Haydn slipped. It was an accident, he explained. He'd attended last night a concert commemorating Wolfgang's work, at 20.15, Viennese time, but the wind gust he'd caught off St. Stephen's high roofs sheered, and he'd wound up in my suburb, Brooklyn Park. It was one unlucky left veer. And except for the winter of '85 (1785), more snow piled on the ground than Haydn had ever seen.

Driving was going to be difficult. My hands already trembled on the wheel, I felt so extremely honored. Why *my* car, I thought.

It was uncanny, he read my mind: Like me, he was getting out of Brooklyn Park. And I was the only driver waiting for the red light at the Fleet Farm corner who knew his name. He also felt a slight connection to me—hadn't I visited the memorial to his brother, Michael, in the Stiftskirche, St. Peter's, last summer? "*Ja, ja,* I know," he said. "You'd really come to see the other memorial, the smaller one, for Wolfgang's sister; still, you doffed your hat to a Haydn."

I asked him if he'd ever met her. He squirmed. He'd had to be discreet in making women friends—the wife, you know—but in the *Mozartin's* case—"Nannerl, they called her, *nicht?*"—he'd never had the opportunity, although—and here he paused to dig among long buried facts—she had a reputation for being a first-class musician, no novelty performer. Lord knows one female oddity was enough on the circuit. "That blind clavierist, Maria Paradis, or that Englishwoman Davies with the harmonium. And her singing sister. Fickle Viennese audience material. The kind, *Gott sei Dank,* Esterhazy didn't hire." Sequestered on a country estate, Haydn had been delivered from dealing with a female musician's temperament.

One could go bankrupt in Vienna, anyhow. England was the place to make real money. Haydn had tried to persuade Wolfgang to do a London season, but he died too soon. Haydn went himself, got the Frau off his back with more take-home pay.

"Why am I telling you these things?" he laughed. The car-capsule echoed, *Tellink chew dees tinks.*

I steered his reverie back to Maria Anna Mozart. "Nannerl's biggest problem was her brother."

He pooh-poohed my bait. "Next to Wolfgang, *all* musicians pale. Let alone a woman, a sister. Now you take, for example, that Martha Silbernagel, the fat one that married a petty clerk. She was one of Wolfgang's best students. . . ."

"Josepha von Auerhammer, you mean?" I suggested a bit coldly.

"That's the one. Good clavierist. Good performer. Toured. Played with Wolfgang."

"Nannerl's former position, before she was retired by her father," I said. "I don't think Josepha had a brother for her father to pin his hopes on."

"And no brother like mine, throwing half his talent after booze. Bah!" He dabbed with a lace-edged hanky a droplet of cloudy spittle on his lower lip. "God keep me from punch."

But he loved my cabriolet. "You are American but you drive no pioneer wagon? *Mein Gott!* She rides so quiet, so smooth, no bumps, no lurches, a cabriolet on velvet."

"*Cars* we call 'em in American," I told him.

He purred the word. "Kar-r-r-rz. A kar-r-r is so warm! Cushiony. Prince Esterhazy, the Empress Maria Theresa would turn green!"

I immediately apologized for mine. "Not everyone likes my car. It's made in Japan," I said. "Up here on Highway 169, Ford and GMC pickup country, bumper stickers read, Jap Cars Suck."

I once got chased off the road in it. When I caught up with the rats at a red light, they flicked their cigarette butts out the window and said, 'Drive American and we'll let you stay on the road.'" Nazi jerks.

"I've driven a lot of cars over the past thirty work years," I confessed to Haydn. "One so small I could park it under the kitchen table; a Bug whose accelerator stuck; a Duster with Look-Ma-No-Brakes; an Oldsmobile whose engine trailed its guts, leaving me to hitchhike in the woods; a LeBaron station wagon, beautiful thing, used to wonder if I should drive it or just look at it: You've not known twentieth century American fear, Herr Haydn, until your motor conks out on the Indiana TriState around Chicago, and the car slows down to thirty in the fourth lane of an eight-lane freeway with semis barreling by at eighty." My palms got clammy, remembering the LeBaron's quirks. Why even bother listing Bel-airs whose carburetor problems I'd nursed through too many winters?

"But now," I told him, brightening, "I feel safe. It's more than the quiet ride and cushions. I love my car. It doesn't matter who made it. This car and I are going to die together, though not in an accident."

His breath did not frost up the window he stared from, horrified at the stream of red-tailed cars we had joined on the freeway. "If a wheel broke," he said, "six or seven coaches would pile up. *Ve voot die!*"

"Cars," I corrected. "No spokes, but flats. Let's not think us into an accident. How about some music?" I punched a button. "Hey!" I exclaimed. "They're playing your Violin Concerto in A Major!"

God. It was gorgeous. No wonder Mozart wrote six songs in tribute to Haydn.

"Sounds good, my music! *Zountz goot, my moosik.* But I don't understand." And now his voice had the fervor, the passion all those German classicists displayed when talking about organs and new pianofortes, carriages and money. "Where on this prairie," he asked, pulling himself closer to my ear, his transparent hands tugging on my headrest, "where is the *Konzert* hall? How have you conjured to appear behind my ears this music?"

"The magic of playing the radio, Herr Haydn!"

"*Ach, ja!*" He immediately wanted to know all about my radio, its balance, tone, the accoustics. He could have cared less that the

Japanese had made it, though he understood about losing jobs and making money. "And *you* have this," he marveled, "even here among the aborigines." I didn't bother to explain how our forefathers had removed that competition.

Thank God, Haydn didn't ask me the intricacies of a tape deck. Last Christmas I was in a music shop looking for a record of "Exultate Jubilate" and the clerk, scratching his nose-ring, respectfully informed me, "Ma'am, they don't make records anymore." If a ghostly Haydn attended concerts, why wouldn't he hover around the taping in some Viennese studio near the Staatsoper, or drop in on a Musikverein to listen to modern period instruments, or compare performances of his work by Barenboim, Muti, Solti, Dohnányi, Mazur?

"Would anyone have believed it!" he suddenly said, shaking his head. His wig curls jiggled. I caught his stare in the rearview mirror. "*You!* Now I place you. The thick bones. The moonface. You're the great-great-granddaughter of Esterhazy's chamber pot emptier, Maria Sophia. Imagine *you* with access to the court's music. And in a coach! A softer, faster, warmer, more wonderful coach than the Prince ever had! Every day, any hour, with a finger push, you are privileged to private performance!"

All my own. My eyes smarted with gratitude. Yes, the traffic, in tandem, was yoked to the hour like a line of plowhorses plodding onto a predictable day, but I sat on a cushioned throne with Haydn behind my shoulder, humming to his work. "Don't stop now, Josef," my lips moved. His fingers conducted his music as I drove my cabriolet, rollingly, south.

The concerto ended on the east side of Wayzata. I glanced into my rearview mirror during the news break. No Haydn. Somewhere between the concerto's last note and the top of the hour, he'd slipped out. No problem. In this suburb he'd easily be able to find a seat in a BMW or Mercedes, heading east on 394, through the Lowry Tunnel to 35W, over the Crosstown to the airport, and back first class to *Wien* and the strains of classicism.

I can imagine him running into Maria Anna Mozart on the Opernring, in that foggy way two spirits collide. "*Entschuldigung!*" He bows, unwinding himself, but because of our conversation, he stops to talk to her. He even joins her at a club admitting women musicians, a salon with a high ceiling, a room where portraits tilt forward on their wires. Where a great time is had by all, playing each other's visions, compositions, and variations, performing in the starlight from the past.

I'll bet those women attend every concert Iona Brown, Comet, Ben-Dor, Dudarova, de-la-Martinez conduct, from Vienna to Hamburg to the Gewandthaus. Who else could be cheering so loudly from the ghostly non-seats in the rear? *Bis, Bis!* they shout. *Bis, Bis!* I echo.

Countdown

The countdown begins
for the long walk into autumn.

Cornbread and acorn squash
hum half-forgotten
songs from childhood.

Cold rain
touches our skin
like a soft drum.

Nestled at the feet
of sweet gums and sugar maples
jack-o'-lanterns
lick their lips and cackle:
happy birthday . . .
happy birthday . . .

And the hunter's moon
offers each and every one of us

a bag of poisoned candy.

....

My Hungry Heart

I was crazed the year I turned thirteen, panicked that life was passing me by, that I'd be stuck forever in Clintock, Georgia, that my zits were permanent, my breasts fried eggs, and that if I didn't get to know Jesus fast, I would burn in hell. Mama favored my twin sister, Myra, called me a heathen, refused to take me to church, and said to forget about my skin, Daddy's side of the family was all pockmarked. My only friend was my little brother, James Taylor, ten years old and ready to turn his smooth, freckled face to me and say, *okay.* You could see the flicker of indecision move through his eyes, but he said yes to truancy, thievery, salvation, to whatever I proposed. At the time I thought he was responding to my brilliance; now I know he said *yes* to my desperation.

So, when I told him we were getting off the school bus in town, he wadded up his lunch bag, stuck it under the seat, and followed me down the stairs. He didn't look back when Myra hollered after us, and neither did I.

"We got to get saved," I explained and pointed to Pilot the preacher waving his Bible at the other end of the square.

"Okay."

"I want to know Jesus," I said.

"Yeah, me too," James Taylor said. "How're we getting home after we're saved?"

"Jesus will provide," the preacher yelled just then.

"That's how," I said and James Taylor nodded.

We were the sole members of the preacher's sidewalk congregation that spring. He was a grizzled old guy in faded army camouflage, called Pilot because he'd flown choppers in Vietnam. Mama said he was crazy, but the preacher had a voice on him.

"You, Girl, you, Boy," he yelled. "Judgment Day is at hand." He flourished a Bible over his head. "Repent, ye sinners, repent!"

James Taylor flinched at every "Repent!" but I liked the sound of the preacher's voice in my head. I'd read about mortification of the flesh somewhere, and it was that mortification I was after and that Mama provided when we got home late every day. We'd stand there with our hair blown back by the wind of her voice, saying "Yes'm" and "sorry" with our fingers crossed behind our back.

"How will we know when we're saved?" James Taylor asked one day when Pilot's harangue rivaled Mama's in vehemence.

"I'll tell you later," I said, but I didn't know. That's when I started looking around for something with more potential than hellfire to play with. I found it at school of all places, a poem, Tennyson's "Ulysses," declaimed in sonorous tones by my English teacher. "All times I have enjoyed / Greatly, have suffered greatly. . . ." Ulysses's words fanned out like clear, bright petals in my head. Pilot the preacher promised a single note of doom, but Ulysses unfolded the epic possibility of greatness, with or without suffering.

James Taylor was gawking at the preacher when I pulled him away. "Bet you never heard of Alfred, Lord Tennyson," I said.

"I thought Jesus was Lord," James Taylor said.

"Alfred is better," I said. "Listen to this." I cleared my throat. "'I cannot rest from travel—I will drink / Life to the lees.'"

"What are lees?"

"*Lees*," I said. "You know, 'I will drink life to the *lees*.' Lees. That means you get every bit, the last drop. Lees are the essence of experience. Listen. He explains it farther down. 'For always roaming with a hungry heart / Much have I seen and known.' That's us. You and me. Roaming with a hungry heart."

James Taylor looked longingly at Pilot, who had reached the lyric peak of his harangue, "I promise you hell or salvation, the choice is thine. . . ."

"'How dull it is to pause,'" I said, "'to make an end, / To rust unburnished, not to shine in use! / As though to breathe were life!' That's it. That's it, James Taylor. We've got to do more than breathe. We've got to live! 'Life piled on life / Were all too little. . . . !'"

He looked at me warily.

"You're my mariner," I said, "and we're roaring with a hungry heart. On to the untraveled worlds!"

By the next week, we'd explored every property in town, every floor of the courthouse, been up the steps of all the churches, covered every inch of the square. We'd been everywhere but in jail.

We stood outside the front entrance of the police station for an hour on Saturday morning, me bullying James Taylor to go in first. I wanted to see what it felt like to be imprisoned, to face the Cyclops. James Taylor said that was crazy and he refused to go unless I stole two sticks of licorice from Bolton's Drugs when Irene, the cashier, wasn't looking. Irene was so mean and into everybody's business that it didn't seem wrong to steal from her. And her daughter, Ray Jean, was still sleeping with our daddy so it was all in the family. Sort of. Anyway I needed the licorice to bribe James Taylor into accompanying me to jail. I slapped the candy in his hand. "Mariners first," I said and pushed him ahead of me. I figured the cops would be more sympathetic to a little boy than they would be to a pimply-faced girl with straight hair and no breasts.

Our first view of the interior of the police station was disappointing. I'd hoped for a counter just inside the front door with a pudgy cop in blue, snarling at all who entered, and the bars of the cells arrayed just behind him. But the door opened onto a corridor with tobacco stains on the floor and a couple of chairs lined up against the wall. I pushed James Taylor down the hall. The first two doors were closed, but the third, on the right, was open. James Taylor stopped in front of the open door. A young woman chewing gum and pecking at a manual typewriter with two fingers sat at one desk. The other two were empty. I cleared my throat but didn't get her attention. I poked James Taylor. "Say something," I hissed.

"Where's the jail?" he said quickly, then sucked in his breath so he wouldn't laugh.

The girl stopped smacking her gum and looked up. She stared at us for a bit, then tossed her head to the right, indicating that we should proceed farther down the corridor. She popped her gum as we walked away.

The hallway curved and we came to a counter more like what we expected, with a couple of closed doors behind it. A man with a complexion as ugly as mine saw us right off. "Hey, there," he said. He was wearing a policeman's hat and a light blue, short-sleeved shirt with a navy tie.

"Hey, yourself," I said.

"Hey," James Taylor said.

A fat policeman I'd seen on the square came out of an open door to see who we were and waited to hear what we wanted.

The pockmarked guy lifted his eyebrows. He had eyes the color of his navy tie that gave him uncommon good looks in spite of his bad complexion. "You kids got trouble?"

James Taylor shook his head vigorously.

The fat guy laughed. "Cat got your tongue?"

I poked James Taylor, but I could see I'd have to do the talking. I smiled straight into the pimply-faced guy's navy blue eyes, seductively, I hoped.

"I'm Carlotta Grant," I said, taking my favorite alias just in case they thought of calling our parents, "and this is my little brother James Taylor Grant. We'd like to see a jail, sir."

"A jail?"

I nodded.

James Taylor nodded.

"Yes, sir. A jail cell, I believe they're called. James Taylor's doing a project on incarceration for school."

James paled at my lying to an officer of the law, but kept quiet.

"It's an assignment and he is supposed to spend twenty-five minutes in a cell, to see what is there and what the experience is like. Of course, his being so young and all, only ten years old, he asked me, his older sister, to accompany him down here to the incarceration tank." I paused imperceptibly. I thought I'd heard cells referred to as tanks in some story or movie, but I got a flash of fish in an aquarium as I said "incarceration tank."

"Incarceration cell," I repeated. I looked around with interest and sophistication. "This is where you keep your cells and criminals and all, isn't it?"

The young guy swung his navy eyes over to the fat guy and back to me again. "Yes, Miss Carlotta Grant, this is where the criminals are at, but I don't know about allowing you kids in there."

"It's for school," I said helpfully, glancing down at James Taylor in what I imagined was a plea for the cop to consider the needs of a young, inquiring mind.

When the young guy smiled enough to show his narrow teeth, I knew we were in. "So you want to see our incarceration tanks?"

"Yes, sir." I smiled winningly. "If you please, what is your name? My mama taught me to know whom I am addressing." She hadn't actually. I'd read it in Emily Post in the school library, how it was gracious to address a stranger by name and that helped you remember their name for the rest of your life.

"Officer Simpson," he said, "and this is Captain Walnut." He indicated the fat man.

"Pleased to meet you both," I said and bent my knees in a quick curtsy. "We'd be much obliged to spend just twenty minutes in jail."

"I thought you said twenty-five," Officer Simpson said.

"Oh, that would be wonderful." I clapped my hands and smiled broadly. My teeth were my best feature. Not a cavity or stain in thirteen years.

Captain Walnut shook his head and stepped through the doorway he'd come out of. Officer Simpson stood up and walked around the counter. "Fifteen minutes," he said. "Follow me."

James Taylor grabbed my hand and we squeezed each other's fingers, then we followed Officer Simpson down a second corridor behind one of the closed doors. Officer Simpson wore navy blue pants the color of his tie and a pistol in a holster on his right hip. He patted the pistol twice as we followed him down the hall. James Taylor pointed at the gun and made firing signs with his hand.

I shot him back with my fingers, then we stuck our hands behind our backs so Simpson wouldn't see us if he suddenly turned around.

....

The Clintock Jail wasn't much. We'd hoped for a series of locked chambers presided over by armed guards, but there was just one cell in Clintock in those days, and it was occupied by a middle-aged man in dirty army fatigues.

"You just got one?" I asked.

Officer Simpson leaned on the desk across from the cell. "Just the preacher here." It was Pilot the preacher.

I nodded to Pilot. "I meant one cell."

"Yeah, just one."

I fell back on Emily Post in my awkwardness. "Well, if this gentleman is using it, sir, we could come back another time."

Simpson looked at his watch. "Naw. The preacher's done for the day. Aren't you, Pilot? Until next time?"

The preacher looked small in real life. He stood up slowly and I caught a whiff of stale tobacco. He stuck his red vinyl Bible under his arm. "I am ready," he said in a voice that was unexpectedly full for his diminished presence. "I am ready," he said again. "I hope you'll be ready, too." He waved the Bible across the air behind the bars like a benediction. I thought he'd recognize us, call me Girl, but he didn't flick an eye in our direction.

Officer Simpson unlocked the cell and held the door open for Pilot to shuffle past him. "Wait up," he said. "You got to sign out." He looked at us. "Go on, you two. Into the incarceration tank. Make yourselves comfortable. I'll be right back."

James Taylor and I walked quickly through the door and Simpson let it close and lock behind us. We were in jail.

"Let's go, Preacher," he said and the two men went back the way we'd come.

The interior of the cell was cement block construction with no facade to make it look like anything else. James Taylor traced his finger around the outline of one of the blocks. "Just like school," he said.

"But cleaner," I said. The painted blocks looked as if they'd been scrubbed with a brush every day for a year. There were thin lines across the white paint and the cell reeked of bleach.

We took off our jackets, looked around for a place to hang them up—there wasn't any—and tossed them on the bunk.

"This *is* kinda cool," James Taylor said and sat on the edge of the cot, bouncing it up and down. "Not too bad," he said.

"It's just a bed," I said. "Come on. Let's do what we came for, pace this thing off before Simpson comes back."

"*Officer* Simpson," James said. "I wonder what it would be like to sleep here."

"Bigger than the crawl space under the bandstand," I said. Pilot the Preacher spent most of his time behind the lattice work that covered the base of the bandstand on the square.

We tried the faucet of the small sink in the corner, one cold water spigot, slow drain, no stopper, no mirror, no towel, a sliver of soap, toilet with no seat and no cover. No window.

"There's no mirror and no towel so the criminals don't kill themselves," I explained to James Taylor.

"How do you kill yourself with a towel?" he said.

I knew but couldn't think of how to explain it to him. "Let's explore."

We walked the perimeter of the cell, up on the cot and down again, eight steps plus five and a half plus eight plus five and a half. Then we measured heel toe, which gave us more steps, seventeen by twelve. The cell was plenty small. "Do the diagonals," I said and James Taylor walked kitty-corner, heel toe, both ways. Nineteen steps.

There wasn't much else to do. We sat on the edge of the cot for a while, staring through the bars, watching the door Officer Simpson would come through to let us out. It was stone quiet in there. No sounds of voices or telephones or typewriters. Not even people's feet moving back and forth in other rooms. An occasional drip from the faucet. I got up and tightened the spigot as much as I could, but I succeeded only in slowing down the drip to one a minute.

"Do you think he's forgotten us?" James Taylor asked after awhile.

"Naw," I said and looked at my wrist even though I didn't own a watch. "Two hairs past a freckle. He'll be here."

James slid back to lean against the wall with his legs stretched straight across the cot. For me, that was too much contact with a bed that had so recently been that of a vagrant crazy-man preacher, so I paced the length of the cell again. Then I paced the breadth for a while. Five steps, turn. Five steps, turn. That's what we'd come there to do, pace it off, walk the edges of the most dangerous place we could think of, jail.

"Wait till I tell the kids I spent the day in jail," James Taylor said.

"Don't tell Mama," I said. I knew he wouldn't but it didn't hurt to remind him. I looked at my wrist again. Fifteen minutes were definitely up. I walked the length of the cell again, alongside the bars, counting them—seventeen bars. I grasped one in my hand. It didn't seem all that thick. An inch at most. I tried to shake it, but it didn't budge—too many crosspieces.

I noticed the cell door had one less crosspiece. The bottom one was missing between the bars of the door, giving a twenty-four-inch gap twelve inches off the floor. I stuck my leg between the bars of the cell, to see if I could wriggle through. My leg and thigh slipped right through and I lowered my torso to get my hips out.

"What do you think you're doing?" James Taylor was stretched out on the cot with our jackets bunched under his head like a pillow, eating his licorice.

"Escaping like Houdini," I said.

"I thought we *wanted* to be in here."

I pulled my leg back inside the cell. "Well, yes, we did. But that's the point of jail. Trying to escape it. Once something's got you, even if it was something you wanted, the next step is getting away. You got to keep moving, James Taylor, to the untraveled worlds. Now that we're in, let's see if we can get out of here."

James sat up and cupped his pale face with both hands. "What if you get caught? Officer Simpson is coming right back."

I'd talked myself into something I hadn't given much thought to—escaping. But I was right. The challenge of jail was getting out. I could see the headlines: *Carlotta Grant (a.k.a. Mona Garrick) Makes Miraculous Escape from Clintock Jail.* I stuck my leg through the bars again.

James Taylor shuddered and fell back on the cot.

I'd developed some womanly padding through the hips in the previous year, but I felt that some combination of sucking in my stomach and angling my hips and butt just right, cheek by cheek, would get me out.

I was one cheek closer to freedom when Officer Simpson and Captain Walnut burst through the door dragging a black kid by the scruff of the neck. He was about my size.

"Stand up, you bastard," Officer Simpson said, "or your filthy black face'll get some rearranging."

James Taylor slid off the cot and stood at attention next to my twisted torso, half in and half out of the cell. I tried to jerk my free leg back in, as if nothing were happening, but it didn't jerk. The bar rubbed hard against my most tender places and I let out a tiny shriek.

"For Christ's sake. What in the hell are you doing?" Captain Walnut yelled. "Well, Wee Willie Simpson, looks like your girlfriend's escaping."

I hated that, being called anybody's girlfriend. I tried to force my leg back through the bars again.

"Ow!" I screamed.

"You got yourself in a real pickle, missy. You coming or going? This here isn't no maximum security facility. You're expected to stay on the inside where we put you."

"The fifteen minutes were up," James Taylor said in a quavery voice. He was as pale as the scrubbed cement blocks. He put a hand on my back.

Captain Walnut had a point. My left leg, thigh, hip, and buttock were outside the cell; my right leg, thigh, hip and buttock plus my upper torso were inside the cell, but bent over because the horizontal crossbar between the vertical bars was only three feet off the ground. I'd injured myself twice in trying to force the left leg back in the cell. Therefore, it seemed prudent to move slowly. "Give me a moment," I said in my most elevated diction. "Even Houdini took a little time."

"Houdini, yet," Captain Walnut laughed.

"If you could look the other way for a second, I'd get out of here easier."

The prisoner had been quiet during all this, but it suddenly occurred to him that he could use my predicament to his advantage. He wrenched his arm away from Simpson and lunged for the revolver on the officer's hip. He actually had it out of the holster when Captain Walnut flew across the room and slammed the kid against the wall. The gun flew out of his hand, bounced off my left leg—the one outside the cell—and landed on the floor. Walnut nailed the prisoner—you wouldn't think a fat man could move so fast. He'd knocked Simpson to the floor, but landed solidly across the skinny prisoner, then grabbed the kid's hand and bent it across his back.

I took a deep breath and used the diversion to concentrate on getting my whole body on the same side of the bars. The smart thing would have been to end up inside where most of me was, but I didn't like the way those two men had been talking to me, assuming I didn't know anything, so I sank down and forced my torso through. The head was tighter than I expected; I came close to ripping off both my ears. When I got my body through, James Taylor bunched up our jackets in his arms and waited at the cell door. His confidence inspired me. I lowered and angled the remaining buttock and hip, pulling gently but firmly until they popped out. I was standing unfettered between the desk and the cell about the time Captain Walnut pulled the prisoner to his feet and slammed him against the wall. Officer Simpson was just getting himself up off the floor. I bent down and picked up the gun by the barrel. It was heavy. "Drop that gun, miss," Captain Walnut ordered and I let it go. It hit hard, clanged against the cell, then lay across my shoe. We all stood staring at each other for an instant. I slid my foot out from under the gun.

"You can let my brother out now," I said.

Simpson swore and pushed the prisoner against the wall as he came around to release James Taylor. He grabbed the gun and jammed it in his holster, then swore as he fumbled through the keys, trying to scare us. The black boy whimpered against the wall, cradling his elbow.

"You broke his arm and I'm going to have a big old bruise on my leg," I said. I stepped closer to the boy to inspect his injury.

The prisoner curled his red lips at me. "How'd you get your pussy through those bars, girl? You can show me that any time."

"Shut up!" Walnut growled and shook him again. The prisoner yelped.

Simpson opened the cell door and James Taylor walked out. Walnut shoved the prisoner in. Simpson hung in the door. "What's your name, boy?"

The kid showed his teeth at that. "Jesus," he said.

James Taylor gasped and I clapped my hand over his mouth. I wanted them to forget about us so we could see what was going to happen. I was interested in this Jesus. I didn't know any black people then. Our school was supposed to be integrated, but wasn't really, and we weren't rich enough to have a maid.

Simpson's wiry neck broke out like he had the hives. "I'll Jesus you," he shouted and he pushed the boy against the back wall of the cell. Jesus hit the wall and for a minute it looked as if he were going to bounce right back in Simpson's face. Simpson slammed the door shut just as the prisoner fell against it. He grabbed the bars with his good hand.

"My name's not Jesus, Cap'n. You know it as well as I do. But I had a vision of His face when you asked me my name and I knew He was here with us. Jesus!" The prisoner spoke in mellifluous tones, as if he were telling a story or singing one of those slow, storytelling hymns that gather strength and high notes word by word. I couldn't take my eyes off him. I wanted to know his real name and wanted to hear him talk more about Jesus. I still wanted to be saved. I wanted to *know* Jesus the way this black kid did.

Walnut herded us to the door.

"Hey," the prisoner yelled. "Leave the red-haired piece of ass here!"

"Out, you kids, out. You seen and heard enough for ten reports." Walnut kept us moving out the door and down the hallway. "You can't write a thing about that nigger in there because he's a minor and his good name is protected by law."

"Jesus?" I said.

Walnut snickered. "That's Caleb Evans' boy. Caleb didn't name none of his kids Jesus." He walked us all the way to the front door and watched us go as we walked back toward the square. I turned around at the corner of Church and Main. Captain Walnut waved, then disappeared through the door.

I felt this tremendous pressure in my chest. "We did it, James Taylor. Went to jail, paced it off, walked the edge *and* the diagonal of that cell, and *escaped!* We did it."

"You did it," James Taylor said. We were standing in front of the drugstore.

"You want a vanilla coke? You got licorice stuff in your teeth."

He shook his head. "How old you reckon that colored boy was?"

"I don't know. Young. Sixteen or seventeen."

"You think he was a stabber?" James Taylor's blue eyes filled his face and the dots of pink on his cheek were spreading.

"No. He wasn't no stabber." I put my arm across his bony shoulders. "Stabbers are just a story Mama made up to scare us. That boy was real."

"My knees were slapping together, but he wasn't afraid at all," James Taylor said.

"Oh, he was scared all right. Didn't you hear his ugly mouth? That meant he was scared to death. Why else would he be shooting those words at us?"

"At you." James Taylor looked across Main Street to the bandstand in the middle of the grassy area of the square. Pilot was yelling at some old woman on the other side of the street. "Hell," we heard him holler. "Burn, I say. Burn in Hell."

"That old preacher slept the night in jail," James Taylor said. "And that Negro kid's going to be there tonight."

"Black kid."

"That black kid was a real prisoner, too. Not for no fifteen, twenty minutes. He'll be there tonight while we're home eating supper."

James Taylor was right. I liked that Jesus Evans too, admired his guts. Going to jail and mouthing off at the same time. Naming what terrified him. He put our mama's sharp tongue in perspective. I wasn't so afraid of her after that, only sad. I was sad for Caleb Evans' boy in jail too. He was everything I wanted: young, tough, and with a tongue in his head that would keep him at the end of a white man's fist his whole life. He'd live life to the lees without even trying. I'd been trying for thirteen years and the best I could do was to pretend I was escaping from something. It wasn't enough.

....

When we got home I went down to the back of the yard where Daddy ran the hose to dig worms for fishing. I turned the water on, and when the soil softened up a bit, I scooped up a handful and spread it on my arms to see how I'd look if I were black. There was too much red clay in that dirt and not enough black topsoil, but I liked the effect—smooth with no freckles. I smeared the mud on my legs, too, let it dry, then brushed it off so I was covered with just a dusting. I didn't have a mirror, so I hollered for James Taylor to come down from the house.

He didn't even smile when he saw me, just shook his head. "You fixing to join that Jesus Evans' family?"

I held out my bronzed arms, then stuck my fists on my hips the way I'd seen a black woman do. "I might," I said. "I just might do that. 'I am a part of all that I have met.'"

He looked at me without speaking.

"Come on, James Taylor. Grab yourself a daub of mud there."

"Ah, Mona," he said. "Let's play something else."

"No," I said. "I can't. I am Carlotta Evelina Annie Ulysses Grant, '. . . strong in will / To strive, to seek, to find, and not to yield.'" My heart was so swollen in my chest that I could hardly breathe. I threw a lump of red clay at James Taylor. He stared at me flat eyed without a flicker behind his lids. I threw another and then another, crying and screaming, "Do it, do it, do it, do it."

The skin of his face was so pale that I could hardly see his freckles or the color of his thin lips. "Do it," I hollered. "It's your last chance."

He bent one knee to the dirt and scooped up a handful of clay and raised it over his head. "Burn, I say!" Tears streaked his face, but he pumped that ball of clay over his head again. I thought he was going to heave it at me, but he smeared it against his skinny arm and rubbed it in, crying, "Burn, burn, burn, burn."

....

A Little Something against the Cold

That my father died in the middle of a long-standing and incredibly complicated quarrel with Jimmy Stanski at Universal Liquors was something my mother could not forgive; and if she could have, she would have called Pop back that spring and ordered him to finish what he'd started.

My husband, Jerry, could not believe that a quarrel could start over dog shit or last, as my father's had with Stanski, for two and a half years. But Jerry was not from the neighborhood. Where Jerry and I live, farther west—toward but not exactly in Hinsdale—quarrels are infrequent; and when they occur, they are patched up quickly. The people where we live are very rational and very liberal, and everyone there knows that grudges are uncivilized.

In the neighborhood where I grew up, sharing a two-flat with another Hungarian family—them upstairs, Mom and Pop and me downstairs—things were different. For example, Mom had a ten-year-old grudge against her neighbor, Mrs. Voss, because Mrs. Voss's magnolia tree shed blossoms into our yard, and even though our yard was only the size of an area rug, Mom was territorial.

Every spring Mom waited for the magnolia tree to bloom. "Pretty," she'd say, "but such a mess." She couldn't enjoy the beauty—wouldn't give Mrs. Voss the satisfaction. When the blossoms fell, she raked conspicuously.

Likewise, *Mr.* Voss, who claimed—mistakenly, Mom said—that the two-foot-wide patch of sandy soil between the garages was part of their lot and dug up the ornamental gourds my mother planted there every spring. Rather than talk it out with Mr. and Mrs. Voss, which was what Jerry and I advised and what they would have done where we lived, Mom raged inwardly and doggedly replanted her gourds, sometimes two or three times a season.

"The American dream," Jerry said. "People fortressed in little stucco houses and fighting over a patch of dandelions."

My mother folded her arms and turned her back. Her standing opinion of my husband is that he is pleasant enough most of the time and not bad looking, but dense, a dummy, educated, she says, but lacking in common sense. Jerry, on the other hand, sees Mom as a museum piece, a classic example of first generation immigrant adaptation. Jerry's a sociologist: U of I, Chicago.

"All I'm saying, Mom," he said to her, "is that it's artificial, this dividing up of lawns. A tree doesn't know where your property line is."

My mother looked at me. "You talk to him," she said.

The quarrel with Stanski began, as near as I can figure out, when Jimmy Stanski took over the liquor business from his father, Herman Stanski. The first thing he did was complain to Pop about the dog shit on what we always called the "parking," the thin strip of ragged grass that ran between the sidewalk and the street. Customers walking across the grass from their cars stepped in it and blamed the liquor store. Jimmy showed Pop examples of the problem. "Help me out, Hank," Jimmy Stanski said.

Pop had been walking his dog, Bags, a basset hound with mournful eyes, on the parking that fronted both Jimmy's store and our house for seven years. Bags wouldn't go anywhere else. It wasn't personal. A dog was a dog. It wasn't anything Pop felt he could change.

"Help me out," Jimmy Stanski coaxed. Pop ignored him.

Jimmy was small, hyper, with thick glasses that made his eyes seem to swim behind the lenses like dark brown fish in a tiny aquarium. To make matters worse, there was *his* mother, who lived with him above the store and who owned a wiry schnauzer that looked like an irate Scotsman. When Bags and the schnauzer met, there was always trouble.

Finally, Jimmy Stanski put up a sign:

Please Do Not Air Dogs Here

My father pointed the sign out to Bags. "To air is human," my father told his basset and walked on.

A week later, Jimmy took the first sign down and put up another one:

No Dogs Allowed on Parking

The Mgt

While my father was amused by the first of Jimmy Stanski's signs, he took great exception to the second, not so much the message as the signature. He and Stanski's father had been friends for twenty-six years. Pop was practically Jimmy Stanski's godfather. It fanned some deep, unacknowledged anger in him that Jimmy Stanski was all grown up and Herman Stanski was dead, and he himself was—he never expressed this, but I know he felt it—no longer Jimmy's funny, generous Uncle Hank, but a used-up person, an old man, a nuisance. Jimmy Stanski was known forever afterward as "The Management," and Pop never lost an opportunity to ridicule him.

My mother's concept of family was such that it was unthinkable, while Pop's quarrel with Jimmy Stanski lasted, for any of us to patronize Universal. This was a heavy censure for Jerry and me, and we went there secretly anyway, like kids sneaking into a dirty movie. We told ourselves that Jimmy's prices were better than the Jewel. Not true. We said—not true—it was more convenient to go there. The fact of the matter was that we liked Jimmy Stanski and his cramped, dusty store full of good, cheap Bulgarian reds and exotic cordials better than we liked the discreet, tasteful liquor stores in our own neighborhood. Jimmy had booze that more efficiently run stores hadn't carried for years.

Then my father died. We didn't even know that he was sick. Even Mom didn't know. She knew but she didn't know. Just like that, he was gone.

I have a brother—much older—who lives in Atlanta, Georgia. His name is Marty; he's not much for fights. And I'm just a girl, so that left it up to Mom to carry on the quarrel with Jimmy Stanski. She felt she owed it to her husband. It was early spring when my father died, just before the magnolia was due to bloom, just about the time Mom began to think about planting her gourds. The conjunction of these three quarrels and her grief over Pop's death boiled inside her through April, and her life took on an embattled, bitter monotony, which she dramatized by standing for hours at a time on our side of the parking, her hands on her hips, scowling into the impassive plate glass windows of Universal and occasionally making seemingly casual remarks about the store's high prices and filthy interior.

"Won't even let you walk your dog," Mom said to no one in particular. "Not even that small courtesy."

Stanski tried to ignore her. Not easy. And we were caught in the middle, Jerry and I. We were modern people, Americans. We had good educations, money, subscriptions to classy magazines, interesting friends. Our grief did not oblige us to carry on the quarrels of the dead; it did not suggest to us that we should boycott Universal.

Of course, we didn't express any of this to Mom. We let her believe, instead, that she had allies. Maybe that was wrong. Anyway, the whole thing blew up one rainy evening in June when we went to Mom's for dinner.

"So where's Jerry?" Mom said. She had a pork roast in the oven and potatoes on to boil.

"He's parking the car."

Jerry, of course, was at Universal, buying a brand of hazelnut liqueur that we couldn't find in the stores in our neighborhood. My job during Jerry's secret forays to Jimmy's was to distract Mom and to keep her from looking out the window, but this time Jerry was gone so long that finally she noticed and said, "So, where's he parking it, De Kalb?"

She sat down at the kitchen table and wiped her face with a dishtowel. "When Herman Stanski and my Hank were alive, you could park any time right in front. You know why?"

"I know."

"Herman marked out a spot for us. Right in front. The customers knew it." She glanced out the window. "Remember that, Bethie?" she said. "He had that big sign, the one in the bucket of concrete, No Parking. He put it right on the curb in front, remember that?"

In fact, I did remember. Universal customers knew that the spot in front of our building belonged to Pop. An unwritten law.

"It's that boy," my mother said. "The Management. Hot shot businessman now that his father's gone. Him and his customers. They park anywhere they please."

"I know, Mom."

"Year in and year out, Hank mowed that parking. You know that, Bethie," Mom said. "He never failed."

"Mom?"

"We don't bother their dog."

"Mom."

"When Herman Stanski and my Hank were alive, we all got along. Friends, you know what I'm saying? And if the dog wanted to shit in the soup bowl, that was his business."

"Mom?"

"I'm only asking for a little consideration."

She began to cry. I don't know why that should have surprised me. I put my arms around her and she bawled like a baby. But when she heard Jerry come in through the back door, she broke away from me.

"Don't let him see me," she said.

Jerry has the painful, self-conscious honesty of all liberals, and when he came in the door, a kid would have known that he hadn't been parking the car.

Mom said nothing. Nothing through the pork roast and potatoes, nothing through the green bean casserole with mushroom soup and the canned onion rings on top. We were, in fact, halfway through the Jell-O with bananas and Cool Whip when Mom said, "So, how's your friend?"

"Friend?" Jerry's eyes locked on his coffee cup.

"Stanski," Mom said. "The Management. Don't tell me you haven't seen him lately."

"Mom," I said.

"Okay," she said, starting to clear the dishes. "You want a ginger snap? You can only have two. I'm saving them for work day at church."

"He's not a friend," Jerry said.

"I should care." Mom whisked Jerry's bowl out from under his spoon. "You fight the good fight, you fight alone."

"Mom," I said. I thought I could head her off.

"That's what your father always said," Mom said, silencing me. "You remember him."

This was the kind of statement/question for which my mother was famous, and before I knew what I was doing, I was pushing back my chair. I stood up. I folded my paper napkin and laid it beside my plate.

"You fight alone," Mom said. "You can't count on anybody. Not your friends, not your kids. That's what Hank always said."

"Why does there have to *be* fighting?" Jerry said. "What has anyone done that's so terrible?"

Mom gave Jerry one of her withering looks. "Bethie," she said. The old guilt trip. "You of all people."

"Let's not get into it," Jerry said.

"Yes, let's not, Mom," I said. "Let's not fight."

She began to run water for the dishes. Steam rose from the sink. "Take his part," she said. "God knows, you never stand up for your own family."

"I'm not taking anybody's part," I said.

"You got a husband," she said. "Me?"

"Stop it," I said.

"No, *you* stop it, missy." She turned and let her anger roll over me. "You stop pretending that you care."

No one said anything for almost a minute.

"Just go," she said. She dropped onto a chair and stared at the floor. "Go on home."

I nodded to Jerry and he went to get our coats.

"You know, Mom," I said, "I've lost someone, too."

She lifted her head and looked me straight in the eye. "Who?" she said.

....

Jerry knew that grieving people punish the ones they love. He showed me books on it. Apparently, it is a common pattern of grief. But, in Mom's case, it was more. In putting me through rituals of obedience, she was imitating Pop, whose love was always measured and circumscribed.

Maybe she was keeping him alive.

Pop gave and he took, an emotional quick march that provided me—and Mom, too—with a sense of security. He gave without asking what and whether you wanted, and then he exacted gratitude in proportion to his gift.

Take the swimming lessons, which required me, at the age of eleven, to take the Oak Park bus from Pershing, transfer, and ride to the end of the line—an hour's travel, at least—to reach the Y.

It was February, bitter cold. I did not want swimming lessons. I hated the water and stood, skinny and shivering, beside the diving board, while the other girls lapped the pool like happy seals. But my father had never had swimming lessons.

He had never had music lessons either, so I had those, five years of piano. My father was on his own at the age of fourteen, working as a busboy at The Berghoff. He became a waiter, which is how he got into the restaurant supply business. He married my mother at nineteen.

Of course, my father never went to college. So I went to college, and whenever I won some prize or got an A on an exam, my father would say, "You know, Bethie, I never had the chance to go to college."

My father had rules, and they were inflexible. If you obeyed the rules, he loved you effusively, and there were treats and pet names, and, although there was never much physical contact between my father and me, a certain glow; a balance filled the house when the rules were acknowledged and obeyed.

My mother was also subject to the rules and looked upon me as a fellow sufferer. She used me both to fantasize escape from the cramped life she had lived with Pop and as a target for jealousy, someone she was proud of whom she despised.

My father did not drink; that was one of the rules. But my mother did. She liked to take what she called "a little something against the cold," usually port, but she never dared to drink in front of Pop. I would find her sometimes late in the afternoon, sitting in the rocker in the back bedroom, cradling a jelly glass of port and staring out at the maze of wooden stairways that connected the flats in the building across the alley. Understand, my mother was not a drinker; she just liked her port, and that half hour in the afternoon was hers.

After Pop died, she denied she ever did this. I'm not sure how the matter came up, but she looked me straight in the eye and said, "There was never a drop of liquor in this house."

"Mom," I said, "I saw it. You used to keep it up in the kitchen cupboard. With the spices. I'll bet it's still there."

"Beth," she said, stopping me from snooping in the cupboard. "You know how your father felt about alcohol."

....

Mom's sister, Bernice, came to stay with her, and that fall they took one of those scenic tours on the Greyhound up to Wisconsin to see the leaves turn gold. She wrote me a card, a very ordinary message in which she documented every town they had passed through and every meal they had eaten on the trip. Then at the end, she added: *Such beauty, Bethie. And, think, from death.* Her cramped, loopy handwriting filled the card and continued up the right edge and around the right-hand corner to the stamp: *Don't feel bad or think I blame you about Daddy. You have your life to live. Bernie sends her love.*

It was typical of my mother that she was able in one stroke both to forgive me and go right on dishing out the guilt. The fact that she didn't blame me somehow implicated me in my father's death. The fact that I had a life to live implied that she did not and was somehow an indication of my indifference and an affirmation once again of what I had always known intuitively, that the only way to escape guilt in my family was to suffer.

While she was gone we took care of Bags, who was getting older and uglier every day. Although my father ironically called him Bags the Wonder Dog, Bags had only one perfected trick in his repertoire. He was capable of balancing a Milk-Bone dog biscuit—the big ones, his favorites—on his nose for five or more seconds while my father, his forefinger uplifted, crooned "Hold, Bags, hold." Or, more to the point, he had been willing to do this, to my father's delight; and perhaps there had been something wonderful in the way Bags's loyalty to my father could overcome his greed.

If he dropped the bone, they started over, my father again raising his finger and Bags again shivering with anticipation. A faint whine would escape Bags at these moments, a sigh of duty, tinged with indulgence.

Then, when the room had sufficiently admired my father's mastery—for he never asked Bags to perform without an audience—my father would snap his fingers and cry, "Release, Bags."

The way that dog slipped his nose from beneath the bone and

caught it deftly in his mouth as it fell was poetry to my father, art itself, a symbol of what love had become between them.

....

I would like to say that there is some dramatic conclusion to this story, but, in fact, the passage of time is the denouement. Time passed, which is the bedrock of all stories, and my fragile family righted itself in the same way a plant will find its own way upward seeking the light.

One evening in the deep of winter my mother brought out a bottle of port after dinner, and we recognized, Jerry and I, the label of an obscure brand that only Stanski carried. My mother did not make a fuss about the fact that my father was finally dead and she was having port with her children after dinner, her own woman now and ready at last to make some decisions.

"A little something against the cold," she said, filling three jelly glasses.

I raised my glass to my mother. "Salut," I said.

We were balanced, the three of us, in my mother's kitchen under bright light, having just finished dinner and holding the moment, a fleeting syncopation before we drank our musty port in a hail and farewell. Bags whined faintly in his sleep on the braided rug in front of the sink, and across time and memory, down all the years, from some safe and final place, I heard my father snap his fingers and whisper softly, "Release."

BARBARA CROW

Journeys

My husband wants difficult things.
Where are my hiking boots, he asks,

and the other blue woolen sock.
He speaks mysteries. I am

unencumbered, lying in bed
this Sunday afternoon. I've been

sick, but he has brought me juices and teas
and breads leaking honey.

Tomorrow, he leaves for the south.
He gets out old maps, fingers

roads that will take him
out of here, then comes

back into bed. I reach down,
pull the covers over

and give up
the poem I was going to write today.

....

Hemispheres

I don't know where to go from here.
Every day the radiant sun
unhinges me. I rise
early, put supper on the table late,
feed and shine the cats, rearrange
their bed and mine. Last night,
at the radio station,
my fingers on the black knobs, setting
things on fire through the airwaves,
I believed myself to be
back in my brother's room in my
old land; saw the cream
cupboard where his clothes
hung, the old tartan
rug, torn green curtains
on windows facing west. I want

to go home. Surrounded by books,
lines I'll never read, the day
progresses. Yearnings come and go.
Our hearts are imperfect and
redeemable. It was my brother who called to say
our mother had died,
held in my sister's arms
in her own bedroom,
a whole perfect
sun streaming in
from the west.

ALAN DAVIS

....

The Women of the Brown Robes

Elaine stood on the steps of the Unitarian Church waiting for Patsy, her best friend, but it was Oscar who appeared first at her side. He tried to give her all the money in his wallet.

She stared at him. "Is this a payoff or what?" She shaded her eyes from the bright sun. In the temple basement, a fellowship service was about to begin, but hours earlier Oscar had done his damnedest to get those long delicate fingers of his under her silk blouse. For years, his fingers had guided Elaine from "Chopsticks" through the various moods of a sonata, but last night he had tried to play a different kind of music on parts of her body that had nothing to do with the piano.

She had been stunned. He was tall and sallow, granted, but quite charming in his old-fashioned way, like an Ichabod Crane kissed by the Pope. There was always a vase of flowers near his piano, and next to it a tray with a pitcher of hot tea, cubes of sugar, and wedges of lemon. A metronome made of mahogany that stood like a pagan sentinel next to the flowers was as heavy as a stone paperweight. "If this is a payoff, Oscar, forget it. The whole thing, I mean, the lessons, the drinks, everything."

"You don't understand," he whispered, glancing at the empty schoolyard on one side of the temple and a parking lot on the other. "I depend for my livelihood on word of mouth. One indiscretion, Elaine, especially in this Peyton Place, and I am doomed. Absolutely doomed." He adjusted his cravat and shrugged to settle the coat around his waist.

Elaine had faith that a good day was a better drug than the antidepressant she sometimes took, and today flowers were bright like decals, the wind was high, and the heavens had the speckled texture of a robin's egg. If she were in Alaska, she thought, she would be standing watch with the Women of the Brown Robes. "Listen to your voice," they would be saying. All of them had given up families, careers, fortunes. Elaine much preferred their imagined company to that of people. She turned from Oscar, shaded her eyes, and squinted, trying to get back to Alaska and those calm voices so hard lately to find inside her head. A bunch of kids across the street were playing "one-two-three red light" in the front yard of a yellow house. A tow-headed youngster, still in his Sunday suit, was "it." Each time he turned, stranded on the sidewalk, the other kids crept closer. He moved fast, but one girl was faster. The boy untucked his shirt, tossed away his tie, even cheated by twisting his neck before shouting the words, but she always stopped a step or two closer with a trickster smile as bright as sunlight on the azaleas.

Elaine was still in love with Kevin, her ex-husband, even though he had moved across the country to California and had fallen in with a cult. She had thought she knew him down to the marrow in his bones, but the voice inside his head these days was one she no longer recognized. His phone calls were about audits and bad thoughts and sweating inside a sauna at the Center, but she could remember a time before they became high school sweethearts, when promise was everything. On a trampoline in the gym, he had performed double-flips and back flips, defying the laws of gravity for her while she leaned against the waxy, folded bleachers, pretending to be indifferent. On their first date, they had drunk Coca-Cola and danced in swirling light in the same gym, one bedecked for the occasion with ribbons and crepe paper that gave the illusion of glamour. Quaint, chivalric, he had docked her at her door after the chaperoned evening while his father waited in the car, eyes averted. He had placed his hands stiffly on her shoulders, probably following the old man's directions. He was a head taller than she was, at that unwieldy age some people take years to suffer through. He rubbed his lips against hers, her first kiss, but she flew away from him, her mind on the trampolines that had been all folded up for the evening along the gym walls behind crepe paper and tinsel. When he had turned away, red faced, his father tapping the horn, she had been relieved, and had jumped high enough to touch the ceiling tiles inside the front entrance.

"You've got to promise you won't quit taking lessons," Oscar said. "I mean, I'm willing to compensate you for any lessons you feel you took under false pretenses. That's fair, isn't it?"

"A bribe, Oscar?" His shirt was never untucked, his cufflinks never undone. Not a single greased strand of thinning hair was ever out of place. He chose his cologne, he once told her, because it had the fragrance of his first piano. "Look," she said, "you made a pass. Big deal." She clicked her tongue. "This is a hard time for me, Oscar. I thought I could depend on you. Instead you pawed me and told me I've been your mental wife for months. What was that supposed to mean?"

"I just drank too much wine," he whispered. "I have a drinking problem. I'm not supposed to drink, it does something to my metabolism. I get crazy." He nodded at several parishioners, who returned his greeting and disappeared into the temple. "You held my hand, didn't you?" he said, his blue eyes going gray. "You don't call that leading me on?"

He turned on his heels and followed the others.

Patsy arrived in a floppy hat the color of tree bark, a loose-brimmed hat two generations old that shimmied in the sunlight, a garage-sale hat. Patsy called it her traveling hat, and used it mostly on days her job as a case worker required house calls. She swept Elaine into the basement, a low-ceilinged room as long as a small gym. The minister, a wiry marathon runner, put them in a circle and opened his arms, as though to enclose everyone in his benevolence. "Let's greet each other with a smile, followed by a handclasp of fellowship," he said. Everyone dutifully followed his instructions. "Good. Now, let's imagine we're in the woods. There's a great waterfall above us." He rocked his hands to simulate ripples. "Can you hear it, cascading down, blotting out anxiety, helping us relax, helping us witness our lives?"

Patsy tickled Elaine's palm, reminding her to hold hands. The real-estate salesman on her right grabbed her fingers so fiercely he almost broke bones. Across the circle, Oscar alternated disdainful stares with beagle-like mooning. There was something odd about him today. He looked as if he had slept in his clothes. Elaine's hands started sweating, as they did whenever anybody wanted something from her. She was not much for fellowship services. Her stories were always outlandish, despite a sincere desire to change. She was always turning some soap opera or movie plot into autobiography. "A Mexican general flew into a mountainside when I left him," she would say in a deadpan voice. "Now, is that tragic or what?"

"I have something to say," Oscar announced, surprising even the minister, who had never quite figured him out. The service sometimes functioned as a forum on a current controversy, but more often someone broke into a crying jag. Everyone would encircle the aggrieved party and the minister would serve up, as though in a chalice, some Emersonian proverb. Because Oscar had little patience with such things, most of the congregation found him repulsive, too much the aesthete, hunching his shoulders in a flinch whenever the language got too rough. But Elaine and Patsy were his students, familiar with the shoe-polish fragrance of his cologne. They valued his predictability. He was the only man they figured they could trust.

"Well, Oscar, let's have it," the minister said.

"Love is everything," Oscar said. He flinched a little and stared at the floor. "Without love, there would be nothing."

Everyone waited, but that was it. "Hey, Oscar," Patsy whispered to Elaine, "how about some of the juicy details?" Elaine studied a piece of bubble gum so ground into the gray carpet that it looked like an old penny.

Everyone surrounded Oscar and lovebombed him, a few parishioners taking sadistic delight in Oscar's discomfort. Patsy told him she loved him in a voice that sounded sincere. She laid a hand on his butt and batted her eyelashes. Oscar grew as pink as the inside of a frankfurter until the group's attention turned to the real-estate salesman. He launched into a diatribe about a lost sale, his anger filling the air like a virus.

"Elaine," the minister finally said, "you have anything this week?" It was her cue for comic relief; he wanted to wind things down.

"I just cannot stand all this light anymore," she said, gesturing broadly to make clear that she did not mean the fluorescent ceiling. "In Alaska, where the Women of the Brown Robes live, their voices are clean and cold. They take vows of poverty."

A few parishioners exchanged glances, but the minister did not mistake her tone. "Elaine, isn't that a little elaborate?"

"No," she said. "That was the message of Christ, to give everything up and follow his voice. Or am I mistaken?" She kept putting her hand on her cheek, as if to hide a birthmark.

"No, not exactly, Elaine, though some choose to do that."

"Well, I so choose. We all of us should so choose. Jesus had himself a clear, clean voice inside his head. Did he not? Alaska is not easy. Azaleas do not grow there. The sun sometimes does not come up at all. Just because the weather is great does not mean we should feel good about the world. When the Women kill an animal in Alaska, they apologize to it. Everything is alive. People, animals, trees. I don't want a lovebomb, I want to *do* something. Why is it that we do not go down to the wrong side of the tracks and listen? Don't any of you get tired of hearing the same voice inside your head each day?"

"Look, Elaine," the minister said, "I'm too tired to deal with this right now. If you're serious, we do need volunteers. For that matter, we have connections far away. You could go with the Habitat people to San Diego and build houses." He rubbed his hands together. "I tell you what. Try not to sell your house before you come see me. We'll talk about it, but let's close for now with a meditation. All anger and fear must be forgotten before it can be surpassed."

Patsy gave Elaine a stricken look. What she liked, Elaine knew, was the tavern where they walked in the shade of maples and oaks to drink something sweet after the service. Usually, Oscar would tell them stories. He read, exclusively, the biographies and critical studies of great composers. The voices inside his head were very dependable. He would have the week's choicest anecdote rehearsed: how Cocteau, Satie, and Picasso collaborated with Diaghilev on a ballet, for instance.

Elaine was not in the mood. "Patsy, I'm lonely," she said when they hit the sidewalk. "I'm lonely all the time. The only people who keep me company are the Women."

"Is that a confession? Should I give you some shit for getting down on yourself or do you just need me to listen?" She was a short woman whose back had an S-curve in it and she trotted to keep up with Elaine.

"I miss Kevin. I wish we were together again."

"Is that possible? Does Kevin want In again or just you?"

Elaine shrugged. "I don't know. He hangs out with people who put little words in his head. He pays tons of money to take courses that any real religion would offer for free. But what do you expect?

The sun is way too bright out there, and it always shines. Whenever I visit, I get migraines." She rubbed her forehead. "The sun isn't even working *here* the way it should. I'm ready for Alaska, Patsy, a different way of life."

"Then do it."

"You are exactly right. I should leave right now. Right this second. I would if I could."

"Shoulda, woulda, coulda," Patsy said, one of her refrains. "You stopped taking your meds, didn't you?"

"Don't play therapist with me," Elaine said.

"Elaine, have you ever been to Alaska? Even on a cruise, I mean? Even for a weekend?" She jogged along in her flats. She could listen to Elaine when Elaine was near tears without bringing them on, and Elaine knew it. Kevin would tighten up, his jaws working, and the minister lapse into his psychobabble, but Patsy let her go on.

"This morning I wanted cigarettes. Kevin and I started smoking unfiltered Lucky Strikes and quit with True. That was *years* ago, Patsy, but this morning I wanted a smoke. I was lonely for a cigarette, for what we used to do. We used to go to the park down the street. Smoke, drink, feed the ducks. There was a dinky playground, park benches, a slide. A few kids tossing a baseball."

Patsy shrugged. She took off her hat and twirled it on a finger. "You're in Waiting. If Kevin wants In, then Waiting is all right. Otherwise, you've got to work on Letting It Go."

"I guess then I'm lucky, right?" Elaine said. "You all could have loved me to death back there instead of Oscar."

"Don't forget, Elaine, I'm a card-carrying member of a helping profession. It's good for the soul."

Elaine stopped before a rosebush to take home a flower as an act of rebellion but got herself stuck by a thorn. A spot of blood appeared on one thumb and grew to the size of a dime before she sucked on it. "That's it," she said. "With me and Kevin, there were never enough thorns. Too much friction, not enough thorns." She clutched Patsy's forearm. "Come to Alaska with me. It will be hard on you. You will find it testing your mettle."

Oscar overtook them. He had his tie in one hand. His neck was blotchy. He was gulping air. "Elaine, may I have a word?"

"Sure, Oscar."

Oscar glared at Patsy. She shrugged and waved them ahead. They crossed a street and walked into a small park with lanes and hedges. "Alaska?" Oscar shivered. "That's just like you, I guess, running off on a fling."

"Not a fling, Oscar. A pilgrimage, a soul-adventure."

"I see." He paused. "But you held my hand, Elaine. When we held hands, I just assumed." He trailed off, as though seeing the flaw in a grand Aristotelian design. "I know you like adventure. You told us about that Mexican general, that fling in Brazil with your Peace Corps friend."

Elaine bit her lip. "Look, Oscar, I make that stuff up. I do not mean to mislead you. Nobody else believes a thing I say."

He frowned. "And you said you wanted to take advantage of your freedom. You said that to me when we were alone, just the two of us. Did you make that up, too? What about those women you talk about all the time?" He gripped her arm fiercely. "Life isn't meant to be taken with a grain of salt," he said. "Salt is bad for the blood. You seduced me and you didn't even mean it. Don't you ever listen to yourself?" He pulled his arm away from her, as if she were the one holding on to him, and stalked off, his head bobbing above the shrubs.

Ah, holding hands, she thought, walking alone in the park. She could remember lying in bed and mooning all night after holding one of Kevin's hands most of the evening. She would scribble the magical name in her notebook, *Kevin Kevin Kevin.* She would place her name next to his—*Kevin Gould Elaine Gould Mrs. Gould*—say it a dozen times for the sound before destroying the page, entrusting to her diary only some cryptic word to mark the ritual: *EG, eleven letters, what if.* Hand-holding for beginners should be a required high school course, she thought. Your palms sweat, your fingers get stubby and stiff like pieces of chalk. Long before she married Kevin, years before the sun got too bright, she would try to figure out when to give him her hand or how long to let him hold it. Much later, the marriage winding down, they would tussle in bed, too full of aggravation for anything else. They would hand-wrestle and forget their latest fight, neither one hurting the other with an accidental-on-purpose slip of a fingernail or a grip too tight for fun; some invisible necklace of affection was still unbroken between them.

Standing on her back porch, she heard her phone ring. She fumbled with her keys and they fell with a clink, small slivers of bright metal. She thought about leaving them there on the stoop, along with the rest of her life, especially the glass that let in too much light. Alaska is cold, she thought, and I'm not used to privation, but there it is. She blushed when she thought of her makeup and perfume and earrings. The Women would take a look and laugh themselves sick.

It was Kevin on the phone. "I'm getting married," he said. "Did I tell you about her? I met her at the Center. She's helping me get rid of all my bad thoughts." When they had lived together, she had yelled all the time, she remembered, screamed about everything, and the most he gave in return was a frown as thin as a Communion wafer.

She poured a glass of tea and garnished it with mint. What would the Women be drinking about now? The snow swirling as they held hands and prayed between sips of hot tea, bitter laced with licorice. Pearls of moisture collected on her own glass. Ice cubes clinked. Ice, she thought. In Alaska, it connects everything. Water, snow, ice, frozen air. It connects land to water, water to air, air to land. She consoled herself with such profound thoughts until the sun went down.

The following Sunday they talked about toxic waste. "I found out they're testing for PCBs in the courthouse where I work," said Frank Holliday, a heavyset man with a homegrown voice. Elaine, sitting next to him, could hear its timbre inside her head. "But what can I do? Quit? I have a family."

Patsy nodded. "Yeah, you all know they checked my office for asbestos? Some men with ladders and a little meter? They won't tell me zilch about the results. We need to get organized. The military used to spray our cities with poison, just to see how the stuff carried in the atmosphere. We need to get radical again. The sixties have to come back."

Across the circle, Oscar smiled like a sheet of shook aluminum foil. "Why don't you shut your mouth, you stupid bitch."

"What?" Patsy said, leaning forward.

His shirt was soaked with sweat. "All I did was touch one of you, just touch you after you led me on, and what happens? I see you smirking. Satans, all of you! Every one."

There was stunned silence. When he left, his shoes echoed on the metal stairs like gunshots. Patsy surged after him in her floppy traveling hat, calling out his name.

The minister stepped forward. "Patsy is a professional," he said, holding out a hand like a traffic cop. "She'll help Oscar find the help he needs. Now, it's time to meditate. We've never had such need of it. Everyone, take a deep, calming breath. Please. Do it now. There's nothing to be afraid of, nothing to worry about. Breathe deeply." He cupped his hands behind his neck to demonstrate a way to breathe from the abdomen. "Let your thoughts move like the tides, like the ocean. Listen to my voice." He lowered his head until his bald spot gleamed in the light like a doorknob. "Close your eyes. Let your mind go wherever it will."

Elaine opened the door and stepped into Alaska.

"Good," the minister said. "Stay there, wherever you choose. Go deeper and relax, as I count to ten."

It was forty below, inky, silent except for the wind. When it stopped whistling, Elaine, with the Women, heard someone outside the cabin cock a rifle, a sound clear like a door snapping shut. She prayed for a quick, clean kill. "So many voices, so many people saying so many things," one of the Women said.

Four, he counted. "Good," he said. "Nowhere to go, nothing to do, not even a reason to ask why."

Five. They lived on prayer, their souls clean like new snow.

She heard Oscar and Patsy, their voices coming to her as if from a great distance.

Six. Seven. Eight.

She stretched her fingers, the same fingers that tried to play the preludes of Chopin. She longed to hold hands with the Women, but her fingers felt plump, sweaty, incapable of grace. She leaned forward as far as she could, holding her stretch in every muscle and bone until the room echoed with footsteps. "Holy shit!" Frank Holliday shouted.

She opened her eyes and took in the scene. Frank Holliday was grimacing, one of his arms dangling uselessly at his side. Patsy sat against a wall. She was staring blankly around the room. The minister was sitting dazed on the floor, holding the side of his head and moaning.

Oscar, staring at Elaine, stood beside the minister. His blue eyes had gone gray. He had his mahogany metronome in one hand and his wallet in the other. "Elaine," he said, and squinted. "That is your name, isn't it?"

"Oscar."

"Elaine," he said. He hurled the metronome wildly in her general direction and it bounced on the carpet with dull thuds. He approached Elaine and raised his wallet over her head; he shook it like a hankie, showering her with dollar bills, credit cards, claim checks, and a single foil packet. When he was finished, the wallet empty, he dropped it and sat down at her feet. He stared up at her. His eyes were blue and placid again like an unruffled lake. His hands were in his lap and his mouth a little open, so that Elaine was dizzy looking down, as though seeing herself in his eyes and hearing for the first time the real voices of rage inside her head, voices as complicated as musical phrases ringing out one against another in a fugue.

....

Keokuk Lock

By then, time and weather had reduced the *Molly Houston* to a relic—a tired stern-wheeler with stacks too tall and an old-fashioned boiler that sent stokers diving over the side in terror. But as all that remained of a beloved era, she was beloved.

As Billy and I watched her ease in for the season's first landing, younger boys of ten or twelve stood by while deck hands made the stern line fast. Hairy forearms of roustabouts moved the boys aside while Jennifer Parsons, dressed in a white cotton dress, red shoes, and a Chicago hat no mother of ours would admire, might step unbothered down the gangplank. Jennifer—only now dare I use her first name—led a pair of sweating draymen to Flynn's boarding house while Billy and I scampered ahead, setting Mrs. Flynn's bony hound yapping with contagious excitement.

At the iron gate Jennifer gazed across the square and down to the vessel rocking against the gentle heave of the river. As we stood there she studied us, our hands in our pockets. She moved her hip slightly, the way a man nudges a horse to free a stirrup, and as her eyes settled on me I thought she meant to speak. But in a flutter of white and red she disappeared inside the house.

....

With the river low, snags spoiled the channels that summer, while algae-coated rocks broke the surface and clams from the bight tasted like mud. River men said you could walk to Cat Island from the Illinois shore.

For years townspeople had dumped excess kittens on the island, reasoning that over there they'd return to nature, happy to hunt field mice and feast on dead carp. Old Jake Samuelson took the kittens across in his white rowboat, collecting a quarter a trip for his trouble.

Billy claimed that Samuelson rowed out of sight and flipped the cats over the side, and that's why he went at night. I didn't believe him, and insisted that some day I'd go over and find out for myself. Not to the island—you needed a yawl and know-how of the shoals for that—but to the Illinois side where the island was closer, and from where if the night was moonlit and if you listened hard enough you might hear, as others claimed to hear, the sound clear as a child's cry and twice as sad. *Meow, meow, meow.*

The deep grass along the limestone blocks near the wharf gave me a place to stretch out, and the nearby box elders offered shade. From there I could see the boarding house. I hid easily, taking up little space, for I've always been diminutive. I watched Jennifer through the window, cradling her own cat like a baby, kissing its ears while she watched the river.

Afraid of home, I dreamed about that river and where it went, seeing in my head the wiggly blue line on the map at school, running to the dot called New Orleans. And I'd picture myself on the *Molly Houston* in her fine days—railings of varnished oak and carpet you could sleep on, a floating heaven where men played cards on felt-covered tables while women who were not their wives stood at their shoulders and fanned themselves.

....

"I had not thought the North should be so hot," Jennifer said the first time she spoke to me. As always it was dark when she stepped outside. The gaslight showed a tiny blue vein pulsing on the side of her forehead.

"You lack height," she said.

I made no reply, for no words would come to me. I'd watched and dreamed of her for days, and she'd become a goddess and an angel.

"Have you no home?" she asked.

"No, ma'am," I said.

Dawn traffic moved on the river—new steelbottoms, diesels with flats of coal, short traders risking the soft mud. An old burner with a split wheel arrived, loaded with hogs and smelling of manure.

"How elegant you'd look in a vest of gabardine," she said.

....

With her first July landing the *Molly Houston* brought to town a scruffy man in a suit and cap who called at the boarding house, provoking much curiosity among the boarders. Mrs. Flynn said the man demanded sherry and smoked a cigar. He sent a message to Jennifer's room, but waited in the parlor alone until the boat's warning whistle drew him away.

In August, General Balderson and his company of Spanish-American War veterans marched around the square. They were aged by then, with fine, white hair and bony chins. But their sabers were sharp, their colors snapped over their guidons, and their caissons moved on wheels that could crush a man's back. I walked beside them, basking in their memories.

....

When she was young and the vessel new, my mother rode the *Molly Houston* to Memphis. Though she held passage all the way to the Gulf, the courtly men of Memphis intervened. They called on her with buttercup bouquets. They took her riding by the river and offered sassafras tea in chipped ice against the heat of Tennessee evenings. She stayed for weeks but clung to the remembrance forever—the finest summer of her life.

Mother drank. Father brought rye whiskey to her in a jug with a broken finger loop, refilled for a half-dollar at John Tattern's. For years, Father spoke of taking her back to Memphis on the *Molly Houston* and on to the sanitarium in New Orleans.

But he waited too long, for now the boat was old and Mother no longer cared.

....

The night of autumn equinox, I carried a message from the *Molly Houston* to Jennifer's room. She accepted the paper, folded it twice on her writing table, and turned her eyes on me, staring. The cat yawned and stretched, working his front claws into a perfumed lap pillow. Sheets the color of cream were turned down on the bed, as if ready for occupation. My mind burned with thoughts of Jennifer lying on the sheets. I turned to go, noticing bracelets and earrings arranged carefully on her dresser.

"Some day when I'm rich I'll have a gold pocket watch with links," I said.

"If you can't have love, have gold," she said.

"Oh, but I'll have both."

She smiled. "Perhaps."

Again I turned. "Wait. Put this on," she said, picking from the bureau a twilled wool riding cap, smelling of cedar shavings. "No, not like that. You must learn to wear a cap. One tucks the hair beneath it on the side. Here, allow me."

She reached around my head, her fingers busy. A trace of moisture cooled my ear. "Ah," she said. "A gorgeous river town man. Now the rest of it."

She laid clothes on the bed: a single-breasted suit, bright blue gabardine, with patch pockets and striped pants—all in a match to the cap. Along with a white shirt and detachable collar it made a fashionable outfit, worn by men of class year-round.

"Go on," she said. "Try it for size."

I looked around. "May I use the closet?"

"No," she said, moving toward the closet door as if to guard it— though a huge brass padlock made entry impossible.

I turned and slid my canvas shirt over my head. She handed me the collar and the clean shirt. The rich, cedar air and my half nakedness stirred me, slightly at first, then visibly. Standing behind me, she helped me with the shirt, then the jacket, tugging at the shoulders, pulling me around to face her.

"Small men," she said almost to herself. "They'll be my death." She shook her head. "But you are so young. Try, like so."

She pushed the back of my head against the wall. The wainscot nudged my spine. "When you walk, imagine the wall follows you," she said. "And come down on your heels, like a man. A bit of pretending can take you far. You see? Now the pants."

I turned to the portrait of Lincoln on the wall. Starched bedding hung to the oiled floorboards. I loosened my trouser stays. She stepped toward me, placing a hand on my chest, lowering it gently. A shudder rolled from my shoulders down to the arches of my feet. I was a young man, overfull with desire. Jennifer touched me for an instant. I pulled away too late and emptied myself in hot surges.

95

In a moment she brought a cloth and water. She coaxed me from the wall, crooked an index finger under my chin, and drew her face to mine.

"You'll never be more of a man," she said.

....

Billy threw pebbles in the dust and watched me stare at the boarding house through Indian Summer days while box elder leaves curled over on themselves from the heat. At night I slept, smelling cedar, wood smoke, and the river. Mornings I awoke to the croak of frogs from the oxbow and watched Jennifer caressing her cat.

Again the man came to call on Jennifer. This time he found his way into her quarters where he stayed for two hours, marking Jennifer in the eyes of the other boarders. I watched him leave, hating him, as he reboarded the *Molly Houston*.

The following day Jennifer sent for me. "My affairs are completed," she said. "I'll depart on the next boat south." Perspiration beaded on her pale forehead. "I've booked passage to New Orleans," she said, shifting her hips. "For two."

I questioned nothing—even when she laid out the conditions: I must pretend to be someone else, and though I would own a paid passage, I would remain hidden aboard for a time. And I must tell not a soul I was leaving.

Jennifer summoned me to her room the evening of departure, with the *Molly Houston* two hours upstream. She appeared so solemn, knitting her brow and speaking hesitantly, I became convinced she'd changed her mind. But she wished only to explain how I was to conceal myself in a locker for an hour after we cast off, and to warn me again that no one should know I was leaving.

"One hour, then come to the stateroom. One last thing you must do," she said. "Take this note to the apothecary. We'll be needing cuprate of mercury."

I was horrified. Cuprate of mercury was what John Tattern used to rid his building of mice. Jennifer's eyes were cold. "I mustn't allow my cat to starve," she said.

I tried to explain about Samuelson and Cat Island.

"Please do your duty," she said, as if not hearing me.

When I returned with the vial—for I could never refuse a request from her—she snatched it from my hand and threw it aside.

"I've changed my mind," she said. She lifted the cat from the bed, kissed him on the head, and handed him to me. "See that he's taken to your island." She opened my hand, dropped coins in my palm, and folded my fingers around them.

I found Samuelson behind John Tattern's store. He accepted the cat and looked at the money without a word. I followed him as far as the old wharf warehouse. He played a fingernail over the cat's skull and rubbed its tummy before dropping it gently inside the office door.

The *Molly Houston* was to cast off in early evening, but a splash-guard came loose upriver, and the crew worked until dark to repair it. I boarded easily in the confusion and hid as directed. From my hiding place I could see the main deck, the ramp, and the wharf of the town where I was born. For an instant I wanted to dash ashore. But shortly after the stage went up on its boom, lines thudded onto deck, and the floor beneath me shuddered as the engine built steam. We were moving.

But we barely made speed before the engine slowed, then stopped. Through a crack I could see the stern coming around. We'd struck a snag, still within sight of town. Shouted orders rolled down from the boiler deck, davits squeaked, and deckhands with broadaxes stood by as the yawl was lowered.

Unsure what to do in the face of this delay I ran to the stateroom to find Jennifer, pale and distraught, pacing the floor from steamer trunk to porthole. "Remain here until I return," she said.

I found that if I leaned out I had a view of the portside promenade. Passengers idled about, no doubt embarrassed to be in such an unromantic predicament so close to town. Jennifer stood near the railing. She touched the arm of one of the officers, a muscular man with a riverboat beard. He opened his pocket watch and held it to her.

Jennifer returned to the room only long enough to tell me I must put the blue gabardine suit on. Her hands fluttered about the steamer trunk, checking the catches, but it was from a smaller trunk beneath the bed that she pulled out shirt, pants, vest, cap. "You must now remain at the window, and remember to keep the cap over your face," she said, steering me to the place she wanted.

In her haste and anxiety over this delay Jennifer left the steamer trunk unlocked. In my curiosity about this trunk, which had taken four men to move, I peeked inside. Below the single layer of Jennifer's long dresses lay a heavy muffler and matching boots. Next were woolens, red and thick. Still deeper my hands touched a rich coat of otter or mink. At the very bottom I touched something else—a hand attached to an arm, attached to a human body, a man with his head tucked between his upward-bent knees, dressed in a bright blue gabardine suit, cold and dead. In a frenzy I repacked the trunk and closed the lid.

Trembling and ill to the core I leaned out the window. The main deck was nearly empty now. I strained to see through the darkness. The town had gone to sleep. Far below, the fire crew's lanterns threw yellow light on the oily waters of the Mississippi. After a time I spotted the bearded officer on his way to the stairs, trailing Jennifer by the wrist behind him. He spoke to her, and she nodded.

By now word circulated among the passengers that we'd be delayed again. The last of the curious began drifting to their staterooms. Soon the promenades were clear. I loosened the door latch and pushed, but it had been locked from the outside. I fought for my breath and began to itch in the suit. I missed Billy. I thought of my mother, drowsy on her mattress but missing me.

As a deckhand yelled from below I went to the window. The yawl was coming up—we must have cleared the snag. The main engine rumbled. Behind us, faint lights from town speckled the hillside. On the distant wharfboat, two tiny squares of brightness shone through the windows where men were playing pinochle and drinking corn whiskey, far from harm.

I fastened the chain on the door and pulled myself through the window and down to the deck planking. The cap fell off. I grabbed it and ran to the railing. The steam was up now, and to the stern the wheel was throwing water in steady cascades that misted the lights of town.

I leaned over the rail and twirled the cap as hard as I could. Then I put a foot up, and half-falling, half-diving, over the side and into the water I went—gabardine suit and all.

I plunged deeper than I expected, feeling the cold, and came to the surface as the wheel wash passed by me. Up on deck a lone man in a banker's hat leaned against the stern railing, dreaming, I imagined, of julep, gulf shrimp in wine sauce, and delicate pastries served on bone china. Above him hung the curved sign with its gingerbread trim: MOLLY HOUSTON.

To my right the cap drifted out of reach, floating nicely on a raft of trapped air. If not caught in a net or a hook, and if it avoided snags and didn't sink, and if it made it through Keokuk lock, it stood a chance to reach New Orleans.

The water smelled of crayfish and the air of coal smoke. I worked my way out of the coat and let it sink as I swam and floated toward the closer shore, the Illinois side. Not until I reached the sandbar did the sound of the *Molly Houston's* engine fade away. I lay there half an hour or more, resting and thinking. My arms never had the feel of Jennifer, only the wish and the memory.

But feet have a memory too, and I started walking, staying above the mud but below the thorns and willows on the bank. I used the courthouse belfry light as a guide, and walked until I knew I was abreast of Cat Island and across from town. There I stopped to rest under a tangle of overhanging roots where flood water gouged a scar against the rock. And that's when I heard it—coming from across the water, mixing with the ripple of the river, the frogs, and the breeze. It was very faint, but it was there, soft and musical. *Meow, meow, meow.*

....

There are few yet alive who remember what happened to the *Molly Houston.* She was above St. Louis and trying to make up time when another snag punched a hole in her bottom. The pilot tried a landing but pushed too hard, and when the boiler blew it split her all the way up to the texas deck.

A twenty-foot section of the guard was the biggest piece intact, and they found an iron stack feather half a mile from water. Maybe twenty aboard died, or so they thought at the time. A second steamer, this one northbound from Memphis, plucked most of the passengers out of the water. A few swam to shore. Clam fishermen rowed to the rescue of others.

The end of the *Molly Houston* left some true stories, plenty of rumors, and a few mysteries. For weeks I checked the newspaper for names. Three lists were kept: Alive, Dead, Missing. Names moved from one list to another and back again, or—as in the case of Jennifer Parsons—never appeared at all.

Now and then through the years I've searched river-town museums for more information, hoping I might even find an old brown-toned photo of her. But no. I've had to imagine it, the familiar forehead, the focused eyes, and the straight-away gaze with the hint of a crooked smile, as if instead of looking at a camera, she stared into the future, and the future amused her.

After the war when the Louisiana Line went bankrupt the archives in New Orleans came into possession of news clippings associated with the disaster. Various of them I'd seen, except for one from the *Times-Picayune:*

> One Genevieve Crabtree, 36, of this city, is now considered among the dead. As reported earlier her husband Theo Crabtree is also presumed to have been lost. Optimism was expressed following the disaster after witnesses reported seeing Mrs. Crabtree aboard a rescue vessel. That report is now understood to have been erroneous. According to friends Mrs. Crabtree had been summering in the North and her husband ventured upriver to accompany her home before cold weather set in. The loss of this upstanding couple shall be hard to sustain. Theo Crabtree (known by all as "Shorty") who was a sugar broker in our fair city has been long regarded a most generous patron of our public institutions. Providence sometimes smiles unkindly and mysteriously on His fairest children.

I considered this the end of the sad affair until years later when a package arrived at our St. Louis office, having been forwarded from my boyhood home. Inside was a fine, elegant timepiece, the case solid gold, with diamonds marking the quarter hours. No note was included, but it had been sent from Basel, Switzerland. I concluded at first it must be a gift from someone seeking business favors from whom I'd hear in time. But upon closer examination I discovered engraved on the bezel and discernible only under a glass, the figure of a cat at rest.

Under the press of other obligations I forced aside my curiosity about the watch until my enterprise took me to Basel. There I made a point of inquiring with the manufacturer. Their agent, a fussy little man whom I discerned at once was poorly disposed toward Americans, determined after much difficulty that the piece had been commissioned and paid for in bouillon by a Genevieve DePriest who represented herself as a traveler from Klondike, Canada, in North America. The warranty along with the receipt that they mailed to her in Canada was returned.

Was Genevieve Crabtree also Jennifer Parsons? Was the dead man in the trunk her husband? Happy am I to go to my grave never having learned the truth.

Idol Construction

Take any one of the things you believe in:
spools, leaf-light, breasts, jars,
buds, shells, brown eyes, ponds,
glass marbles, a live firefly, the penis—
and repeat:
I believe in the penis as the soul of creation,
the stiff center of the tower of all
that makes us choose to live.
O, penis-eye-god defend me.
Then.
Then the Everything-else-eye-goddess,
raises you up, up, up—
sucks you like ripe fruit off the rotten pit of self.

SUSAN FIRER

Driving Home after the Funeral

We stopped outside Lake Geneva.
At a plywood produce-stand,
we asked to go into
the pumpkin field. The three of us
stood there in our holy confused lives
in the tripping vines,
among the startling
brilliant shapes and
oranges of pumpkins. Grief
is a toll road, a large field. If you listen
closely, each pumpkin speaks a name.
We stood raw with loss
in the erupting fields of color
under the still warm, late October
sun. (October, the month of rosaries.)
Our feet released the songs of the buried.
We were greedy with loss, grabbing
the pumpkins by their prickly stems
and loving the pain of it. We stopped
there in the wilderness of loss and pumpkins.
We had just buried your mother.
Our son, and you, and I were the only
people in the weekday pumpkin field.
We were separating
pumpkins from their vines.
We were snapping
the prickly stems
from their tangled vines.
We were taking more than we needed.

We held the pumpkins close to our bodies,
loving their awkward weight and dirt smell.
We held the odd Laurel
and Hardy shaped ones, the movie
starlet perfect ones, the accordion
pleated pumpkins, the green
ones, the candle-flame-colored
ones, the pumpkins that flat leaned
to the dirt they came from, and
the pumpkins that grew lonely
next to the papery cornstalks at the edge
of the field. It was so windy
our hair whipped our faces. It seemed
the wind was blowing the world away. All,
except the pumpkins and us who stood
loss-full, wrapping ourselves around the beautiful
flesh and seeds of autumn
held in the fields of pumpkins.

....

In the Burrito

Layla lived in the *burrito,* as she called it, with her husband, Saldo. Deglazing the ham, refrying the potatoes. He wasn't really her husband. But he was her man and his children were her stepchildren.

At first she'd had a husband. Not the father of her children. But her husband had married her and been a father to her children. They'd even had a child, who lived with him now. But what thought had he had in his head? She finally left from boredom in the fireless marriage.

Her father had made sure she had what she wanted. He'd provided. When she left her husband, she moved in with her father. After her mother died.

Layla'd never married the father of her children. He was the father of most of them, anyway. He wasn't the man for her. He kept hanging around, yes. A hang-around-the-fort. As long as it was convenient. She wasn't being fair. Just angry.

Then he stopped coming around.

At first it didn't hurt.

But after a while, Layla climbed the walls.

She moved in with her father again. By then, he had another wife, who let her know the house was crowded.

Then she lived with a girlfriend. But their kids fought. So did they.

Then she'd had relationships. But they never worked.

Now she lived with Saldo in a low bungalow with blue print curtains and a front porch roof like a frown.

How did she get there? One wrong turn after another.

Then there was a freak snow.

She saw the old woman across the street crawling on her hands and knees in her yard. Her old hound dog baying. Had she fallen? Her blue dress, boots, her wool jacket, a scarf around her head. The old woman looked confused. Quickly, Layla threw a blanket over her shoulders, ran out, and saved her.

Their picture was in the paper. The old woman and the hound dog and Layla and Saldo and her children and stepchildren and her former husband, who was a firefighter.

After their picture was in the paper, the ardor returned.

Layla cooked that Mexican sausage, *chorizo con huevos,* wrapped with beans and chilies in a flour tortilla.

Mole.

She remembered grade school fevers. High school sunburns. The smell of wildfire burning in the field, sparked from lightning. She remembered the comets. The book burnings.

The salsa.

The traffic of boyfriends and lovers, husbands and former husbands, children and stepchildren, girlfriends and their children, mothers and stepmothers.

She'd wanted a simple life. Where had the clutter come from? Their blankets folded over them. All their lives inside.

Visitation Rites

Mama didn't like Chinese food. She never cooked it and she never ate it, but whenever we went on vacation, which was the long drive across the prairie from Michigan where we lived, to Livingston, Montana, where my father lived, she insisted we stop for meals at Chinese restaurants. She ordered shrimp, no sauce, and white rice. When possible she ordered fried chicken.

"The food's cheap and the Chinas keep a clean kitchen," she said as we combed the streets of Blue Earth, Minnesota, in search of a restaurant.

She pointed an instructive finger at me where I sat with my head resting against the glass of the passenger window. "Their bathrooms sparkle." She rolled her window down a touch and lit a cigarette. "It's not easy to find a clean biffy on the road," she said.

Well, it wasn't easy to find a Chinese restaurant in that little Corn Belt town either, but it didn't stop Mama from looking. Eventually she gave up and we made a dinner of apples and Oreos.

Soon we were crossing South Dakota. The prairie passed, hour by hour. Mama lowered her window again and lit another cigarette. I got carsick on long rides and Mama's smoke turned me green. I made a big show of rolling my own window all the way down and hanging my head out. I played with the side mirror and adjusted it until I could see my own face. I crossed my eyes, stuck out my tongue, and folded my upper lip under. When I felt Mama looking in my direction I pretended to vomit convulsively.

At sunset we pulled off the road again, cruising the main drag of Chamberlain, South Dakota, until Mama found a tavern she liked the look of. Inside, I drank Coke and swept the bar counter with the ragged, wispy end of my braid.

"Gem," Mama scolded. "Get that hair off the table."

"What table?"

"Don't get smart with me, young lady." She sipped at her screwdriver, as she did every night on the road, and complained about her canker sores.

"Oo," she said. "Gosh darn," she said. She was working her inner cheek with her tongue. "Remind me tomorrow to pick up some . . . what do they call it . . . not Preparation H, that's for hemorrhoids. . . ."

"Cankaid," I said.

"Yes. Remind me tomorrow morning to pick up some Cankaid."

"I reminded you *this* morning," I said sulkily, looking at her over my shoulder with the God-you're-stupid look I'd learned that summer. I was just ten but had picked up sarcasm and superiority easily, and it made that particular trip difficult for Mama. She stared at me and sighed, a long what-am-I-going-to-do-with-you sigh.

We sat that way every night on the road, in some little beer-smelling honky tonk. If a man talked to Mama she slid ready quarters in my direction and I lowered myself from the bar stool and went to play pinball.

Mama looked so pretty when the men talked to her. She crossed her legs where she sat at the bar and held her cigarette in the air like a movie star. She puckered her pink lips, tilted her blond head back, and blew smoke high and even as steam from a whistling tea kettle. Sometimes she left her stool to play pool, or dance to the jukebox, and there were other times when I worried she'd leave the bar altogether. But she never did. She didn't want any of those cowboys. We were on our way to Montana where my father lived, the only man she ever really wanted. Every summer we made this pilgrimage to Livingston, so my father could exercise his visitation rights.

"And it's a vacation for us," she said.

But I hated the long, dusty drive across the prairie, and by the time I was ten I realized my father wasn't exercising his visitation rights at all, my mother was enforcing them.

My father faithfully sent us money every month, which made him godly in my mother's eyes. And every month Mama set aside a bit of this check for our summer vacation. They'd never been married. Our summer visits, I believe, were meant to correct that, or to at least give them a chance to get to know one another, something they'd neglected to do before conceiving me. I knew this through overheard conversations and playground cruelties. Once Jesse Baker even called Mama a "waitress whore," and though I didn't know what it meant, I sensed it was a very bad thing, too bad to ever repeat to Mama.

The next morning, driving again, Mama looked away from the road and studied me. "You'll be a young lady soon, you'll need a proper haircut."

I grabbed at the sides of my head and gripped each braid tight in my fists. I hadn't reached my goal yet, which was to get my braids all the way down to my butt.

Mama smiled. "One day you'll be ready. You'll see. No hurry," she said. "Maybe we could at least cut you some bangs."

I scowled at her. Only the prissies wore that neat little fringe over their foreheads. I parted my dark hair straight down the middle and Mama spent a bit of each hurried morning weaving it into the thick long braids I was so possessive of.

"Draperies," Mama said. "Pulled so severe to the sides like that, you look like you're wearing Grandma's living room drapes on your head."

"No bangs," I said loudly, and put an end to it.

....

My father was in the yard when we passed through his split rail fence and pulled in on the gravel driveway. He waved at us and walked toward the car with his big white-toothed ranch smile.

"All the ranchers have beautiful teeth," my mother whispered, still in the privacy of our car. "You pay attention. You'll see. I think it's all the minerals in the water out here."

My father was a hired ranch hand, and lived alone in a small rambler that he owned just outside of town. It was situated in a cozy valley not far from the ranch where he worked. He had a spotted springer spaniel, Pepper, and a horse, Cindy, that I had named on one of my earlier visits when Cindy and I were both very new. She was a rich caramel-colored horse named after a baby-sitter I adored who cared for me on the nights Mama waited tables at the supper club. That was her second job. Though it was only part-time, it wore her out. "But the tips are so good I'd be a fool to give it up," she sighed routinely after work, as if it were part of the job, the way she closed up for the night.

"Well, you made it," my father said, opening my door, which I realize now was an insult to Mama. He tugged my braids, took a long look at me, and hugged me toward him with one arm.

"Frank," Mama said. "We made it all right. I swear that drive gets longer every year." The gravel crackled under her feet as she turned to reach in the back of our Pinto for her bag.

"Marlys," my father said, and walked around the car to greet her with something that resembled a hug, but it was clear to all of us that the gesture didn't come easily.

"Well," Mama said, fidgeting in her discomfort. She set her bag on his Montana soil with a thud. "Here we are." She lifted her pale, bare arms and spun herself around, sniffing the country air. The yellow skirt of her sundress blossomed as she turned.

"I got us some steaks," he said. "Hope you're hungry. You like steak, Gem?"

"Mm-hmm," I nodded.

"That sounds wonderful," Mama said. "We haven't had a decent meal since Michigan." Mama liked uncomplicated foods, and uncomplicated living in general.

Mama freshened up inside, I played with Pepper, while Frank started the grill and fussed with our meal. We ate quietly at a picnic table on the deck. It was a time of adjustment. Only Mama disturbed the quiet with silly nervous questions, as if she were afraid silence would erase her. "How old is Cindy now? You still working at the Gregg Ranch, Frank? It sure is a beautiful evening isn't it, Frank? How do you keep everything up so nice, a man alone? And where'd you learn to cook so good? Gem, can you imagine, a man cooked this wonderful meal?" Her questions were like needles poking endlessly, trying to stitch us together with conversation.

I ate silently and noticed how beautifully blue Montana was—hazy, dark mountains, periwinkle sky.

....

My father always planned every day of our visit, like camp. He had a schedule of his plans near the phone in the kitchen, which even included alternate outings for rainy days. It made me a little sad to read it, as if he might not know what to do with me if he lost it. The week passed with trail riding, white water rafting, a visit to a Grizzly museum, a rodeo, and a swimming trip to the hot spring pools at Chico Lodge. Frank invited Mama to join us on some of the quieter excursions.

At the rodeo, I sat between Mama and Frank with a blanket across our knees after dark. Frank drank beer and Mama and I ate popcorn. As the night grew cold we huddled our legs tight for warmth, just as if we'd all been roped together. Mama covered her eyes every time a cowboy was tossed into the air.

"I don't see how you can watch those men hit the dirt like that," she said, shuddering. "It's a wonder they don't break their necks. And it's terrible the way they upset the animals so. Poor things," she cooed.

Frank laughed, "You're out West now, Marlys. Life is rock hard out here."

I liked sitting between them while their words floated across me, light and comforting as mountain air.

At Chico, Mama drank daiquiris and soaked in the hot pool. In her trim yellow swimsuit, with her blond ponytail curling down her neck, she reminded me of a pretty lily shimmering in the water. My father and I tossed a beach ball in the big pool and drifted on air mattresses under the hot sun. I felt so fancy, afloat like that, wearing the bright pink sunglasses Frank bought me. Mama laughed when I got out. "With your braids waving on top of the water and those giant glasses, you look like a rain forest bug."

I raced to the mirror. I giggled so hard I thought I'd pee my swimsuit. Mama was right; she always was.

We all ate burgers at the bar, and Mama and Frank played pool. I played the winner and I believe Frank was a little surprised when that turned out to be Mama. "I'll be damned," he said, shaking his head and handing his cue over to me. "Your mama's good."

"Yep," I said.

"Yep," Mama said, and gave me a secretive wink. We both saw that Frank was just a lousy pool player. It was a real vacation that day, for all of us.

I don't know what Mama and Frank did after I went to bed at night. I'd hear music and their low voices. Once I got up to use the bathroom and saw them dancing in each other's arms. I stood and watched a while from around the corner. Mama looked so relaxed with her eyes closed and her head against Frank's shoulder. Her pink lips were fixed in a small smile. I was happy for her, happy that she had a week away from waiting tables.

....

On our last morning Frank took me fishing, leaving Mama behind in the luxury of his air-conditioned living room.

"You two have fun," Mama said. "I'll have dinner for you when you get back."

"That'd be nice," Frank said. "Make yourself at home."

So my father and I went trout fishing in a stream in Yellowstone Park. On the drive there he pointed out buffalo and mule deer. Then one lonely moose standing majestic and dumb up to its knees in a swamp. We stopped to gawk at him a while. He lowered his head in the water, then raised it again and shook his antlers dry. The low early morning sun seemed to hold each droplet bright and still in the air.

Driving again, Frank asked, "You like fishing, Gem?"

"Sure." I looked out the window of his pickup as if to study my honesty on the mountainside, and soon corrected my answer. "Well, I'm not really sure, I've never done it. It sounds fun." I tossed a long braid out and pretended to reel it in. Frank laughed, showing all his big, white, friendly teeth. He was handsome. I'd never noticed that before. I had his dark hair and his high forehead that Mama called a sign of intelligence.

It was a cool sunny morning. Frank pulled the car off the road and we climbed down the bank to a quick little river. The wind in the pines made the same shushing sound as the river, and I sat on the rocky bank and listened to the noisy mountain quiet while Frank got our poles ready. He didn't say anything, just threaded line and tied knots and fingered through his tackle box. I tossed a rock into the river with a plunk and Frank startled and turned to me. "Hey," he shook his head. "Don't scare the fish."

I set down the rock I had ready to throw next. He hadn't scolded me exactly, but I felt I had failed at fishing, something I knew was important to him. It must have shown on my face.

"It doesn't really matter," he said. "The fish we're going to catch aren't even here yet."

"Really?"

He nodded. I picked my stone back up and pitched it. My father winced, then laughed. "They *are* on their way, Gem. No more rocks, okay?"

"Sorry," I said.

My father fished the way my grandma did her needlework, carefully, surely, and yet absent-mindedly. He made small talk with me as he tugged and cast and fiddled with his line. Sometimes I thought when he was done he would pull a completed tapestry up from the water and not a fish. But he did pull in fish, with a matter-of-fact pride that I admired. Big ones he placed in a net he kept in the water, and little ones he threw back. "We'll catch him next year," he said, skillfully and tenderly removing the hook from the slow, pulsing mouth of a tiny one. He didn't toss it back, but gently lowered the fish into the water and sent it swimming away.

Every time he caught a fish I dropped my own pole and went running to his side, sticking my face up close, inches from their filmy eyes. I moved in so tight to my father's work it's a wonder he could work at all, but he never minded, never slowed down the task or pulled away from my curiosity and amazement.

I caught the biggest fish that day, a rainbow trout that my father greeted happily. "That's not only a keeper, Gem. That's a prize. A fine fish you got there. A real fine one."

We admired my trout turning slowly in the air on the end of my line. We looked at his mouth and gills, then studied his bright sparkling belly.

"These are clever and evasive fish, Gem." My father shook his head at my beginner's luck. "It's not easy to trick one of these guys onto your line." Suddenly he lifted my fish high in the air and declared, "Dinner." He patted my back. "We can go home now."

Back at the house Frank put our fish in a big cooler on ice outside, and we returned our gear to the shed.

"Gem caught us dinner," he announced, walking into the kitchen.

My mother was unpacking groceries at the counter. She had what I recognized to be the fixings for pork roast and stuffing, a meal she took pride in. I knew it was meant to impress Frank, a farewell meal.

"You've been shopping," my father said cheerfully, but still managed to sound a little disheartened.

"Well, yes, but we don't have to eat this today," Mama said. Her hip was against the counter and her face looked fragile. We did have to have it that day, though, because the next morning we would leave for Michigan.

"It'd be nice if Gem could eat her catch," Frank said, with a delicacy that embarrassed me for Mama.

"Oh, sure," Mama said. "This here's nothing. We'll just throw it in the freezer and you can fix it some other time."

At home she always complained about the price of pork roast and only fixed it for special occasions.

"Well, no," Frank said. "I can see you've got something special in mind."

"There is nothing more special than fresh trout," Mama said, but I could tell she didn't have her heart in it. She pushed the groceries to the back of the counter, as if we wouldn't notice them there, as if she suddenly wanted nothing to do with them.

"Let's make the fish for lunch," I chimed in.

"Oh, honey, your father doesn't have time to sit around and eat meals with me all day and into the night." I realized she was feeling ignored. Frank and I had taken off on a different adventure every day, usually leaving Mama behind to do who-knows-what, read magazines, smoke, watch TV, all things she could have done just as well at home.

Frank abruptly went outside. Mama and I watched from where we stood as he walked around the yard picking up things that had been lying out there all week, an empty flower pot, a fallen branch. Finally he sat in a lawn chair and folded his hands in his lap.

I started toward the door. "Your father's not used to having folks around all the time, Gem. Let him pout this out alone." Her voice was stiff with irritation. She turned and went down the hall.

Pout? What had just happened? We came home happy. It was the first time I had an inkling that their relationship reached beyond me.

That night we had fried fish and pork roast for dinner. My father filled up on the fish and took only a polite sample of Mama's meal.

Later, on that last night in Montana, I packed my suitcase and said good night. I had forgotten to say good night to Pepper and climbed out of bed to find him. My parents were in the living room sipping drinks in the dark. My mother's shoes lay on the floor near her chair.

"You've done a fine job with Gem," Frank said.

"Well, she's a good kid," Mama said, and poked at her shoe with her toe. She gave a demure shrug, just as if he'd said she was the prettiest thing at the dance.

"And won't she be a beauty?" Mama said, "with your long legs and dark hair?"

My father smiled at his contribution. "And she's got spunk," he said.

"Well, she sure does have that," Mama said. "And you might as well know, it is not always so easy to appreciate."

Frank laughed. They were sitting in dim lamplight. Frank set his drink down and said seriously, "I know it hasn't been easy for you, Marlys."

Mama sipped her drink and looked at him expectantly.

"I'd like to see more of her," he said.

"We could do that," she said. "Maybe we could come at Christmas."

"Well, I was wondering . . ." he said. "Wondering if you think Gem's old enough to travel alone now."

Mama stared at him a long time without even blinking.

"If I sent her a plane ticket, I mean," he said.

Mama looked dumbfounded. I don't think she'd ever imagined the visits carrying on without her.

"I'm thankful that you kept us in touch all these years," he continued. "You knew something about blood that I never learned." He paused but Mama had nothing to add. "I'm grateful," he said.

There is nothing more interesting to a ten year old than a conversation solely about that ten year old. I was thrilled at the notion of traveling alone. I twisted a braid around my finger and held my breath, waiting to hear Mama's answer.

"I'd like to be a real father to her," Frank said, leaning earnestly toward Mama.

Mama set her drink down. "A *real* father lives in the same house, at least the same state," she said. She shoved her feet into her shoes and stared at them. They sat in silence for a moment. My father stood and walked to the window, gazing out into the dark.

Mama was sitting straight up, her back stiff and her feet set firmly together on the floor, staring at Frank's back.

Still facing the outside darkness, he said, "Well, I can't be that real."

"I didn't think so," Mama said, with a voice that made it sound as if my father had failed at something.

"I'm afraid you won't let her visit," he said.

"That's not what you're afraid of," she said.

He studied the dark night while a stillness grew up around them, thick and stiff as a pine forest.

It was Mama who finally spoke. "She can visit, Frank. She'd want to. I won't keep that from her."

He turned back from his stubborn silence. "Thank you."

....

The next morning we loaded the car. I said good-bye to Cindy and Pepper. I set my bag in the back seat and hugged my father.

"Maybe you could come out for Christmas," he said. "You could fly on an airplane."

"Sure," I said, but I knew I wouldn't. It wouldn't be Christmas without Mama.

Frank walked around the car and hugged my mother. "Good-bye, Marlys," he said. "I'll be in touch." He held her a long time in his arms. Mama rested her cheek on his chest. He kissed the top of her head and smoothed her hair. "I'll be in touch," he said again.

Mama got behind the wheel and gave him a long, full-armed wave from her window, a sweeping wave that took in Frank and all of Montana. The gravel turned and crunched beneath the tires of the Pinto.

We started home. Mama's eyes were ringed red and her hair was pulled into the quick ponytail she wore around the house. I realized then as we wound our way out of the mountains that it was never me, or at least not only me, that Mama longed for my father to love, and I hurt for her, as if I'd stolen something from her, something that was meant to keep her young and hopeful. There'd been a hole in the sky all my life that she'd been trying to wriggle into and I closed it that summer simply by growing up. It was as if all her years of dreaming had just been swiftly and carelessly whittled away.

Though I knew it was unkind, I couldn't help myself, I wondered aloud about my next visit, when I would take my first flight to Montana alone. "What is airplane food like? Can you flush the toilets up there? I couldn't possibly go at Christmas, Mama. I'd miss you."

"Let me have some peace and quiet," she said softly. She looked so tired.

She sat heavily back against her seat as if she were being pushed home unwillingly. Many times she looked across at me and smiled a kind, sad smile that I was helpless in front of, a smile that made me feel flimsy all through.

"You are my best work, Gemmy," she said, and delicately traced her eyes with a finger tip.

I scooted across the seat, rested my head on her shoulder, and curled toward her. I tied my long braids around her thin, bare arm and gripped her with both hands on the place where her muscle should have been. We took our last trip together that way, side by side in the Pinto, back across the dry, empty prairie.

....

Still, Falling

To a photograph by Sarah Charlesworth

As the woman falls
past other open windows,
her skirt flies up
to hide her torso,
so her legs seem roots,
her waist a stem,
and her skirt a blossom
velocity has forced to bloom
in the wind of her descent.

We contemplate her passage
down a chute of air,
study her open mouth
as it fills with sky.

We cannot know the reason
she is there, suspended
above some pitted sidewalk;
we can only stare, our shoulders
aching with the weight
of her inevitable arrival
just beyond our reach.

MARGARET HASSE

Bean Fields

They labor along the straight lines of their
parallel rows, the farm boy, the town girl
earning an hourly wage for her college fund,
weeding, staying even with each other,
learning they like each other's smell.

He has the slight acrid burn of green leaves.
She, catnip—residue of shampoo—
her hair streaked shades of brown
like the fizzy tassels at the top of corn.
His tom body yowls in the back yard

of his brain that he wants that minty weed.
She, too, longs for the end of the row
when they will sit in the bed of the dirty truck
against warm rubber tires, drink
lemonade with tongues so keen

you could map the exact spot where
the sugar of desire does its dream business,
where the lemon pulp—call it
her education plan, his religious training—
persists in its tart denial.

A bean in its ripe casing hangs on a stem,
three fuzzy lumps in its throat. One for the boy,
one for the girl, and one for how the hinge
of what might happen to us swings slightly,
opening here, closing there.

....

Bathroom Horror Stories from the End of a Century

Story # 1.

A man comes into the rest room of a department store—a well-known national chain. An older man. Mid-to-late sixties. When he's seated and going about his business, the toilet inexplicably flushes, filling the bowl to the rim. Unaware of the impending disaster, he remains seated, jumping up only after a shock of cold water reaches his buttocks. He pulls the last three inches of paper from the tube, but, to his dismay, the back-up roll does not tumble into place. (Note: he had, as men his age will, judiciously checked on an adequate supply of paper before selecting a stall.) Spying no feet in the neighboring booth, he decides to seek relief there, but in order to get there without having cold water run down his legs and into his new pair of suede shoes—purchased earlier that same day at the Florsheim shoe store—he has to dismount from the seat and remain in a squatting position. He duckwalks between booths. I mind my task.

Story # 2.

McDonald's. Same mall. A Thursday afternoon. Daniel Allison, a sixteen-year-old distributive education student, is carrying out his duties, which include cleaning the rest rooms twice during his shift. He discovers a triangular-shaped wedge of cooked hamburger floating in the two urinals and in all four toilets. Each wedge is about the size of a quarter and has been cut precisely, as if by machine. He fishes them out with a slotted spoon and then proceeds to complete his duties.
We do not speak.

Story # 3.

Spend enough time in the bathroom and you soon realize that, when it comes to toilets, one size does not fit all. A maintenance man with whom I have had need to become personally acquainted confides in me that on a daily basis persons like you and me—ordinary people with no more ill intent than a firefly—are regularly blocking up the apparatus (as he prefers to call it) because, really, they need much bigger openings and more water pressure. He assures me that the majority of these people—men and women both—are not flushing anything particularly exotic down there—although he has freed things from pipes that he claims would gross out the world's most jaded adolescent. He says that mostly these are just plain folks, except for the fact that their business (another term of art) comes out bigger. He says that doctors have a name for this—megacolon—and that there should be a special section in the plumbing supply store for patrons with this condition. He speaks with great conviction and claims to be able to identify every toilet in the mall by the sound of its flush alone.

I am not a pervert. It is important to me that this be understood up front. I am talking about love here.

An anniversary approached. I was broke. As you will see, that is the point of the whole thing.

I am an aspiring (read: unemployed) musician involved in a difficult relationship with an impossible woman who just happens to be a graduate student in psychology. According to Trish, the aforementioned impossible woman, the reason that I am unemployed is that music is a feminine attribute and that as your average gender-repressed African American male I have allowed my subconscious creative life to be stymied for fear of being classified in my own head as something less than a man. Trish is always saying things like this, often in response to questions like "Have you heard the new album by the Dave Matthews Band?" and "What should I wear to the audition?"

Trish is, of course, the reason I have been frequenting various men's rooms at a large suburban shopping mall that shall, to protect both me and the "integrity" of her research, remain nameless.

If you have ever yourself had more than a little time on your hands (read: been unemployed) you can well imagine how I got into this mess. Let's all say the line together, shall we:

"As long as you're not doing anything...."

Why people should assume that sleeping until noon, eating a big breakfast of Doritos, assorted cold cuts, and domestic beer, and spending the afternoon hoping that today is the day that *Days of Our Lives'* Sammi finally gets hers is "doing nothing" is beyond me. It's the nineties: there are more of us out here than people would like to imagine, purposefully frittering away our afternoons. You can see us every day, sipping our lattes in Calhoun Square, catching a matinee at the multiplex. You say to yourself, how can these people stand to be doing nothing? How can they afford to? Or, you best believe if that were my son, I'd light a fire under his ass. But this misses the point, really—this worrying about idleness and lack of ambition. Americans! Being an artist is hard work! Sometimes a person has to sit on his butt for a spell and let the well refill. (I might suggest you mind your own business, but, as we shall see, such is hardly my prerogative.)

I've digressed.

Trish and I were sitting in Annie's Parlor, a burger joint not far from the building where she pursues her studies. I had just come off what I thought would be a promising audition with a band named Dutch Elm Disease, a group that claimed in the local trade rag to be looking for "hip dudes with unusual instrumentation to round out progressive sound." With my dreadlocks and my aspiration to be a rock-and-roll violinist, I figured I'd hit pay dirt. I'd fantasized fast cash, instant millions, an ostentatious anniversary present for my beloved. Speaking of whom, she'd asked me to meet her for a late supper.

"I've had a breakthrough," she said to me, crunching her Caesar, mucus-colored dressing dripping from her upheld fork. "This is the research that will establish my career!"

I scarfed my bacon smoky cheddar cheeseburger as if hordes of starved refugees from nearby undergraduate dorms would at any moment storm down Fourth Street and snatch it from my callused fingertips. I smiled. I was happy that she was happy. Her good mood somehow made me feel less guilty for the anniversary trinkets and tokens that, alas, did not appear forthcoming. The audition had been a bust. "Unusual instrumentation" turned out to mean shop vacs, chain saws, and other high decibel garage appliances.

Trish dropped her fork on the table and sat up straight in the wooden-backed booth in a way that thrust her rather ample breasts toward me in what I thought was an intimidating and aggressive fashion. "I have come upon the dissertation topic of the decade," she announced.

"Congratulations," I said through a mouth full of medium rare meat. I nodded, fake enthusiasm vibrating the length of each 'lock. Trish was always coming up with "dissertation topics of the decade." All of them had some sort of militant, if tangentially feminist, slant. In the year we have been together she has triumphantly announced and then rejected theses on "Thumb Sucking and Bed-Wetting by Males in Matriarchal Households: An Analysis," "The Hostile Remote Control: An Extension of the Male Ego," and "Power Rangers, Ninja Turtles, and GI Joe: Action Figures and Bisexuality Among Preadolescent Boys." Suffice it to say that for one bizarrely complex reason or another, those projects petered out, no pun intended. So I had no reason to expect that on this particular night I would be hearing anything promising.

"George," she said to me, "I've gone down a lot of dead ends, but this time I'm on to something."

And then she got all misty eyed and held her hands in front of her mouth, the way they all do when they're about to share some turgid little secret or start in on some crap about how you haven't been picking up your gym socks from the floor or scrubbing out the sink after you do the dishes.

"I'm gonna need a lot of love and support," she said, blinking back the tears and biting on her lower lip in that way that drives me crazy. So crazy, in fact, I was temporarily distracted, was not paying attention to the details. My by-this-point well-honed instinctive response should have been, "Oh, shit," but instead I said, "I'm there for you, babe. You know that."

"Good!" she chirped, and she smiled and then ordered herself one of those humongous hot fudge sundaes, which we shared. Lip biting.

Hot fudge. Who doesn't love a woman with a good appetite! My distraction was complete. I figured I wouldn't be hearing any more about "the dissertation topic of the decade" until she ran into some kind of snag with it, and frankly, my dear, I didn't give a damn.

Imagine my chagrin when later that night—post-coitus, as they say in the literature—the whole idea in all its sordid psychotic glory got sprung on me.

Now I don't know about you guys, but when I'm done, I'm done, if you know what I'm saying. It's like when the last sperm heads by on its way to the exit, it flips the switch to the brain that says "closed for repairs." I'm out! And there, by the way, would be a research project for you. So, I'm laying beside her, well down the road to never-never land, and she's curled up next to me, and this is her idea of a good time to announce:

"I've got this theory."

"Mmm," I replied, which I also would have responded to "Here's a million dollars," or, "How would you like an audition for Hootie and the Blowfish?"

"It goes like this," she said, or at least I think she said that. I take no responsibility for the accuracy of her words. She says, "You know how you guys in the bathroom have those urinals lined up on the walls? And how in the row there's always three that are at a regular height and then there's one that's down lower than the others?"

"Mmm," I said.

"So, I ask myself. I say, Trish, how is it that you guys decide which one to pick when you walk in the door? That's assuming, you know, that they're all available for use and everything. So, the theory is that the guys with the big, like, you know, the big . . . penises, choose the tall ones, and the other guys with the like, you know, small ones, you know—the ones with the self-esteem problems and everything—will go to the little one. How about that?"

To reiterate, this is what I *believe* her to have said. "That's great, honey," I mumbled in reply. Or something to that effect. And then she probably said something about how much she loved her Georgie-bear and then the next thing I knew it was morning.

That is more or less how I find myself a regular frequenter of public rest rooms.

Story # 4.

This guy brings his son into the bathroom. A little tow-head. About two.

"Ready, slugger," Dad says. He rolls down Junior's tiny stretch pants and his didy and then holds the little man up in front of the urinal and tells him to "go for it."

"I don't want to go in that one!" Junior wails.

"Okey dokey," Dad says, and steps to his right, holding the kid in front of the next convenience.

"I don't want to go in that one!" the kid wails.

Dad works his way around the room and eventually runs out of options. "There are no more choices, son," he sighs with exasperation. Junior, who is pants-down on display like some deviated ventriloquist's dummy, has been unceremoniously releasing dribs and drabs of urine while being carried through his stations of trial.

"I want to sink the circles!" the kid cries.

"Aha!" says Superdad. "I believe I can accommodate," and he reaches into a pocket and throws a handful of brown stuff into the urinal, after which Junior does his business like the champ we all knew he was. Later, I take a look in there and find the porcelain dotted with what appear to be Honey Nut Cheerios.

....

So the next day at breakfast time—hers not mine—I am gotten up and told that "as long as I'm not doing anything" and since I have sworn to support her on her difficult journey, she expects me in her office this afternoon for data collection training.

I yawned, smiled, took a big slug of coffee, and told her, sure, I'd be there. It just so happened I was fresh out of pressing engagements. I was also fresh out of cash, desperate for whatever bit of spending money this "job" might bring. There were clubs to hit, networks to net, agents to schmooze. (And that annoying business about an anniversary present.)

It was the ringing of cash registers, I guess, that drowned out another sound in my head—the buzzing of a gnat of suspicion worrying its way around the back of the brain, biting here and there, reminding me to watch my step. I had a vague notion there was something to be cautious about, but at certain times of the morning and night—like just before or just after sleep—the line between my waking world and sleeping world has been at best dotted. Reality means nothing, and forget about logic. I had spent many childhood midnights convinced that Martians were right outside my bedroom window, sucking people into the earth and planting chips in their necks—just like in the movies. I can still, after a late night at the bar with the boys, be convinced that that's true.

Trish shares an office with another grad student in one of those nondescript, circa 1940s behemoths in the middle of the main campus of the U. I peddled my bike over there at the appointed time and sauntered down the jury-rigged corridor where they stashed teaching assistants and junior faculty members. The whole building stank of reheated coffee, sawdust, and a scent I can only describe as academic despair.

Seated in her office was a woman a few years younger than us—early twenties—with the fresh-faced look of the dairy princesses at the Minnesota State Fair. With her sharp blonde Scandehoovian good looks, one could certainly imagine her carved out of a couple of hundred pounds of freshly churned butter.

"This is Brigid Johnson," Trish announced.

Brigid would have been my third choice. After Ingrid or Heidi.

"Brigid's going to conduct the interview portion of our study."

I told her I was pleased to meet her. Brigid was wearing a very chaste-looking blouse and skirt, and, over that, a white lab coat. Her hair had been pulled back into a severe bun and her mouth set primly in a pout. I felt the stirrings of lust and the stirrings of other things less esoteric, more specifically things located in my pants. Ms. Johnson was a knockout.

"Let's get started," said Trish, crisply. She slammed a clipboard onto my lap—directly onto my stirrings, as a matter of fact—and gave me a look that let me know that at some time in the not too distant future there would be hell to pay for ogling this white girl.

Trish caressed the back of her Afro and turned a page on her own clipboard. She closed her eyes, thrust her nose in the air, and, reopening them, emerged as doctoral candidate Patricia Banks-Summers, specialist in human communications and gender psychology.

"As you know," she began in this somewhat stentorian pitch, "proper methodology is the key to successful social science research, and at the heart of its methods is the art of data collection."

Brigid nodded. And since, with her lab coat and her shellacked-looking hair, she appeared to be the sort who knew what she was doing, I nodded, too.

"Ladies and gentleman, I don't think I can emphasize to you enough how critical your jobs are, so in this, the first of our inservices, my goals are as follows . . ."

Inservices, I says to myself, emphasizing in my head the plural just the way I'd heard her emphasize it out loud. No doubt for my benefit. And like this could go on longer than, say, your average fast food meal. I raised my hand.

"How long?" I asked, glancing at my watch and waving the other hand in the air for emphasis.

"Save your questions," she snapped, and then proceeded for the next hour and a half to give us a lecture on the entire history of anecdotal research in the twentieth century.

I zoned out. I entertained various fantasies if only for the purpose of keeping my brain alive and not falling asleep on the spot. I tried to imagine myself on stage at the Orpheum Theater, bowing away, smack in the middle of a bunch of guys who had some talent and some musical integrity. I tried not to imagine Brigid, naked, posing for a horny and deranged butter sculptor in the dairy barn at the State Fair. I have never had a thing for white girls, even back in high school, where white girl fever among young African American males can sometimes be more contagious than herpes. Yet there was something appealing to me about her cool honey-blonde good looks, the way they contrasted with her tough—and I thought feigned—I'll-not-hesitate-to-remove-your-masculinity-with-this-nail-file demeanor. I made a mental note to not accidentally find myself in a discussion about any of this with the future Dr. Banks-Summers.

"Mr. Randal, for example," Trish said, and I looked around for my father, who is the only person I know with that name. I realized it was me she was referring to, and that I had no idea what the current thread of the discussion was.

"If, in the men's room, you were, say, to go up to one of the research subjects before he established his trajectory, or, let's say your own position as observer were to place you in such a location so as to unwittingly influence the subject's positional decision-making set, well this is what is meant by contamination."

So, I says to her, I say, "I beg your pardon," and she said to me, "It's just an example for Ms. Johnson. We'll continue, if it's not too much trouble for you." And she and Ms. Johnson gave each other a look and Ms. Johnson rolled her eyes and Dr. Banks-Summers inclined her head in concurrence.

The trouble, it seemed, was only beginning.

Story # 5.

Brigid, it turns out, gotten away from the colloidal confines of the University, is a hoot, a regular Roseanne. In addition to a whole repertoire of mostly unrepeatable in polite company stories about "farm life," she tells me her own personal bathroom faux pas.

In the story, a pre-university Brigid had just returned from Washington, DC, from some sort of future farm wives' conference— which she described as an excuse to "get a bunch of small town broads to the big city so they could really party their asses off." She arrived back at the Twin Cities airport on a Sunday night and was "righteously hung over" and had to make an important detour to the john on her way to pick up her luggage. Upon exiting, she found herself the subject of many odd looks. A man at the luggage carousel said to her, "Excuse me, Miss, I don't mean to be fresh, but you have your dress caught in your panty hose." She claims to have—in order to really give the girls something to talk about back home—fished her dress out of her panties right there for the whole world to see.

This story makes me crave a butter and sugar sandwich.

Back at the apartment, after the "inservice," Trish removed her University frock (a shapeless paisley job that looked like something that might have escaped from one of those love-ins from back in the old hippie times) and went into what can best be described as a classic black-woman-rage-fit.

As is often the case, "Why do I put up with this?" was the first line out of her mouth. I sat on the couch with my head sort of pulled in like a turtle's might be, waiting for this tantrum to run its course. I learned this coping mechanism at a young age at my father's side. Growing up in a house with a mother and two sisters—all of them black women—I knew better than to do much more than to hope that no knives or other sharp objects crossed her line of vision before the storm passed. Following Daddy's careful example, every once in a while I cleared my throat and said, "Now, honey, let's talk about this."

"Talk about this! Now the nigger wants to talk. Of course, when Trish wants to talk it's a different story, isn't it? Isn't it?"

In full fit, Trish always refers to herself in the third person. Most of them do this. They also, of course, have to lean right up in your face for the "isn't it? isn't it?" part. Research on the best practices tells us to sort of suck our teeth and shrug and say "Well . . . ."

And if you're lucky at this point—as I was—the response will be a rapid intake of air and a storming out of the room to the tune of "Why do I bother?"

I sank down with my beer into our support-sprung couch, my knees up to my neck and with the depressing realization that there was now no way I would be getting out of becoming a public rest room surveyor.

And at that moment, should there have been any doubt about the general direction of things, a stifled, strangled scream came from the kitchen, and I thought, Uh-oh.

"Is this the last beer? Is it?"

"Well, yes, I guess," I said. "If you don't count this one." I held up my almost empty.

"Not even bread to eat in this house," she screamed, and she started in on the long expected tirade # 2.

"Where do people think food comes from?" she asked the air. My father had also been known to go off on this particular fit. In his case it was usually triggered by me or one of my siblings making the mistake of asking for an advance on our allowance. Trish ranted and raved for a good ten minutes about the high cost of everything.

And then, just when I assumed she was finished for the night, just then, she dropped the big one.

"Not that certain people have any money to buy food with," she said.

Under different circumstances I would have called a foul here. She'd gone for the sorest spot of all, the tenderest of the tender. What had I done to deserve such rancor? Well, of course, we all know what I did, and, as if on divine cue, it was time in her remonstrations to put it on the table. Her big bomb. Her ace.

"And I saw where your eyes were this afternoon. Don't think I didn't notice."

As always, I opened my mouth and raised both hands in innocence and surrender.

"Don't you dare deny it," she said. "And a professional colleague, too." Trish put a hand to her head, gently, just as if it were made of the most fragile new-spun silk and she were afraid of destroying it with her touch. She seemed to pant slightly, almost as if she had been underwater. She set her beer down and looked at me with a hand on one hip.

"You wasn't really looking at that ugly scrawny thing, was you?"

"Oh, baby, no!" I said. And I beckoned her with my arms.

She sashayed over all sassy, hand still on her hip. "Better not have been," she told me. Her eyes were squinched shut, but a sly smile was etched across her face.

The situation, as it was, called for a little private in-servicing, if you know what I mean.

As they say in the movies, fade to black.

Story # 6.

The custodian of that large department store tells me that one just wouldn't believe the things people flush down the toilet. Rings, receipts, false teeth, cosmetics. He says that apparently people have no conception that there's a pipe underneath there and a very sharp turn early in the journey. Occasionally, he says, people will stand over his shoulder waiting for him to fish out some treasure that they have impulsively flushed and then changed their minds about. Once, a rich lady flushed a strand of real pearls and then came to him begging to get them back. Luck would have it an end had snagged at the first joint and he was able to pull them back without too much trouble. He reported that the woman clutched the filth-covered pearls to her bosom and cast her eyes to the heavens.

"Old girl didn't give me a tip or nothing," he concludes, eliciting my deep sympathy.

The maintenance man's name is Murray. We've gotten close. It's the circumstances, you understand.

....

As you can imagine, when you are standing around a bathroom all day with a clipboard, people tend to get the wrong impression. Pretty quick I learned the importance of befriending the store manager and the security people. And Murray. Brigid is the saving grace—we have sort of a tag team thing going where I do what you might call the on-the-spot visual survey and she stands outside the door and button-holes them for the big interview.

While I refer to the guys who come through the "research station" as "the one in the trenchcoat" or "the bald guy," Brigid likes to refer to her subjects as johns. A bombshell with a sense of irony, a punster par excellence.

She says, "You know that third john that came through last hour? Boy, was that guy a card."

Now, you'd think guys wouldn't want to discuss their bathroom habits with some woman loitering outside the men's room, but Brigid has her ways. She uses her breathy little prairie voice to stop them—that is if they aren't already stopped by her Nordic good looks. And also, even though you wouldn't think so, most men are apparently perfectly happy to answer question # 18, which is where Brigid gets to inquire as to whether they would describe their penises as being small, smaller than average, average, larger than average, or large. Brigid is a diligent researcher. At the end of a good day, she hands over to Trish manila folders full of raw data.

"I hope we get enough of a sample to support my research," Trish said.

I told her I thought we were doing okay, that Brigid said we were hustling four or five johns per hour.

"Excuse me," she said to me, and I thought, Oops.

"It's kind of what she calls them," I told her.

"George Randal! That is a lie. I pay that girl good cash money to act professionally and I know she would do no such thing."

Rather than argue the point, I seized the opportunity to once more explore our most sensitive turf. Since a large part of being a musician is spending a certain amount of time in seedy joints listening to the competition and commiserating with the boys between sets, one needs a stake to stay in the game. (And then there was that anniversary gift thing.)

"Speaking of money," I said. I raised my eyebrows.

"Yes," she said. The woman gave no quarter. Literally.

"Evidently Brigid's been paid?"

"Yes."

"And, well, basically Brigid and I are working together?"

"Yes."

There would be no mercy.

Coincidentally, I first met Trish in one of those aforementioned seedy bars. I was playing a gig with the band I was in—the Rancid Oreos—shortly before we broke up over what is commonly understood to be artistic differences (which is the preferred euphemism for what happens when the people in the group who suck get resentful over being told so).

We were jamming when out of the corner of my eye I spied the finest hunk of black womanhood I had laid my eyes on in years. She was a healthy looking girl with one of those big old-fashioned Angela Davis Afros that haven't quite come back into style just yet—the hairdo from the posters we all had in our bedrooms when we were babies. I sauntered over real casual and struck up a conversation. I introduced myself as a struggling musician. She presented herself as a young academic who was doing quite well, thank you very much, with a full-ride graduate fellowship and a generous living stipend. To make a long story short, I have basically been here at her place ever since. Our one year anniversary approaches. One ought at the very least to get the woman a little trinket or something, oughtn't one?

Story # 7.

When I was little I always wanted to know what the inside of the girls' bathroom looked like. This is really important information when you are in second grade. In Miss Dahl's class a whole mythology grew up around that other room. Jimmy Schmid told us that it was very plush in there. He said that it was painted pink and that there were couches in there for the girls to lie down on, and they needed those couches because they were girls and sometimes, because of the way girls were built differently than boys, girls needed to lie down. Randy Berneisen said that Jimmy Schmid was a liar and that the girls' room was nastier and smellier than the boys', and he had two sisters and thus living proof that girls were pigs. Randy insisted that in the same way the boys' room had urinals lined up against one wall, the girls' room had a wooden bench with holes in it that could seat ten girls at a time. When you are seven and whispering with a bunch of fellows about something as important as this you do not worry about evidence or contradictions. Both stories are from reliable sources and therefore true. One lingers at the drinking fountain across from the girls' room door hoping to get a peek inside. There is nothing to see but a wall of glazed beige bricks. The real story is on the other side of those bricks, but no one has nerve enough to actually run in and look around. And besides—if you were seen, the girls would tell. They always tell. Everything. Miss Dahl patrols vigorously at the fountain outside the girls' room. She has taught second grade for twenty-seven years and knows what boys are like. No one dares turn around.

In third grade Miss Hagar took the boys and girls on separate tours to visit the various lavatories. Apparently our class was notorious and she thought it prudent to squelch the rumors once and for all. Everyone giggled a lot, but in reality we were all deeply disappointed.

....

"Check out this doofus," says Brigid. An obese man is striding toward our men's room with a definite purpose in his gait. Brigid and I are returning from a lunch break in one of those ubiquitous

133

and frighteningly identical food courts that have sprouted in shopping malls like so many diseased mushrooms. Through her kewpie doll lips Brigid sucks up the remnants of a thick vanilla shake. Despite what you've heard, there is no correlation between glamour and food intake. Only a teenage boy with a tapeworm could pack in more food than this gal.

"Dude walks like he has syphilis," Brigid says of the big man, and my mind immediately jumps to the logical question: what could this woman possibly know about the way men with venereal diseases walk. But, alas, our Brigid is a complicated woman. Don't let the peaches-and-cream exterior confuse you. She has lived, I tell you. Lived.

She says, "I'm thinking of buying Harvey some of those silk pajamas they have over in that lingerie store. Black. Maybe red. What do you think? Would you ever wear something like that?"

Harvey is Brigid's "old man"—some guy from her home town that she claims to have hooked by the short hairs and dragged to the Cities to be househusband and father to her kids.

"I prefer to sleep naked," I tell her, and a noise comes from her throat that sounds like the sort of thing that might come from the mother vulture to call her young ones to supper.

"You don't look like the type," she cackled, and then ordered me to "get my ass in the john and see where fat boy did his business."

I complied.

At home that night Trish is in another state. A fit is imminent. One of her sisters had been on the phone again.

"You! Men!" she says to me as I come in the door.

"Us," I say in reply.

Apparently another one of the Banks-Summers sisters had again washed up on the rocky shores of love. Five black women, single, gorgeous. Such calls came as regularly as invitations to switch phone companies.

"Which one is it?" I asked.

"Tamara," Trish sputtered in rage.

"And what happened this time?"

"Oh, you know," she responded, exasperation dripping from her lips like acid.

And I did know, I guess. He was shiftless, untrustworthy, cheating, the possessor of unspeakable personal hygiene traits.

"I'm sorry to hear this," I offered. "Tamara will bounce back. She's a strong girl."

"But how many more times?" Trish wondered. "How many more times."

At our next-day research site I encountered Murray polishing the chrome to a high shine. I figured maybe he had some answers.

"You married?" I asked him.

"Twenty-two years and counting," he answered, and I wondered who was doing the counting and just what was being kept track of.

I told him that twenty-two years was a lot of time and asked him what was the secret.

"Secret. Secret," he said, scratching his frowzy chin. I might just as well have asked for the recipe for Coca-Cola. He polished around and made a lot of those contemplative *Hmm*-ing noises. He left and Brigid and I turned a couple of tricks.

I passed Murray on our way out of his store. Brigid and I were headed across the mall to work a fresh patch.

"A good marinara sauce," he said. "I think that's the ticket."

Story # 8.

My own personal contribution. It isn't pretty but it goes something like this.

In college I hung out with a bunch of guys. Artists and musician types. Folks like me. We had the same cynicism as other cultured types our age had, including the requisite disrespect for authority. We knew everything, had all the answers, and were harsh critics of those who didn't toe the party line. Nothing drove us more crazy than pomposity—those pseudoscientific creeps who trotted out their little facts, a solution often scavenged from an obscure academic journal, or, worse, from a twenty years out-of-date textbook. And while I could go on about the various brands of self-righteousness we subscribed to, I won't stray from our theme—which relates directly to what we did to those who dared cross our path. There were a whole series of cruelties, actually. All kinds of "noogies," and a range of caustic arm "burns" and "titty twisters," many named after various ethnic groups who had supposedly perfected the torture to punish their enemies, all involving painful skin-on-skin abrasion. We were fond of "wedgies," too, an obnoxious process whereby one grabbed a handful of the label side of a fellow's underdrawers and proceeded to yank upward. (For an "atomic wedgie," one suspended the victim by his underwear from a clothes hook or any other convenient hanging device.)

We were, of course, young men, all of us still teenagers, acne-scarred, hormonally-challenged, each one badly needing to get laid. These are the sorts of things boys do.

And worse.

There was this one fellow. A cellist. Very talented and everyone knew so. He has a first chair at a prominent symphony, and if I called his name some of you would no doubt know who he was. He was also, like many prodigies, abrasive, rude, and arrogant. Thought he was, knew he was, better than the rest of us, regardless of our chosen fields. He would lord his gift over us, sputtering through his lips, dismissing our every feeling or belief. One night in the lounge, we were discussing determinism or fusion or some other topic that seems pressing when you're nineteen.

"How sophomoric," the cellist said. I can't recall the specific context, the words or idea that set him off, and really, they aren't even important. But that is exactly what he said. How sophomoric. And at that point there was no signal amongst the rest of the guys. We just got up, en masse. We picked up the cellist, five or six of us, and we carried him as if he were a canoe to the bathroom where we chose the grossest empty stall we could find. (A men's bathroom in a college dorm—need I detail gross?) We upended him over the commode, aiming his head toward the chilly pool of water there in its porcelain bay.

"No," was what he said. "No, please." He did not struggle and he did not scream out for help. Only said, "No."

We lowered his head ever so gently to the water. And then we flushed. That's all.

This is what's known as a swirly shampoo.

We uprighted the cellist and let him go. He wrapped his hands around his face almost as if to create blinders. He sank to a crouching position and remained there shivering. We stood and watched. Waiting. Nothing happened. With his plastered-down hair and wet frame we could see that he was no more than a kid. A lot like the rest of us, I guess. Scared. Cold. Humiliated. Eventually we left him there and wandered back to the lounge, back to the usual BS.

After that night we didn't hear much more from his sorry ass.

....

"Damn, damn, damn!" Trish curses and sweeps the pile of surveys to the floor. "Anomalies, coincidences, pointed exaggeration: there's not one thing here I can use."

I stand behind her and rub her shoulders. "Don't be discouraged," I tell her, though I know that she is.

"I need more data," she says under her breath. But I know better.

We've been down blind alleys before. Frequently. It's only a matter of time before she sees this for herself. I'll spare her what pain I can. In a week or so I'll bring up again what will ultimately be her actual thesis topic: her synthesis on the state of black men and women in America. The ongoing battle. Our wishes, fears, and dreams, and our hope for one another.

"Too facile," she'll protest. Then there'll be another big fit.

Trish believes it is her destiny to discover some original truth about the world. That will never happen.

"Just a little more data. There's something going on in those men's rooms. I just know it!"

It is the end of the millenium. All the good topics have been taken. Everything there is to know about the turgid lives of men and women has already been ingested, digested, regurgitated, and examined under a thousand microscopes. Still she persists.

"I'll stand in the toilet for the rest of my life for you, honey," I tell her, and she tells me how sweet I am. I chill us up a bottle of that cheap champagne and light a bunch of candles in the bedroom. I slip one of those Grover Washington, Jr., CDs into the box and I make her forget there ever was such a thing in the world as a false paradigm.

In the morning there are five twenties on the dresser and a note thanking me for being her little Georgie-bear. The things we do for money and the things we do for love.

Story # 9.

There actually was one other time in my life I was authorized to go into the ladies' room. Other than second grade, that is. It was when I was the night closer at the college library. I had to go in to make sure no one was hiding in the stalls, someone who might later try to hoard extra reserve materials, throw books out the windows to avoid the theft detector, party, sleep, or—God forbid—study. I always knocked and announced myself before going in. At first I had pretty much the same feeling as in second grade—disappointment. Then I started reading what was written in the stalls. I confess that up to that point in my life I had never read such smut. I was shocked and even now a few years later my brown face turns a shade of red at what I discovered there.

....

And so, students, as my Trish might say—my darling, my sweetie, my employer, my love—what is it, after all, that has been learned? Well:

First, industrial toilet paper is very chafing.

And, air freshener is a sedative.

And, water comes in other colors besides clear.

And, all shit stinks and all little boys want to make pee pee in the big one.

A man walks in the door. He plucks a booger from a clump of nose hair and gives himself a self-satisfied smile.

A child wanders the stalls aimlessly. His mother cracks open the door and inquires as to whether we are finished. From my vantage point, at least, we have yet to begin.

Who knows what it is makes a man choose one woman over another. Or vice versa, for that matter. In a world full of choices what is it that drew me to the one with the clipboard, the mouth, the somewhat disordered academic mind? The one with the living stipend and with the heart that knows no limit. Perhaps it is that butter clogs arteries and the other choices—well, the other choices are more often than not just plain boring.

In the discount jewelry store at the mall where we work—Brigid and I—I dropped a good portion of the hundred on a fairly tasteful but cheap tennis bracelet. The rest I saved for a night at the club with the boys. A man has to earn a living, does he not.

So I am kept. Most of us are. It's the real thing you learn in the men's room, but don't tell that to Trish. It is the metamessage of the graffiti, it is what is whispered in our brains while our pants are around our ankles and our vulnerable parts are exposed.

I stand, clipboard at the ready to take the measure of my fellow man. Enter, kind sir, and be of good cheer. There are six well-maintained stalls at the ready, and, just now, there is no waiting.

JOHN HERSCHEL

To an Orange Cat

Warren, I've been sleeping badly.
I'm awakened by my own breathing
like the whap of lug nuts
at the Discount Tire Store.

And you sleep so well, so soundly,
I can even see your dreams
undulating under your fur,
like all the birds you never caught,
gliding and drifting
and crossing inside you.

GREG HEWETT

Unnatural Acts

Somewhere along the line
of highway I lost nature

maybe finally coming to
the understanding

I am nature
even amid green

destination signs and
six lanes of asphalt

where anything wild gets cut
so far back the country seems

distant as the broken Lakota
outside Sioux City

hitching a ride
who didn't want

my company
just the ride and I can't say

I blame him
I have the luxury

of talking
about the nature

of things and what
I feel as I

drive a Toyota for hours
naturally

just to see
prairie in a park because

that's the only place left
and because every

once in a while
I need or think

I need to watch
clouds moving

into each other
uninterrupted

and I think I need to feel
the sun tan my forehead

and think the prairie needs me
to witness cactus

rise exhausted from winter
or antelope speed away

to the purpling ridge
called Blue Mounds

where I burn
sage to purify

some vague spirit
or conjure an Indian

holy vision before retiring
to the Sunset

Motel that doesn't
even face west

in a room where I'll recount
buffalo I counted

from the bison-
viewing platform as I fall

into dreams of stampede
in which I find myself

naked riding bareback
bow poised just like a sculpture

by Remington or a western
only instead of the noble

giant's eye blessing me
it simply reflects

my whole world
as the shaggy

horned head
says to me *You're going out*

in style, baby,
one thing you've got is style,

heh-heh,
style, style, style . . .

....

What Speaks to Me Now

I'm talking with my roommate, who continues with
a man I predict will destroy her. She stares past
my words as if destruction were just another noun
such as Denver or Detroit, a place she might visit

and easily leave with her same pink skin. I hear her
on the phone in the next room, *okay, okay, okay,*
a small bird fluttering in a silver cage strung
with her own wounded desire. Outside, our two cars,

held hostage by the cold, won't take us anywhere.
The ugly grind of metal in twenty-five below
creates a simple loss. It's as if the part of us
that craved the world finally brittled and now

refuses our stupid ideas about need and want.
So, we putter in the apartment, small tasks
now important, two women waiting to love
something right. I am older and more sensible.

Everyone knows this, but mostly it's gotten me alone.
She says, *he's my best friend.* Fine. I drop it.
But it's amazing how death and life can simply be
a matter of perspective. Behold, the corpse

of healthy relationships stinking on the sofa:
Look, it's breathing. No, it's not. So, she places
a mirror above those lips that grabs a little
lung mist. I agree in part. Someone is exhaling.

Someone knows what's going on. This cold is
a terrible symbol, a wave of dangerous feeling
that will shake us blue, all our deficiencies scattered
across the kitchen floor. What speaks to me now

is the present tense: *Hougen, this is what you've got
to work with and tonight when you cry, you'll cry
alone, the idea of your God-Husband swimming
above the bed, salting your face.* It's not a complex life really.

Sometimes I feel it coming, Deity between my ribs,
clearing his immense throat. A certain kind of rapture.

Aftermath

The morning is like others:
the blinds open the eyes of the house,
cars in a blue silence paused like animals
at the curb. Somewhere in the city,
small murders occur but not here in the aftermath
of teaching, people, the fabric's small tears.
The hour is calm, as in childhood with its measurable
desires. December snow is a kind of tenderness,
a white mitten pressed against the heart
stilled to the wingbeats of the Holy Ghost.
In the kitchen, the kind hands of Bach still say
yes, rising from drafty rooms in old Germany.
Earlier, I watched my face in the bathroom mirror,
decided I was here, tasted the sacred
packed into everything. Beside the big window,
amid slow huffs of coffee, the sun widens
the lake above an open book, the ice breathes
in the light where fish are scraps
of cold silk, and the healing snows spread out
their workbench. In this music, I learn
to see the world again, a motor grumbles
to life, the pen gives its ink.

SUSU JEFFREY

....

I Call the Hill

After Joy Harjo

An earth breast
in the west
where the year stretches
from aurora borealis
to midsummer,
each sunset an Appaloosa
prances the fire
out.

That hill I inherited
after years of looking:
three trees, a horse
the wind.
I rediscover
the hill
holds time.

I plant trees
on a rectangle
in a city.
On paper, I own
this land.
This land owns me.

But the hill
I own like my skin,
my story.
The land is her own.

After D. H. Lawrence

died, it took a long time
for someone to love
trees as much as he did.

It took a long time for
the larch to stop its mourning,
for the little variegated elder
to snap out of it, grow up
into the sky.

The copper beech felt sick,
totally sick, made vain
by Lawrence he could not
become humble again for
fifty years.

Painters and writers
movie makers and photographers
kept busy choosing trees to do,
but to do is not to love.

Arbor Day became a sham,
no one taught the children
to love the trees they planted
so the trees were on their own,
roots stamped down by little feet,
a placid circle of cocoa shells
around the trunk sending up
a scent the trees could not place,
having never been given a cup
of cocoa in their lives.

D. H. Lawrence was so tormented
in his humanness he gave all
holiness and wisdom to the trees,
and the trees accepted—which of them
might have resisted such honor
from such a tangled genius?

Slowly we learn to love trees again,
as the century closes its heart to us.
Slowly we stroke the bark, or drive
a benign stake into the elm, pump
the medicine in, slowly we learn
to feed the birds so they will stay,
make their homes in trees we tend
as the planet shudders.
Trees breathe. We want their beautiful
breath on our skin.

....

Little Photograph

From a distance, a father stands in the sunshine with two little girls. All three are wearing bathing suits, and even in a black and white snapshot, the big meadow and tree-covered hillside beyond are lush with summer green. It is middle-class America. The grass is cut, and all the bare feet rest safely among its blades.

The dad holds his daughters with an open hand pressed flat on each girl's body. I can remember the gorge rising in my throat from that pressure. It did not make me feel protected. Sometimes I couldn't hold in my urgent desire to squirm. If I were without my sister, he would hold me with two hands, pulling my shoulders back to straighten me, his fingers digging into the flesh just below the shoulder knobs.

Years later, at my house in Brooklyn, my father would grab at our cat to stop her from coming in the house. He grabbed her at the shoulders in almost the same way and she bit him deeply in the soft space between thumb and first finger.

In this photo, my sister clasps her hands affectionately around the hand on her chest. I'm the smaller one, with hands rigid at my sides and my knees locked.

My father, already bald, looks very young. He was twenty-eight when he married my mother. Charlotte is about eight in this picture, making him perhaps thirty-seven. My parents' marriage was precipitated by Charlotte's conception. Would they have married anyway?

My mother had a leather jewelry case with a false bottom in which she kept a dried rosebud, from her wedding bouquet she told me, and a letter, folded up, which I never read. Years later my sister was shocked that I never had. The letter was from our dad, said Charlotte. He wrote how he would have asked her to marry him regardless of the circumstances.

But would she have been willing to marry him?

My father is staring at the camera, which must have been held by his sister, our Aunt Bim. She has placed us well. The sun slants from the left so no one has to squint into the light. We are at Camp Allegheny in West Virginia, where my sister is a camper and Bim an administrator and keeper of the camp store. I'm a visitor, along with our dad. Our brother was born earlier this summer, and our mother is still in Charlottesville, with her mother.

It's wartime—the summer of 1942. People talk a lot about "the war" and live placid lives with summer vacations. My dad and I have come on the train from Lynchburg, where his parents live. It's a two-hour trip and I think we go back late this night. I don't remember staying over. Not until three years later when I'm old enough to go to camp, and Charlotte is no longer interested, do I remember the big canvas tents the camp provided, the plank walkways, and the night-long insect noises.

Come in closer on this picture: I look up unwillingly. My stomach sticks out, stretching my shiny bathing suit, while my sister's stomach is flat. I was already tagged fat or potentially fat by my socially-conscious mother, who lost her place at the edges of New York society when she married a middle-class intellectual from the South. This loss may not have been fully apparent to her at the time this photograph was taken. During the winters, we lived in New York on the Upper East Side where my sister and I attended a famous progressive private school. But a fiction about our different-ness had already been instituted.

My knees are locked and my thigh muscles bulge from the tension. I already need to run away. By the following year, I will have divorced my parents. Beginning in these months, just after my brother's birth, I snapped the bond of belief in their authority. This happened because I permitted myself awareness that the bond was shabby, untrustworthy. This happened because I saw—with knife-sharp clarity—what was missing in their relationship with their new baby, my brother. So often, a betrayal of love is blinding, numbing, but for me it was not. It was a blazing recognition demanding response. The precocious wrench—my divorce—drained more energy from me than I could have imagined at three times the age of five, and has taken me a lifetime to recover from.

Here, in the photograph, I am yet in hand; that is, in a sunny meadow a big hand pushes against my chest. My Aunt Bim is speaking. I hold still. I do not smile.

....

Milk Run

"*Geh doch! Schnell.* Get going." My mother's hands shoved me out of the door. Her voice followed me across the yard. "And get him home by noon."

The pickup truck lurched away from the barn. The flat morning sun hit the scratched windshield so he didn't see me until the truck was almost on me. The brakes grabbed and the milk cans bumped across the metal truck bed and slammed into the back of the cab. He looked angry but I jumped in anyway.

"I just want to go along for the ride."

His large head swung over to glare at my mother. He stared down at his red hands.

"Shoulda said something before. You could have been run over— like a dog in the road."

It was eight o'clock. The empty ten-gallon buttermilk cans bounced in the back of the truck. The two full cans of milk were still. That was all we were getting, two cans. We used to have eighteen cans a day before we lost the herd. Then he liked having me count them; now he didn't bother.

We turned off the bumpy gravel and glided onto the smooth black tar headed for town. A tractor was making its first cut on a field of young green alfalfa. A parade of sleek black-and-white cows ambled in a long line back to pasture after the morning milking. He tried hard not to look.

The town looked deserted. Our two cans clattered down the rollers of the can-chute into the creamery. Dad talked to the butter-maker as I filled the buttermilk cans from the holding tank inside. We got back into the truck. Dad looked over at me.

"Time for a quick one," he said.

There were two saloons in the town of seventy-seven people. We'd go to Kellner's because Jimmy'd been one of our hired men. I liked it better than Walter's. The bar was fifty feet long, brown and shiny, curved at one end like a big hook. The bar stools were all silver chrome with shiny red seats. I hooked my heels in the rungs of the stool and spun around. I tried for three complete turns. Two-and-a-half was the best I'd done so far. Two-and-a-half turns faced me away from the bar and toward the light. Above the big poker table the words Kellner Bros. Saloon & Dance Hall appeared backward on the huge window. Last month I watched the sign-painter paint every word of it. My father ordered his second beer. Ten cents. I got a Butterfinger, a small one. It was dark and cool inside. Outside, the light had a faint yellow glow from the yellow grocery store across the street.

Herb, our neighbor from two farms over, came in for a beer. He had a repair over at the blacksmith's. Eldred, the barkeep, stood washing last night's glasses. On a fluffy white towel he set the shiny glasses in perfect rows. He wiped them and asked about the previous Sunday's game.

"*Was hast du mit dei' Geld gemacht?* What'd you do with the money?" Eldred was in charge of foul balls at the town team's base-ball games. I shagged them for him for five cents apiece. His brother Jimmy was the town pitcher. Jimmy kept all the balls and bats in the trunk of his car when he worked for us. He'd let us play with them during the week.

Herb pulled his pocket watch from his bib overalls, looked, then left.

"Let's go, Dad. I want to leave, too." He wasn't moving. I watched the Hamm's beer sign to figure out how it worked. There was a waterfall and the shadow of a bear passed across the pond in front of it. I watched the clock. The hand moved toward ten. If we weren't out of there by ten, it'd be at least noon.

The first beer-truck arrived at 10:14. I didn't have to turn around to see which one. Eldred reached for Dad's half-empty glass and poured it in the sink and set up a bottle of Cold Spring beer. It was free. The barkeepers liked to make the drivers feel at home. I held the screen door as he wheeled the cart. Full cases in first, out with the empties. Then the big kegs, as big as the ones they had at weddings.

The driver bought a round. He knew what I wanted: a Payday bar, the big one.

Dad talked about his string of luck. He'd always been lucky. You peeled back the label of a Cold Spring and if there was a red number printed there you'd get a free case. In June he found three numbers in one case. He got the three free cases and found four more in them. In July two cases. Mom didn't think it was good luck. The Grain Belt truck pulled in. I collected a Baby Ruth, another big one. My teeth ached.

Everybody moved to the curved end of the bar. The Grain Belt driver was trying to talk German, too, but he sounded Luxemburgish. Dad, the drivers, and Eldred played wahoo. It's like the crazy eights we kids played except jacks were wild. They played for money. I watched and rubbed the smooth cigarette burns in the bar. Dad wasn't so quiet anymore. He had two Cold Springs and a Grain Belt lined up. I went over to the big window and looked out. A few town kids walked by. I ducked down so they couldn't see me. They'd started to make fun of me for being in town so much. They were saying stuff about my dad. At least I didn't live in town; being a town kid was really low. I stacked the poker chips and looked at the pictures on the wall, a bunch of dogs in clothes, playing cards. There was a strange dog with a pushed-in nose—I'd never seen one of those.

A truck roared up to the front of the saloon and Lester staggered in, his face all twisted up and red, his cap cockeyed over one ear. He'd gotten an early start. The town drunk, they called him behind his back. He didn't live in town, though; he was a farmer, too. Tuesdays he'd drive to the brewery for a load of mash to feed his cows. They said he got a head on before he left the brewery, drinking free beer in the tap room there. Sometimes it would take him all day to drive the eighteen miles home. He stopped as often as the beer-truck drivers did. The brew-water leaked through the cracks in the trailer-box and ran down the slope toward Stifter's Blacksmith. I went out the door and followed the track of water. Anton smiled as I walked up the concrete ramp into the cool dark shop.

"*Ja, Bubchen, da kommst du wieder.* Yeah, here you are again. Your dad at the saloon?" I nodded.

Anton was pounding out the points on plowshares for the fall plowing. A couple of them had been sharpened so often he had to cut back the point and resharpen it. He ran the grinder and the hot sparks fell dead at his feet. The windows were so dirty the light went out instead of in.

He nodded and I turned on the bellows. The belt swayed from the electric motor mounted near the ceiling. He shoved the plowshare into the heat with tongs. The sudden glow lit his heavy apron and smoothed the leathery face behind the dusty lenses of his wire-rimmed glasses. The tiny scars on his bare arms looked blacker than his skin.

I liked to look at all the horseshoes. The west wall was covered with shoes of all sizes—little pony shoes up to shoes for the largest work-horses. I could always find a new one I hadn't seen before. There was a new one—big flanges on the sides, something to fix a faulty gait, I guessed. I wished I'd seen him shoe horses but he hadn't had to in a few years. He was sure horses would be back. I told him it was 1951— too late for horses. He gave me a long slow look before he spoke.

"Angelus bell's gonna ring soon—maybe you ought to get your dad on the road." He stopped. "*Neh, bleib doch.* No, stay a while," he said. He smiled and tried to be nice; he never had any kids.

We talked about iron lug-wheels and the new rubber-tired machinery. Anton was welding now. It was hard not to watch the flash of the white arc. I liked the way his shadow jackrabbitted around the dusty corners and high black reaches of the rafters. He told me again I'd ruin my eyes, so I sat on the high sill of the back door. I looked at his iron bar-stock all stacked in rows against the back wall, protected by the slope of the overhang. There was a barn-yard right out the back door. Over to one side was Payter's new house, one of those modern ones—no upstairs, just one floor. It had a pic-ture window, the first one anybody had ever seen.

The previous fall we had come to town one night for a Forester's meeting and it turned out that it was Halloween, too. The town kids told us about trick or treat. We'd never heard about it before. A cou-ple of them had paper masks, a few had peck-sacks with holes for their eyes. They wanted us to make our faces black with a cork that had been burnt with a match. We wouldn't do it. We went to Payter's house back there behind Anton's shop. They'd just built the house that summer. Trick or treat we yelled but no one came out. The town kids swore they could see Payter peeping around a corner to see who was there. We yelled again, trick or treat. We went back to Walter's and bought a root beer, shook it up, and sprayed that window until the root beer ran down the new siding.

The back door slammed and we ran to the street. Payter was coming at us, a dark shotgun in his hand. I was imagining trying to explain to Dad how I'd gotten shot—over a dirty window yet! We ran across the road, stumbling through the tangled brush behind the creamery and into the trees that filled the back yards of all the buildings on the west side of the road. *C'mon, run.* Over the machinery behind the garage, past Walter's saloon, through another farm yard, and up past the church. Low branches whipped at our faces. Payter was still behind us. We crossed to the ball diamond and headed back to Kellner's through the mown back yards of the east side of the road. Behind the dance hall we hid in the weeds by the prickly plum trees until we heard his door slam again. We schnaufed like work horses, we were so out of breath. The light from the Grain Belt sign made it easier to find the cockleburs in our clothes. We headed over to Walter's and sat at the bar real quiet until Dad was ready to go.

....

The sun was too hot in the doorway so I watched the welding again until Anton flipped back the black hood that covered his head and caught me. I went back to the saloon. The sun was right overhead. I sat on the cool side of the steps. If I hunched up against the wall I could sit in the shade of the overhang. I saw Cletus walking down the middle of the road through the waves of heat above the tar. He looked as if his bottom half was melting. He turned at the church sidewalk and disappeared behind the church hedge. I heard the big door slam. I could almost see him turn the corner and enter the little corner with the swaying ropes. He'd untie the big loops that kept the bell-pulls out of us kids' reach. The Angelus bell rang out. It was noon. "The Angel of the Lord declared unto Mary. . . ."

I stood up too fast and had to grab the door. I was swaying like a drunk. I thought, is this what it feels like? Once I was inside my eyes adjusted. The Grain Belt man heard the bells, too. He slapped his huge belly. "Gotta go, lot of stops." He ordered one more round, a Baby Ruth. I wondered if that was his own money or did the brewery give him money for the road? Dad had three beers in front of him. Cold Spring must've left while I was at Anton's.

"C'mon, Dad, let's go. I'm hungry. Mom's got dinner on the table."

He growled, "Let 'er wait. Want some ice cream?" I nodded. Eldred knew what kind. I'd been eating on that five gallons of chocolate-marshmallow ice cream all summer. Must have been nobody knew about it but me. Triple dip. Fifteen cents.

Dad was getting louder now. He was starting to swear. I moved down a few stools. He noticed.

"Too good to sit next to me? Think you're better than me?"

I was glad when Lester distracted him with another last round. Another Payday. As Lester left I watched him rev up his truck. He popped the clutch and a dark stream of water wet the dry pavement under the trailer. The water left trails that raised little welts in the dust. His truck backfired a good-bye.

As soon as he left there was lot of talk about Lester—all the cars he'd wrecked, about fishing, how Lester'd holler at the fish. He'd show the fish how it was done—he ate a worm right out of the can. "Remember that time he had ten of 'em dangling out his mouth? Ugh!" Lots of head shaking and big smiles. Everybody there knew they were better than Lester.

We used to fish with Lester sometimes. It was never boring. Dad said we needed the fish. The bangs thing hit Dad pretty hard. He acted like we'd lost everything, that it was his fault. Then they were talking about how Lester caught a perch and quick bit the head off it. I'd heard that one before. Then there was a new story about how they hauled him up to the jack-farm, that's a mental hospital, to dry out. Lester was crying in the back seat when nobody would play poker with him. Two big guys were back there to make sure he didn't hurt himself. He had lost his driver's license but later he talked the sheriff into a produce-license so he could haul his eggs. He always kept a case of eggs in the back there as an excuse. It didn't work, though. They don't let you haul eggs forty miles from home. Now, once again, he was back on the road without a license.

I looked out the window at our truck. The covers of the buttermilk cans in back had popped in the heat. The curds pushed up the lids and spilled down the rusted sides onto the truck bed. We were buying buttermilk from the creamery to feed the hogs that were supposed to pick up the slack and make us some money after we lost the cattle. We weren't starving.

I was fed up. When I said I didn't want a third ice cream cone I got a mean look and he turned away. He was waiting for someone else to come in. It was hot and Lester's smoke was still hanging in the sloping blue-gray sunlight over by the poker table. I could've eaten another ice cream cone but I thought I better not. I had to show him I wanted to leave. Eldred left when his brother Jimmy came in for the afternoon and evening. His fresh white shirt glowed like a candle in the mirrors behind the bar. I liked Jimmy. As soon as he saw me he gave me a pack of gum. He was feeling sorry for me. The phone rang—it was Mom. Jimmy said *"Ja, ist schon fort.* He's on his way." But he wasn't.

I asked Jimmy if I could go into the dance hall. It was dark and musty; the big flaps over the screened windows had been down all week. The stale-beer air was stuck in there until Friday morning when Eldred raised the flaps and propped them open with long poles. I liked the fringe that was all but hidden in the darkness of the ceiling. The fringe started at the center and went out in a big thick spiral. It was like Christmas tinsel, but longer and wider. It swayed back and forth, silver, blue, and red, as if it were alive. They had dances there every Friday night except during Lent. The bishop didn't allow Saturday dances. Last Mass was at ten on Sunday and the bishop didn't want anyone to miss it. During Lent Jimmy had roller skating instead. Maybe the bishop didn't think roller skating was fun.

I pumped the player piano and the same old polka echoed through the empty hall. There was only one old yellow roll—a "Whoopee John."

At Christmas the Catholic Aid had a party there. The year before, the new teacher, the one with the big ideas, got up the town kids in three-cornered hats and a bunch of them danced on the stage singing "Mien Hut hat drei Ecken." It was her first big success. It was Nicklaus Tag, December 6, so right after the drei Ecken dance St. Nick and his two black helpers came in with big gunny sacks on their backs. Everybody called them his niggers. We all lined up for the brown paper bags of candy and peanuts that Nicklaus passed out. The two helpers, burnt cork on their faces and hands, were giving the bags to Nicklaus when I recognized my father's fat red hands and looked past the white beard into his smiling eyes. He gave me two bags. I don't know why no one else recognized him. I liked him that way. I remembered my job and went back to the saloon.

The door swung open and one of the town kids, younger than me, came in. In his hand he had Stoltz's half-gallon fruit jar with the handle on it. He'd come for the shoemaker's beer. It must be four o'clock, I thought, that's when Stoltz sends him. The kid stared at my pack of gum as he got on the stool next to me. I gave him a piece. First I thought he wouldn't take it. They think they're better than us farm kids. The heavy jar almost slipped out of his hand as he gave Jimmy the quarter and dime. The shoemaker lived across the street but the heat made his feet swell so he couldn't walk. He was old. They called him the Schuster but he hadn't made any shoes in a long time.

Dad was getting quiet again, his face set. He didn't like Jimmy telling him to go home so he just sat there. His cheeks were all red from windburn. He stared at his blackened thumbnail and swirled the glass on the wet bar. He had switched to the big schooners now. Fifteen cents. A fly buzzed by. The ice cream freezer stopped. Silence. We listened to a crow cry in a tree out back. Two flies buzzed as they fought on the dusty window sill. My jaws were sore. I had all the empty wrappers folded up to look like a full pack, except for the one I gave away. Two salesmen off the highway walked in but they didn't stay long. Bump and a beer, Bump and a beer. Jimmy was banging away at the flies over by the poker table. He was wading through the hanging smoke up to his armpits, sending those flies off to hell.

I laid my head on the bar and rocked back and forth. I moved to a new stool. It felt cooler but the red cover was cracked. I restacked the poker chips, red, blue, white, red, blue, white. Jimmy gave me a look and said to straighten them out. Then Cletus rang the six o'clock Angelus. Finally. We were leaving. One more stop at the can. I looked up at the little window then down at the little salt blocks. My stomach hurt. It was my own fault.

We stood on the steps, blinking like badgers. The heat was intense from the wall that faced the afternoon sun. We could smell the hot buttermilk from the steps. Dad adjusted his pants and took a long look at the stinking cans, at the buzzing black horde of flies adrift in the slop. And then he crossed over to Walter's, the saloon across the street. "Aw, c'mon, Dad! Let's go home! No, I won't go in. I won't! I'll wait in the truck."

"Suit yourself." The screen door slammed.

I opened the truck door. The handle burned in my hand. The heat was rolling out, must have been two hundred degrees. I can't sit there, I thought. I crossed over to the shaded bench in front of the grocery store. It was cooler there. The sharp smell from the stack of binder twine prickled my nose. I swung my legs and watched a car pass down the main street that was also the state highway. I didn't recognize the people. Right away Berthold, the grocer, came out to join me. He must have been watching me from behind the window. We didn't say much, talked about binder twine, mostly, how they make it at the prison, twine and license plates, how it doesn't sell like it used to. All the farmers were selling their threshing machines and buying combines. He was selling more barbed wire though—to farmers trying to keep their diseased cattle. Berthold went back in.

The sharp smell of the binder twine faded and I remembered the foul smell of burning hair from the previous spring. Coming home from school, I could hear the commotion in the barn from a hundred yards away. I ran into the barn. The cows were bellering and slamming their heads against the stanchions. The air was filled with dust from the straw, making little halos around each light bulb. Two government men in striped coveralls were hunkered over in the curved manger, trying to attach a steel nosehold to one of the first-calf heifers. They cursed and jerked her head upward. The rope raised puffs of dust as it snaked over the water pipes. The short guy grabbed an electric branding iron and stamped a large B into the jowl of her upraised head. Her eyes rolled upward and out of sight and the heifer crumpled to the floor, her neck held tight by the pain of the nosehold.

The B was for bangs, the two government men call it brucellosis. The brand marked diseased animals that had to be killed. A stream of smoke came off the sizzle of the branding iron. I ran to my dad who was waiting across the barn near the silo door. "Bangs," he said, and he tugged his cap down lower over his eyes. He looked like he was shriveling up, like he was watching his life going up in smoke.

We lost most of our milk cows that day. They had been aborting by themselves the previous fall—that's what bangs does—the calves are born dead with tiny bodies and slimy blunt heads. Farmers didn't have any choice. They had to sell them or put up double fences to make sure the cattle never got out. Even that wasn't legal if water ran through the pasture, as it did through ours.

So we called Werner, the trucker in town. We loaded them in his trucks. I remember when Werner came back from South St. Paul, he handed my father the check without looking at him. The government doesn't pay much for diseased cattle.

We had five cows left, not enough to make it worth the trouble. We kept them, though—it was Dad's excuse to go into town with the few cans of milk. Maybe we should have shot the rest. It'd have been better than this.

I used to get a funny taste in my mouth—just thinking about that smell of burning hair. We were in the pickup truck on our way to see Kempfer's barn that'd been hit by lightning the night before. It caught fire with two crops of hay in the mow. The barn practically exploded.

We rattled up the gravel to the tar road. A fine shimmer of dust rose between us from the holes in the truck floor. We drove into the sun, squinting through the fan-shaped scratches left by our worn-out windshield wipers. It'd been an early harvest that year and the fields of dew-covered oatstubble were shining in the sunlight. I pointed to the curl of smoke above Kempfer's grove a half a mile away. Through the trees, we could see the squat hulk of the smoldering barn. It was surrounded by cars and trucks, two with the doors still open. Tractors with front-end loaders tugged at the charred timbers scattered in the yard. The cupola from the roof, all huge and broken, was lying near the windmill. It used to look so small up there on the peak of the barn. There was an old shotgun hole in it and hundreds of bird-shot dents from shooting pigeons.

It was early August but the big box elder tree next to the barn looked like October—bare, withered, a few brown leaves and a scorched trunk. The swing seat was still smoking where it fell; the blackened swing ropes swayed quietly above it. Only the lower walls of the barn were left. They were made of concrete blocks. The air was still cool after the storm so our windows were rolled up. Dad pulled up behind a couple of pickups and we just stared. Through the blackened windows and doorways I could see the outline of stanchions buckled by the heat. The metal stalls sagged as if they were made of wax. I looked for the hay mow where the twins and I found a dried-out old cat. The hay mow was gone.

We jerked the door handles and stepped out. The rotten smells of burnt flesh and hide grabbed me and wrenched my insides out. Before my foot hit the ground I was heaving my guts out in a patch of bull thistle next to the truck. The stench of burned carcasses rolled past me like some horrible sin. With one hand I hung onto the door handle, my cap at my feet. My father and brother pretended not to notice and walked away. Ashamed, I picked up my cap and wiped my mouth on the short sleeve of my shirt. I staggered after them. My knees wobbled under me like an empty inner tube.

I forced myself to peer into a window. Its wood frame still gave off a wisp of smoke. Inside were the twisted, hairless forms of trapped animals cooked to twice their size by the intense heat. I noticed that cows are all the same color when you burn the hair off: their insides trying to get out through the cracks.

Right in front of me I saw Richard, one of the neighbor kids, fling open a hot stanchion. He yelped as his hand bounced off the hot metal handle. The cow's head was wedged at the bottom of the narrow V-shaped end. The hairless, eyeless head flopped into the manger. I doubled up again and had to lean on the hot blocks. Dragging a wrecked bag of bones, a tractor went slowly by. A wet trail followed the leaking carcass. On my neck I felt a firm hand that took me back to the truck. The door slammed and trapped the smell in there with me. I realized how my nose and mouth are connected to each other. Sitting there in the heat I dozed off.

I woke up when the door opened. I had a raw taste in my mouth. My head bounced against the seat-back until the smooth tar-road slid under our wheels. We didn't stay to clean up—they had a lot of help already. No one mentioned what had happened back there.

We drove home in silence, and I got to sit by the window. Afterward we heard that Kempfer hung himself on the metal windmill, next to where the carcasses were piled for the dead-animal truck from the rendering plant. He did it the quick way. My dad was doing it slow.

....

An old green coupe pulled up in front of Walter's. Three strangers. A lot of strangers came to Walter's, mostly Protestants from the dry county to the southwest. They'd vote their county dry, but they bought their liquor from us Catholics. Werner, the guy who took our bangs cattle to South St. Paul, used to wash the cow shit out of his truck and haul in cases and cases of liquor for Walter's saloon. We Catholics were shocked at how much they'd buy at one time, Scotch and other stuff we didn't drink. From a shopping list, yet.

Another car pulled up. It was Tommy who worked for the railroad. They called him Tommy the half-breed. He was the only Indian around here. He'd get real mad when the kids called him Tommyhawk. Once when my older brother was in town to have the manure spreader welded at Anton's, a couple of town kids pulled the cables off Tommy's battery and blamed it on my brother. Tommy came after him with an ax. I wish I'd seen that. He didn't get him, though, because my brother ran into the saloon.

Now Tommy was coming out of the saloon, a two-bottle bag in his arms.

I knew it was late when the jukebox started up. Nobody ever played the jukebox in the daytime. It sounded like Eddy Arnold. I was really getting sick of it. I went in. Dad had snuff dribbled on his shirt. He looked ready to fight. I remembered how he reached through a car window once and knocked somebody out at the Sportsmen's Club smelt-fry.

I was really thirsty but I wouldn't drink the orange pop he put in front of me. I went to sit in the old dining room off the main barroom. That's where we had our Forester meetings, Catholic Order of Foresters. We had shirts and everything but you had to buy their insurance, life insurance for kids. I sat at the piano but there was no roll to pump through so I just sat quietly. I must've dozed off—my head jerked up and I heard angry voices in the next room. I listened to Dad argue with everybody about anything. You name it, religion, cows, the town team. He was even talking English to the Protestants. That did it. I'd had as much as I could take. I walked in through all the smoke and I told him I was walking home. He knew I wouldn't but he drank up. As we were leaving he pulled on the screen door when he was supposed to push. It made him even madder.

I had the windows cranked down and the front-opening windshield cranked forward. I was sitting next to the window. We couldn't smell the buttermilk anymore. The cool wind blew in my face. I was awake now. It was two and a half miles home. I wondered how I'd get all my candy into the house without Mom seeing it. Home by noon— I felt sick.

The sky to the east was already dark. The trees by Herb's farm threw long, quiet shadows across the road. I looked toward the east. There it was, just like last week—that same little star in the same place, and all that empty space wheeling around it but not touching it at all. There was no one there but me.

The wind was blowing across the newly-cut alfalfa field and the sweet smell covered the smell of stale beer on his clothes. He slowed down to make the curve. I was hoping we wouldn't go on to the next town.

"*Pass auf.* Careful, we're in that guy's lane."

"What's the matter," he said, "think I can't drive?" He slowed to make the left turn. We weren't heading for another saloon like last week. The sun had set behind the grove. The light was bouncing all pink off the vane of the windmill. The pickup rattled over the washboardy road. The two eight-gallon cans were bouncing now, the reeking buttermilk cans were still. We drove past our five cows who turned their heads to watch us pass. Dad wouldn't look at them.

NICHOLAS KOLUMBAN

Morning Report on Health

You just came home from the hospital.
Your hands are I.V. blue,
shaky calves.
The bravery of being a patient.
Now they brought us a fruit basket,
honoring you—
a taste of Valentine in an altered form.
We're surrounded by plums
but live without trees.
Please eat. Eat in winter,
store a sweet planet inside you
for the times when you'll be abandoned
again.

IAN GRAHAM LEASK

When We Die

For Ewan and Ingrid

It was a Friday, lunchtime, in late October, and Calum Leith was raking leaves in the front yard with his three year-old-daughter, Fiona. The heavily wooded neighborhood was a wasteland of fallen leaves. Some of the trees had shed completely while others had yet to drop any leaves at all. The red sugar maples blazed next to yellow lindens and bare-branched elms; oak leaves were piled into dunes. Where lawns had been raked the grass was long and dark and damp with dew. The sky was very blue.

Calum's five-year-old son, Harry, was due home any minute from the kindergarten around the corner. The teacher would see him across the road and the little boy, reveling in his independence, would run home on his own. He resented it when his parents went to meet him. Calum would try to do something every day in the front yard so that he could see Harry turn the corner at the end of the road.

Little Fiona played in a pile of leaves from the huge trees on either side of the yard. Calum was not thinking so much about his children today, but about relations with his wife, Laura, which had deteriorated beyond toleration; everything was a struggle; there was no cooperation, no energy between them. She was driving him nuts.

The little girl broke into his thoughts, saying, "Daddy?"

He looked around, unable to see her, and said, "Are you hiding?"

"I'm hiding," she said in her funny deep voice.

"You've got me beat," he said, "I give up."

A burst of laughter came out of the leaves. "You can't find me," she sang.

"You're a mistress of disguise," he said, raking more leaves over her. Some of the leaves he threw onto the pile were wet and heavy, some were light and crisp and fluttered slowly down onto the pile like mummified butterflies. The leaves were still for a moment as he stood back and looked at the huge fragrant pile somewhere in which he imagined his daughter to be grinning out at him.

The pile burst open and the child, sobbing, flew to him and up into his arms. His heart felt as though it were caught in his throat. "Sweetie pie, calm down," he said, holding her tightly, "what on earth's got into you?"

Between sobs, one word at a time, she told him that she did not want to die. She did not want to be buried under the ground or burned up in a box. Calum went cold all over; that old debilitating fear of death came flooding back to him. "What made you think of this?" he asked. She could only sob. Then she told him that Harry, her big brother, had been talking about it.

The family cat was dying and Harry, apparently, had a lot to say about it.

"This isn't something for you to concern yourself with," Calum told Fiona, but she merely blinked at him. "You're not going to leave here for a very long time, little pie," he said, "All you have to do is play and be happy."

Calum didn't know what else to say, so he forced a jovial tone and told Fiona to run down the block and meet Harry. He followed her to the sidewalk and watched her sprint away. He had the cellular phone in his pocket and dialed his wife's work number. As the dial tone clicked his son rounded the corner at the end of the block and waved, his mop of fair hair catching the sunlight as he broke into a run toward his sister. A receptionist answered the call and put Calum on hold while she paged his wife. When his wife came on the line he said, "It's me. Fiona just freaked out about death." The kids were holding hands and looking at something in the pile of leaves in the gutter.

"Oh, yeah," Laura said, "Harry's been concerned with it the last few days. Because of the cat. Fiona's picking up on that, I guess."

"You didn't tell me."

There was a silence, then: "Something else I'm wrong about?"

"Come on, you vacuous little Yank, don't you think I should've been told about that?"

"You know the cat's dying."

"No, Christ, I mean Harry being upset by it."

"You can keep track of them just as well as me, you dumb limey."

"I've been in Chicago all week. How the hell am I supposed to monitor the children's mental state? You should've told me."

"Yes, oh yes, you've been so damn busy—certainly too busy to listen to anything I have to say. And besides, what can you do about it? That's life, everyone's afraid of death."

"I'm trying to work on the busy-ness."

"I know you are."

"So what do we do?"

"What can you do? It's the human condition. I've got clients to see. I'll be home early afternoon. Bye."

He put the telephone back in his pocket and watched the children approach along the sidewalk. They were not smiling. Fiona let go of Harry's hand and ran forward, shouting, "Daddy, there's a dead thing."

"Oh, no," Calum muttered, "perfect timing."

They walked back to the pile of leaves fifty yards from their lot and found a dead squirrel. It was plump, had a healthy pelt and no sign of injury. There were ants crawling on it. "How did it die, Daddy?" said Harry.

"Don't know, maneen. Maybe old age."

"He's sleeping!" cried the little girl.

"No, honey. He's dead."

....

Once inside, Harry went to his room and closed the door. Fiona played with her Barbies in front of the fire. Calum went to Harry's door and asked if he was all right. No answer. He was hesitant to just barge in. He'd been trying to give his son privacy now that school had started. He was trying to create stages of growing up, something that had not been done for him by his parents, the lack of which he felt, on many levels, was still affecting him. The cat, however, had picked the dark, dusty corner under Harry's bed as its death spot and Calum felt the need to check on it. "Is Kitty still under your bed, little man?" he said.

He heard Harry get off the bed, then a few seconds later the door opened and the little boy looked up at him with wide, moist eyes. "Is Kitty going to die under my bed, Daddy?"

"She may. It seems to be the place where she feels most comfortable."

Calum lifted up the corner of the Ghostbusters bedspread and, getting awkwardly onto his knees, looked under the bed. He called gently to the cat, then whistled quietly. The cat's ears pricked and it turned its head slowly to look at him. Its eyes shone. It was his cat; it had gone for walks with him like a dog; in fact, it had fought dogs and won—a great cat. He hadn't been looking after it lately, he'd been so busy, and his wife hadn't been brushing the cat's long fine fur so that it had balled up into ridges along its back and around the ruff of its neck. She kept promising to keep up with the brushing but she never could. The children treated it roughly, carrying it around by the neck and swinging it like a snake, and, even now that the cat was mortally ill, Fiona was likely to grab its fur and hug it vigorously. It was rather like making Miss Haversham break dance, Calum had told Laura, but she wasn't amused.

Calum put his hand on the top of Harry's head and said, "Poor Kitty doesn't look to be doing too well."

"I don't want her to die under my bed," said Harry. "That would be yucky."

"Go and get a cardboard box from the basement and we'll make her comfortable and put her in the bathroom."

"No, I'm not going in the basement."

"Oh, don't be such a . . ." but Calum caught himself—he remembered that terror, that there were invisible powers in dark places. "I'll come down with you then," Calum said.

They got a suitable box and then had to move the bed to get at the cat. They put newspaper in the box and then an old green towel and laid Kitty in there and put her in the bathroom with a dish of water. Fiona watched, sucking her thumb, and asked, "When can I play with her again?"

"Not ever," said Harry.

"She's going to die, honey bunch. We have to be very gentle and kind when someone is about to die, so let's be very nice to her."

Calum lit a candle and put it on the toilet cistern and turned out the overhead light. "There," he said, "that'll be more comfortable for her. She'll be able to dream all about her life without that glare, but the candle will give off enough light so she'll know where she is."

The children wanted to stay in the candlelight with the dying cat. Calum told them that Mummy would be home soon and that they would all have a nice lunch together.

"We don't want lunch," moaned Harry.

"We want to watch Kitty die," pleaded Fiona.

....

Calum remembered how hard the concept of death was for him to comprehend as a child. It hadn't settled on him as early as it was on Harry; he supposed it had attacked him around the age of nine or ten. He remembered the dry-throated, debilitating terror when he would awake in his bed at night and know that one day he would die. He remembered being amazed that everyone wasn't racing around in a state of panic.

Harry wasn't in a panic yet; he wasn't quite six and he believed in everything. He was proud of being a Leith and loved the family stories Calum told him about the British Isles. Harry's life was a rich mixture of British and American child culture: Teenage Mutant Ninja Turtles, Rupert the Bear, Superman, Thomas the Tank Engine, Mr. Rogers, Wallace & Gromit, Sesame Street, Postman Pat; he had every Walt Disney video and the numerous family in England would send kid videos at Christmas and birthdays.

As Calum stood in the kitchen waiting for the kettle to boil for his tea he was struck by the fact that his little boy's head was by now a computer full of stories, and for some reason he thought of leaves— leaves falling from huge trees for millions of years, rotting, laying down humus, making earth for other trees to grow in. He shuddered in his bones, understanding that that was the best kind of mortality a body could expect. A little voice on his shoulder said, *But what about the soul!* He laughed at himself and flicked the imaginary creature— something resembling a Cockney Jiminy Cricket—into the sink.

Sometimes Calum worried that Harry was ill equipped for the world he was entering; he had been brought up quietly and with care.

When he fought some older boys down the street who were bullying him he wept and got his little plastic sword and challenged them. They kicked it out of his hand and broke it; he came home red in the face and asked for the sword to be fixed with tape so that he could go back and fight again. Although this broke Calum's heart, he was proud of his son's courage. He could not remember being as brave when he was a child.

....

Fiona was in her room napping. Harry was in his room with his television on low. The cat was barely breathing. Calum went outside and got a spade and dug a hole close to the house. He found himself close to tears as he dug through the black topsoil, setting it carefully aside. Beneath the black top, a foot or so down, lay sand and gravel that smelled like a beach; he dug a foot into this too, piling it on the other side of the hole.

Laura walked around the side of the house, blazer in one hand, briefcase in the other, looking overheated. "It's too warm," she said, and then, "What are you doing?"

"Kitty's about done."

"Are you sure you want to put her this close to the house?"

"It's her garden. She used to hide in these raspberry bushes and ambush stupid birds."

Shaking her head, Laura went inside, saying, "I'll check on her. Poor thing." Calum was squaring off the floor of the hole when Laura opened the door quietly. "Cal," she said, "She's gone, I think."

He came inside and found both children standing in the bathroom looking at the dead cat. Laura told them to say good-bye, and they both bent down and stroked Kitty's head. Calum had to go into the hallway and put his forehead on the wall. He went back into the bathroom and curled the cat into her usual sleeping position. She was stiffening but he was able to push her eyelids closed. She felt light and bony in his hands, almost like a dead bird, as he settled her back onto the green towel.

Harry went into his room and closed the door while Fiona went into the living room and did one of her little dances. Then Fiona wanted to be in her brother's room and he let her and they closed the door. "Poor little things," Laura said, "Shall we bury her now, Cal? Get it over with?"

"Let's wait a bit," he replied, frowning, "I want them to see it all, have some kind of . . ."

"Closure," Laura said. "Yes, that I agree with."

They closed the bathroom door and went into the kitchen to make tea. The phone rang—it was Laura's work, Calum ate a pear, the kettle boiled, the tea was steeped and poured, sugar and milk added. Calum and Laura stood against the counters in the kitchen and drank their tea without conversing. Then the children reappeared, wanting to know what would happen to the cat now.

"Harry," said Calum, "you go and get the stapler out of my desk. And Fiona, you go and get a grocery bag from off the porch and I'll show you how comfortable we're going to make Kitty."

Calum opened the grocery bag on the dining table and placed the green towel inside it while Laura held the cat. Harry handed him the cat's earthenware drinking bowl and Calum put that at the back of the bag, then he took the cat from Laura and held it in his hands for the children to kiss good-bye. He put the cat into the bag and stapled it shut. Then they went outside and laid the grocery bag gently in the hole. "When did you dig that hole, Daddy?" said Harry.

"When you were moping in your room, matey. We'll put her by the house so she'll be near."

Fiona said, pointing, "A black pile of dirt, and a yellow pile of dirt."

Harry said, "What if we move? Or you guys get divorced?"

"Never mind that, silly," said Laura. "Would you like to help Daddy push the dirt into the hole?"

Harry shook his head. Fiona jumped into the raspberry patch, shouting, "I will, I will." And as Fiona and Calum buried the cat, Harry moved his hands over the cat's grave like a sorcerer and chanted, "In the name of the father, son, and the mouldy ghost, and in the hole you go!"

"Where does he get this stuff?" Laura frowned.

....

Harry went back into his room, closed the door. The sound of television came from inside the room. Fiona wanted to help Laura fix tea. "Oh, Fiona, just let Mama do it, okay? Say, Cal, you'd better do something about Harry, I don't like the look of this. Fiona, you can help me tomorrow, honey."

Calum went to Harry's door, knocked, and said, "Hey, little man, you want to come out in the back garden and play some cricket?"

There was a sudden thumping on the floor and the door flew open and Harry stood holding a junior-sized cricket bat that Calum had brought back from a recent trip home to England. On the child's face was a serious, strained expression. "Come on then, laddie. We'll put up the stumps and I'll bowl you a few."

Harry said nothing but went and got his stumps, gloves, balls. Calum took the stumps from him and winked at Laura as he passed through the kitchen. The little boy was plodding behind. Calum stopped at the top of the stairs and asked, "What's for dinner, then?"

Laura looked up from a pot she was stirring and smiled, "I told you this morning. Linguine with experimental fish sauce."

"Yuk," said Harry.

"Why's that yucky?"

"I don't like mental fish."

"Experimental fish," Laura corrected.

"That's yucky."

"It'll be tasty," said Calum. "Come on, let's go outside."

....

Calum knocked in the stumps with the base of the bat handle. Harry stood to the side, turning the hard red ball in his fingers. "Daddy," he said, "Galen said that when you die it hurts forever and ever and you don't see your parents ever again."

"Who the Hell's Galen?"

"My friend from Sunday School."

"Well, he's talking rubbish. He's probably heard some fool talking about Hell, which is a sick concept that the Christians invented to try and control people's behavior. It doesn't exist and you don't have to worry about such nonsense."

"Sean's mommy told him that when you die it's like being in a deep sleep forever."

"And what do you think of that?"

174

Harry's face contorted. "I don't want to be in a deep sleep forever, I want to be alive. I don't want to be like those kids on TV or the one's at Sean's mommy's hospital." He was holding back tears.

"Wait a minute, wait a minute." Calum held Harry in his arms and the boy leaned into him. "What did you see on television that upset you?"

"Those children that went in the trains."

"What children? You need to tell me more so I understand."

"The thing Mommy likes to watch when the men separate the daddies from the mommies and the kids and they never see each other again. And the kids all have to die and be burned up by the bad men."

"Oh God, she let you see that? That's ridiculous."

"It's not ridiculous. I watch TV with Mommy."

"I know, matey. That's okay."

"Why did the children die then?'

"It's hard to explain to you just now because you're a bit too young. But there are wicked people in the world who do things to people to be cruel. Sometimes they know they're being wicked and sometimes they don't."

"Why do they want to kill children?"

"I don't know. I've never understood that."

"They won't kill me, will they?"

"No. I won't let anything happen to you."

"And Sean's mommy works at the hospital where children die. Do you die when you go to the hospital?"

"Only sometimes if you're very sick. Most people are made better in the hospital. When I had to take you to the hospital once you got better quite soon, didn't you?"

"Yes, but they put a needle in me and I cried."

"You were very brave."

"No, I wasn't."

"Okay, but you don't need to worry about all this stuff right now. Your job is to be a little boy."

Calum looked at Harry's face to see if anything else was coming, then said, "Shall we pound those stumps?"

"But I don't want to die."

Calum found himself tempted to pull out all the old church nonsense that had filtered into him during his life, but he resisted it, knowing in his bones that it was wrong and would do more harm than good. And he found himself thinking of his father. What would Dad have said? he thought. And he realized suddenly, and was taken aback by the realization, that his father died twenty-five years ago. He looked at the little boy and smiled. "No one wants to die," he said, "but we all have to. It's normal. You don't have to be afraid of it, and most of the time it comes at the right time, although it seldom seems like the right time. Wars and accidents are never the right time."

Calum tapped in the third stump. His father's voice emerged in his mind and he could see his father's dead body lying in the bed by the window. He remembered the things his father said about death: *I don't give a damn about what you do with me when I'm dead, you can chop me up in little bits and flush me down the toilet, for all I care.*

The terror that had given him! He was sixteen. He had a raving atheist father; even on a deathbed the hard man: no priests, no gods, no salvation—no comfort. He was sixteen, he needed comfort. This little chap of mine's only five, he thought. How do I hold off the fear until he's strong enough to handle it?

Calum had known the truth since he was sixteen. He saw it in his dead father's eyes, and he'd seen it before his father died, the certainty. Yet he wished he'd been at the old man's side, held his hand, but he'd been out with his girlfriend buying the latest Beatles album, *Rubber Soul*. He wished he'd watched his father's soul go. The soul is a myth, yet in his mind's eye he fancied that his father, even now, twenty-five years on, was struggling in a rowboat in rough gray seas off the coast of Cornwall, struggling to get to a spot of land in the far distance, but the wind and tide keep him out at sea. It was a peculiar thought, one he had often, and couldn't place why he had it.

Harry said, "I don't want to play cricket now. I want to go in the truck. I want to go to the lake."

"I just got this stump straightened up perfectly, you little muggins."

"I want to go in the truck to the lake and walk along that path."

"Maybe we'll leave these up and play a bit when we get back."

"All right."

"You'll have to hold the meal on us, Laura," Calum said, "We're going to the lake."

"Shit, look at all this food I've got on."

"I know. Sorry."

Fiona was already in her high chair. Calum bent over her and kissed her forehead. "Come wif," was her response.

"No, honey, not this time. Harry and I have a thing to talk about."

"You think you're the only one who can do this," Laura said.

"I don't know what you mean."

"I guess I don't either," she said, and shook her head.

"I remember that fear when I was a kid. It was excruciating. I have to help him."

"And what are you going to do? Oh, well," she sighed, "fill me in when you get back."

"I have no idea what I'm doing."

....

In the truck, Harry was unusually quiet. Calum thought of his own father; the image of the open boat in rough weather had taken hold in his mind—he couldn't shift it, he kept wondering where it came from. He kept vaguely wishing his father had a helper, someone strong to row the boat with him, and the thought made him emotional as though his father in reality was still being punished for the way he'd lived his life. And when the image of a boatman struck him, he remembered his grandfather, very dimly, telling a story that he loved, and on the back of that memory he remembered his father telling him not to listen to such stories because they were rubbish. Calum's old anger rose against his father, and, aloud, he said, "That's why you're still at sea in the open boat, you stupid old bastard."

"Daddy," said Harry, "you sweared."

They parked at the south end of the lake where the skyline of downtown Minneapolis pushes into the sky like the glass monoliths of Oz. The parking lot was swarming with people taking advantage of the unseasonably warm weather. There were a few swimmers and windsurfers on the beach but no lifeguards on duty that time of year. Harry ran to the lifeguards' chair and climbed up. "Daddy, come up here!"

Calum climbed up into the chair and Harry shifted over so that they were sitting tightly together, looking over the blue lake toward downtown. As was often the case when he was alone with his son, Calum felt a burst of heartbreaking homesickness that prompted him to blurt out the first thing that came into his mind, "When we're out here we're in America, but in our own back yard, that's Britain."

"What?"

"Nothing. I'm talking rubbish. Tell me, how do you like it up here?"

"I'm the king of the castle."

"You are, you dirty rascal."

"Daddy?"

"Harry?"

"What does *lifeguard* mean?"

"What it says," answered Calum. "A lifeguard sits up here to watch over the lives of the swimmers. If they're drowning, he or she has to leap into the water to save their lives, or guard their lives. Do you understand?'

"Yes."

"Are you thinking it might mean something else?"

"Don't know."

A DC10 went over and a man on roller blades danced behind them with a boom box playing loud rap music. When the plane and the rollerblader had gone a woman with massively teased hair parked her convertible near the lifeguard stand and played her radio loudly while shouting to her boyfriend over the noise.

"Daddy, when you die do they put you in a box full of worms?"

"You've got it bad, haven't you? Are you thinking about this a lot and getting scared?"

"Yes."

"I had that too when I was little. I have it now sometimes. It's part of being alive—looking over your shoulder at death. That's what makes humans different from other animals. We can think and get all the wonderful benefits from the special brains we have, but with that understanding comes the drawback of knowing that one day we'll die. That's frightening to just about everyone. Animals probably don't think much about death."

"Is that why animals are happy?"

"What makes you think animals are happy?"

"Because they sing."

"Oh, yeah, you mean in cartoons?"

"Yes."

"Those aren't real animals."

"Yes, they are."

Calum could see how appealing and easy lies have been about this subject over the ages. People need cartoons. He'd been hard all his life toward what he felt was religion's role as a panacea for human fear— ever since his father's death he had maintained, at worst, that man's atheism and, at best, his own brand of skeptical agnosticism—but now, confronted with his own son's terror, he felt like giving up the long-held conviction that human beings could handle their own mortality and by doing so would create a better world; he simply couldn't bear to see the little boy in that sort of pain.

"You've heard all about Heaven, of course?"

"Yes, but what is it?"

"I don't know. Some people believe that the thinking part of a person, the spirit part of you, goes to a place called Heaven after you die. Sort of like a ghost that lives in a machine and makes it work but when the machine breaks the ghost flies back to where it came from."

"Grandma says that if you're naughty you go to a different place."

"Some people believe that."

"Daddy, do you believe that?"

Calum paused for a moment, but he couldn't do as he'd intended. "No," he said finally, "actually, I don't. Not the way people like your granny do, anyway. I think the Hell thing is a very nasty myth. A myth is usually a story that helps people live. Usually. There are all kinds of myths. Sometimes they're stories that we've forgotten the meaning of but we keep telling them because they're just plain good stories."

"Like the stories you tell me."

"Sometimes, but they're usually just for fun. Myths can be a bit more serious."

"Like the story about Magnus the Fiddler who went into the mountain to play for the fairies and stayed a hundred years and then came out and turned into dust when the first person spoke to him? Tell that one."

"That's not what I mean by myth, Harry, although I suppose it is in a way. I'm not sure how much that one helps us to live."

"It made the fiddler die. Tell it."

"You wanted to know about myths."

"All right."

Calum was about to begin and then found he had nothing to say. There wasn't a myth that helped him about death. He was his father's son, a realist, willing to take the pain of mortality in exchange for the freedom to be a full-blooded man; yet he immediately saw the image of his father again struggling in the open boat in the rough gray sea.

Harry looked up at him.

Without thinking what he was saying, Calum said, "My grandfather used to tell me a story about what happens to members of his family when they die. My dad told it as well, but his version was more of a joke."

"Is a myth a joke?"

"Some myths become jokes, but my grandfather, Robbie, told the myth in a way that it helped a little boy get to sleep at night and not waste valuable rest worrying about things he could do nothing about. You've been lying awake at night, haven't you?"

"Yes. Scared."

"Same. I used to be surprised when I got up in the morning and found everything normal. I couldn't understand why everyone wasn't running around shouting 'Holy shit, my ass is grass!'"

The little boy put his hand over his mouth and laughed.

"But like you, I was terrified. I was a bit older; I'm surprised you have this already—it's too soon. Granddad remembered how it was for him, I suppose, and told a little thing that had been handed down from when the Leiths lived in the Orkney Islands in the far north, off the coast of Scotland. When you're older you may be able to see where the story comes from."

"Daddy?"

"Yes."

"Is my ass grass?"

"It will be if you use naughty language."

Harry squealed with laughter.

"All right. Well, once upon a time there was a little boy with a crippled leg. He loved his father very much and his father loved him. They lived in a croft by the sea on Papa Westray with the rest of a big family of Leiths. It's very windy there, and usually big gray clouds come down close to the green land and the sea pounds angrily against the brown rocks.

"The little boy was the youngest of seven brothers but he couldn't work on the land like his six brothers on account of his bad leg, so he'd go every day in the fishing boat with his father and that's how they got so close—they spent every day together and the father taught the little boy everything he knew about the world.

"Now, the little boy was quite special. He'd been granted two lives, probably on account of having so much bad luck with that leg. Maybe also so he could explain a thing or two to the family.

"One day when his father was quite old, and there was famine and bad weather, the pair of them, the little boy with the bad leg and the old father, sailed out of their little harbor to try and catch some fish. They didn't get far out to sea when a big wave swept over their boat and smashed it against the rocks. The father and the son tried desperately to save each other but the sea was too strong for them and, although they clung to each other tightly, the both of them drowned.

"Quite suddenly, they were on a beautiful beach with calm waves lapping against golden sand. The boy was walking, holding his father's hand, when ahead of them he saw a boat, pulled up on the shore with a big red-headed oarsman leaning against it, smoking his pipe.

"The father and son said good morning to the oarsman and he made room for them in the boat and pushed it into the sea and jumped in behind them. They sat together in the prow of the boat as the oarsman rowed them west and they looked back at the land and hoped their loved ones wouldn't grieve too long.

"After a long time the oarsman smiled and pointed and they could see land in the distance. 'The land of the young,' the oarsman explained. And they landed on the beach there and said good-bye to the oarsman and walked up a little path through the cliffs to the meadows above, and across a rich plain they went and into a forest that nestled at the foot of a mountain, and they walked through the trees along the edge of a laughing stream and climbed higher into the wooded mountain until they smelled wood smoke.

"Through the trees in a green meadow full of buttercups they saw the great dilapidated mansion of the Leiths spreading out over many acres. They could hear music coming from the open windows. All around, the snow-covered mountain peaks looked down on the valley.

"They went to the big front door and knocked and the door was flung open and the people inside rushed forward, cheering and welcoming. The little boy's grandfather emerged through the throng and threw his arms around his son, the little boy's father. They held each other tightly as though they would never let go again. The music was playing and people were dancing in celebration—all the generations of Leiths, and their spouses, and the foster children and the bastards, and all the family pets.

"At last the grandfather let go of the little boy's father and looked down at the little boy with a curious expression on his face. 'Ah hah,' he said, 'this is the laddie with two lives that we've all been curious about. So you've seen what it's like in the Hall of Leiths, but you can't stay because you've got a second chance to do well in the world. And when you're ready to come back we'll be here and your Da will greet you at the door. Now be off with you and we'll see you again in sixty years.' And everyone was smiling and touching the little boy, laying good fortune on him, and the little boy held desperately tight to his father's hand but to no avail because as suddenly as he'd left it he was back in the cold, roaring surf holding onto his father. The sea tried to overwhelm him, crashing him around in the rocks, but he wouldn't let go of his father's hand. He kicked and beat the water like a giant and overcame the waves and pulled his father to shore where his brothers and other islanders were waiting.

"The father had drowned and the brothers couldn't understand what had happened. And neither could they understand why their little brother stood so tall and light-eyed and was no longer crippled by a withered leg. He told them about the Hall of Leiths and after the funeral he moved to the mainland and brought many more Leiths into the world."

Calum was quiet. Harry's mouth gaped. Boom boxes pulsed and two cars driven by teenage boys screeched their wheels in the parking lot, burning rubber, while on the other side of the lake a police siren wailed. The sun was low in the west and the glass buildings of downtown Minneapolis blazed with reflected golden light.

"Tell it again," said Harry.

"You must be joking, maneen."

"Please, Da. Tell it again."

"It's exhausting. Another time perhaps."

"Daddy, did your daddy tell the story or was it your grandpa?"

"I'm not sure where it comes from, to be honest. I might've made most of it up. But my dad's version was a little different."

"Tell it. Tell it. It's the joking one!"

"Well, we lived in London. And he said that when a Leith died in London you'd have to catch the 9:15 from Paddington to Bristol and then take a coal boat on the River Severn. When you get to the Hall of the Leiths it's full of wine, women, and song, and you play cricket all afternoon and sleep in in the mornings. There's a waterfall of whiskey nearby and nobody works. Without the waterfall, he said, you'd have to name it the Hell of the Leiths. He was a cynical sod, my dad."

"Is your daddy in the Hall of the Leiths?"

"If he is, I wouldn't mind betting he had to row his own boat to get there. The bloody fool's probably still rowing."

Harry thought for a moment, his eyes looking to the side, picking up the last blue of the lake. "When I go to the Hall of the Leiths I'll see your daddy. I'll play cricket with him."

"Just don't drink whiskey with him."

"Whiskey killed your daddy."

"Yes."

"You mustn't drink whiskey, Daddy."

"I won't, laddie."

"And will Kitty be at the Hall of the Leiths?"

"I imagine so—I'm sure there's plenty of crunchy birds for her to catch."

"I want to play cricket now."

"Let's make a move, then."

....

183

Calum bowled a few balls gently to Harry, who swung with intermediary strokes between cricket and baseball and seldom connected with the ball. The ball would thud against the garage siding. After a while Calum started seriously aiming at the stumps—he wanted a turn at bat. Everything he bowled on target the little boy blocked—sometimes with his leg.

"Hey, you can be called 'out' for doing that. They call it LBW—leg before wicket."

Harry threw down the bat and ran and got the ball. "You bat now, Daddy." And he tried to bowl the ball but it went everywhere but near the wicket. While the little boy was hurling the ball then running to retrieve it, Calum thought again of his own father lying dead on the day bed. Calum was sixteen again, right there in the room with the orange carpet. His father had been rowing that boat in rough seas all his life but he'd disguised it and made it look like competence and courageousness. And there he was, dead on the bed with long white legs as thin as a woman's, and his dead blue eyes staring at nothing.

"If only I'd known how to help him," Calum said.

"What?" asked Harry.

"I was thinking out loud about when my daddy died."

"Were you sad when your daddy died? Were you in England?"

"Yes, and yes. When he passed away he was all alone. That was wrong. Someone should always be with the dying person."

The little boy nodded his head and said, "To tell them about the Hall of the Leiths?"

"Why, yes. That would be a good thing. I suppose when you're sick and ready to die, you're probably in a pretty receptive state of mind. When I'm an old man and you're the age I am now, I hope you'll sit beside me and remind me how to get to the Hall of the Leiths."

"And you'll see your daddy there?" the little boy asked brightly.

Calum's heart was beating so hard he could hear it in his mouth. He had to control himself to keep from letting the emotion burst forth and alarm the child. "I hope I will see him there, little man."

"And the boy with the bad leg?"

"Him, too."

"And I can come there?"

"Yes, matey. I'll be waiting for you. We'll all be waiting for you. So you can go ahead and be a little boy and not worry about this any-more."

"All right."

Calum picked up the cricket ball, and, holding the bat in one hand, tossed the ball and swung at it. It thunked on the oiled willow wood and sailed over next door's giant maple.

"Daddy!" said the little boy. "You lost my ball."

"We'll find it tomorrow."

Laura leaned on the windowsill, looking through the screen at them. "I don't know who is the bigger kid," she said.

"Mummy," said the boy, "Did you see Daddy? He hit the ball right over the tree. And he told me all about the Hall of the Leiths where we go when we die. It's nice there, it's where Kitty lives now."

"Come in and eat something, boys," Laura said, and moved away from the window.

Inside, Calum saw that the dining table was set for four people and that two had already eaten. Fiona was by the fireplace exchanging the heads of her Barbies. Laura spooned pasta into Harry's dish and took it to the microwave. With her back to Calum, she said, "So you've solved man's great fear of death?"

"I told him an old story of my granddad's. A Valhalla sort of thing, only just for family. It helped him."

"You're pleased with yourself," she said, "but there'll be hell to pay when he starts spouting it at church. My mom already thinks you have cloven feet." She came back, holding a carton of chocolate milk, banged it down beside Harry, then looked at Calum as he scraped the remains of the serving dish onto a dinner plate. Without looking at her he said, "You're mother's a bloated half-wit."

Laura raised her eyebrows and squeezed her lips thin over her teeth, "And you're always saying I'm turning into her."

Calum held the plate above the sink and spooned a forkful of pasta into his mouth. As he chewed the bland food, he said, "Despite your infuriatingly theatrical facial gestures, I don't want to be drawn into another round of irrational name-calling. Okay?"

"Okay," she shrugged, "but too bad you can't find some old family myth to save marriages."

Calum shrugged, "I'm just a dumb old Brit, I suppose," and

glanced sideways at Laura. He became acutely aware of the mimetic nature of that glance; that setting of the eyes, that startled blueness was the same expression his father used when Calum's mother sent one of her verbal barbs into him, usually comments or criticisms so nonsensical that the response could only be fury or silence. His father and mother had stuck together; he couldn't understand why. That old look of his father's had always puzzled him, but it made sense now: its ambiguity-veiled rage, shame, and frustration.

The little cockney Jiminy Cricket that sometimes sat on his shoulder was yelling, *Tell her now. Get Out! Tell her now.* Laura pushed past him at the sink and threw cutlery into the soapy washing-up water. Calum put his plate down and the words just came, "Laura, I love being a father to these children, but I've got to tell you that trying to be a husband to you no longer holds any joy. It's making a bad guy of me."

She stood with her back to him, her hands holding the sink. He might have been doing her an injustice, but if he could read her mind he would bet his life that she was already figuring out what to tell her mother.

....

Excerpt from *Down-River People*

Fung Jung-ho awakened reluctantly in the little room behind the shop. It was very hot. He wasn't ready for another day, but light was coming through the cracks between the shutters. It was time to open the shop and get to work. To support the family by hand sewing meant that he must use every hour of daylight, even if his muscles ached and his eyes grew dim.

Pulling on his loose cotton pants, he slipped outside to take down the heavy shutters. He gave no thought to the three men walking up the lane until they closed in and seized him.

"Quiet! Just come with us."

"What do you want? I have no money."

"Just shut up and come. Old Chiang wants you."

Fung cried out, but received a warning blow on the head.

"Any more noise and you'll really get it. You're a soldier now."

Jin-lan, awakened by the noise, rushed out in time to see her husband being dragged off. She screamed and ran after him, but the men pushed him into a waiting truck and drove away.

She returned to the shop. Only half the shutters were down and they were too heavy for her to handle. Dazed, she sat down to assess the situation. By law, her husband, sole supporter of the family, should not have been taken, but she knew that laws counted for little against facts. To protest to the authorities, even if she knew how, might only make things worse.

What had she left? If she couldn't pay the rent on the shop, she and the children would have to get out. Where could she go? A foreign style dress was half-finished. She tried to work on it, but didn't know how the pieces fitted together. There were two finished orders. They would bring in some money, but not much.

Checking her supplies, she found that she had enough rice for three days, a jar of brined vegetables, and some dried bean curd. There were several pounds of charcoal for cooking. In a little leather bag under the mattress was the money they had saved toward the rent. Trying not to wake the children, she pulled it out and counted it. A little over five thousand *kluai*. Not enough for the rent. Not enough to feed them for more than a few days.

What could she do?

If she were alone, or with one child, she could hire out as a helper, but who would take a helper with three children?

They might have to beg. Her gentle soul shrank from the thought.

What could she do? The question beat on her mind. She had always left decisions to her man, who was smart and hardworking and had always taken good care of the family. Now she put questions aside and took refuge in familiar routines. She made a charcoal fire in the little clay stove, like a flower pot with a grate on it, and put rice to boil with plenty of water, to make a thin gruel for breakfast. She pulled out a turnip from the brine jar and cut it into shreds. When breakfast was ready she woke the children and called them to eat.

"Where's Baba?" asked ten-year-old Bin.

"He had to go somewhere," said Jin-lan, trying to put off facing facts.

"It's funny he left the shutters like that."

"He had to leave in a hurry." Jin-lan tried to sound casual, but despair welled up and she burst into sobs.

"Will he come back?"

"I don't know. I've heard of men being taken like that for the army, and they were never seen again."

"What will we do?"

"I don't know. We can get along a few days with what we have. I must try to find work. If I can't, we may have to beg." Jin-lan's tears became a storm, shaking her thin body.

"We'll find some way," said the boy, "but I wish I knew what was happening to Baba. I hope he's all right."

With that, he began to cry, as well, and the other children joined in. They all crept into Jin-lan's arms looking for comfort, and she had none to give.

....

The events of that day were always a blur in Fung's mind. His hands and feet were tied, and he jounced helplessly in the dark truck. Several times it stopped, and another struggling passenger was pushed in. After some time, they came to a place where they got out. They received baggy, old, cotton uniforms, and a bowl of thin rice. Guards roped them together by the right arms and made them stand side by side. A doctor looked at each man, then stepped close, pulled up the shirt, and listened with his bare ear to the chest. One crooked-backed scarecrow of a fellow was turned loose to find his way home.

An officer with a smart uniform and a raspy voice harangued them about the glory of being a soldier. It was their proud duty to defend the country against the dwarf devils, who killed women and children, and who burned their villages.

Then they were herded out to the road and began a nightmare march.

Days passed, one like another, as they walked doggedly on sore feet, stopping for bowls of ill-cooked rice, sometimes with a few vegetables. They slept on the ground, falling where they were at the end of the day and escaping into sleep. Sometimes Fung had dreams of home, but more often of fear, hunger, and hopelessness. He twitched and moaned in his sleep.

Before many days had passed, most of the men were suffering from scabies, which itched intolerably. Dysentery was prevalent. A few men became ill and had to be released, but not until they were really unable to get to their feet and stagger on. Three times men near Fung in the line could not be roused even by kicks, and were untied and left where they lay.

After a few days the ropes were removed. They were now too far from home to escape easily in their uniforms. The daily harangues were making them feel more like a unit. Most began to accept the idea that they were soldiers. At last, those who could still walk reached a training camp where they would learn to fight the dwarf devils.

They were up at dawn, drilling and marching. They learned the savage shout that goes with a bayonet thrust, and the rousing war songs that developed their lungs as they marched. They drilled with wooden guns, and groups of six at a time learned to handle a real rifle. They had to take turns tending a large flock of ducklings that, when grown, would provide meat for the officers. When it became known that Fung was a tailor, he had to mend torn uniforms.

Fung made a show of accepting his lot, but he was always thinking of escape. It would be hard in uniform, and he had no access to other clothing. His only hope lay in a wooded area some distance to the west. If he could reach that, he might be able to hide by day and go on by night until he was at a safe distance from the camp. It would all depend on the people he would meet. Would they hide him and give him plain clothing, or would they report him? It was a risk he had to take.

One day, Fung was assigned to tend the ducklings. Leaving them in a rice field, he slipped away to the woods, where he left his uniform under a brush pile and went on naked with a branch to hide behind. He walked as far as he could under cover of the trees, and then hid until nightfall and walked all night. In the early morning, he came to a charcoal burner's hut. He waited until two men came out to greet the day, and then showed himself and asked for help.

The older man, Old Chang, nodded understandingly. "You may stay here. I'll lend you something to wear. I'll hide you, and pay you a little for helping as long as you work for me. If you run away, I'll report you."

"But I'm a tailor!" Fung protested. "I know nothing about burning charcoal. I could make more money at my own trade."

"You'll do as I say," said Chang with finality. "On rainy days, when we can't burn charcoal, you can sew for my wife."

Fung saw no choice. If he were reported and caught, the punishment didn't bear thinking about. He agreed to the terms, still holding the thought of escape in his mind.

He learned to cut wood to the proper length and stack it carefully in the pit for burning, so that the air would reach all parts of the pile evenly. He was not allowed to go out to gather wood unless Chang was with him. Chang himself, with the precision born of long experience, watched over the burning piles and signaled the moment to pour on the waiting pails of water. If this were done too soon, the charcoal would smoke when burned. Too late, and it would have little heating power.

Good days for burning were few. When it rained, Chang took Fung to his home in the village, where he sewed new clothes for the whole family. When that was done, neighbors paid well for his excellent work. Old Chang took the money, giving Fung a few *kluai* for himself.

In one home where he worked, the man of the house took an interest in him and learned his story. He said that he had pony pack trains running to Kuanglo, and he could take Fung as a driver if he could slip away from Old Chang. He warned, however, that to go home could be dangerous, as neighbors would know that he was an escaped conscript, and someone might turn him in. To be without identity papers was also dangerous. Fung ignored the warnings. His compulsion to get back to his family outweighed everything.

They arranged that he should sew for his benefactor whenever possible. The first time there was a pack train leaving when he was there, he would go with it, and would be reported to Chang as having disappeared. Clad in a dirty, white felt cloak and hat, cracking his whip at the ponies, he would be hard to identify. It would take several days to reach Kuanglo.

....

When Jin-lan's tears subsided, she spoke seriously to Bin. "You are the head of the family now. You must be like a father to the others. I'll have to try to find work, and I'll have to leave you in charge here. There are many things you must know how to do. Today I'll teach you, since I have to wait for the customers to pick up their orders."

"I know how to do everything," said Bin. "I've watched how you do. Let me try, and you see if I do right."

Under Jin-lan's watchful eye, Bin made a fire and cooked and washed dishes and paid the water carrier, and even washed some clothes. Eight-year-old Mei-mei swept the floor and kept an eye on six-year-old Dee-dee. Between Bin and Jin-lan, they managed to put up the shutters, leaving only one open to admit light and customers. At night they closed that one, too.

By the next day the orders had been picked up, and the money for them was safe in the leather bag, which Jin-lan now wore tied under her clothes.

Early the next morning, she walked with little Dee-dee to the place in the vegetable market where she had seen women waiting to be hired. Questioning the others, she learned the rules. Hiring of helpers was on a three-day probation. If she did not like the job, and left within three days, she would receive no pay. After three days she would be paid for however long she had worked.

She listened as they chatted of good and bad situations they had known. The bad stories far outweighed the good, but maybe that was because the ones who found good jobs didn't come back to the hiring place.

Jin-lan compared herself to the others. She was clean and soft-spoken, as many of them were not. She was skilled in housekeeping at her own modest level, but would have much to learn in a home of affluence. She believed she could learn quickly. The only problem was the children. Bin was a responsible lad, but awfully young to be left in charge. After the end of the month there wouldn't be any place to leave him.

A nice-looking woman approached Jin-lan. "Would you do general work for a family of four? Do you have references from previous employers?"

"I've never worked before. I must support my children because my husband was taken to the army."

"Children? How many?"

"Three, including the one with me. The boy of ten would make himself useful. The others are very quiet and good."

"Sorry. I like your looks, but there is no room in my house for so many."

This became a pattern. The next few days passed the same way. Once she took all three children with her, and no one even spoke to her. She toyed with the idea of letting Bin and Mei-mei live alone, but even if they had any place to stay when the rent ran out, the money she could earn as a helper wouldn't buy even the simplest food for them.

One day when she came home, Bin, clean and proud, gave her a little money.

"You said we might have to beg," he said, "so today we tried it. I'd been watching beggars, so I knew how. I smeared us with dirt, and slapped Mei-mei because she looked too happy, and we went up to people and said, 'Do a good deed.' Sometimes they gave us something."

Jin-lan swallowed hard. She had put the thought of begging out of her mind. She couldn't imagine herself doing it. But here was enough money to buy a little rice, and the children were pleased with themselves. Her store of money was nearly gone.

"I'll try once more to get work," she said, "and if I fail we'll all try this new way. You may do it again tomorrow."

The next day, when she came home the children were gone. She made dinner and waited. A neighbor woman came.

"The children were taken by the police," she said. "They were found begging in the street. The policeman brought them home, and when he found no one here to care for them, he took them away."

"Do you know where he took them?"

"No, I know only what I saw."

Jin-lan's head swam. She sat hugging Dee-dee and trying not to think. She was afraid to go to the police. She thought of the Soongs, but had no idea how to find them.

Surely someone will tell me where they are.

She gave Dee-dee his food and put him to bed. Then she sat waiting until the neighborhood was dark and quiet. She could not close the heavy shutter without Bin's help. As she lay down to sleep she thought, *Tomorrow I must stay here in case anyone comes, but the money and food will soon be gone. What can I do?*

The next day and the day after passed like a gray fog. She left home only long enough to buy a little cabbage. Otherwise she just sat hugging Dee-dee until the child rebelled at sitting still so long, and went to play by himself. She still clung to the one thought: *Surely someone will come to tell me where they are.*

She forgot to cook rice. Dee-dee was hungry, but she couldn't force herself to move. The fog in her mind was growing thicker. On the third day, a policeman came to the door.

"Where are my children?" Jin-lan asked him.

"They were taken to the orphanage because you didn't take care of them. Now I see there is another who is not being cared for. I must take him, too."

He picked up Dee-dee, saying, "Would you like to go find your brother and sister and have good food to eat?"

Deedee smiled, but Jin-lan flung herself upon the man.

"Give me back my children," she shrieked.

"I have to take them because you do not take care of them. It is Madame Chiang's order that children must be cared for."

Pulling away from her, he strode down the lane and up the street. Jinlan ran after him in vain. When he was out of sight she sat down in the shadow of a stone lion at the entrance to a park, and there she stayed.

The gray veil that had covered everything since the children were taken became thickened. She sat in a dense fog of her own making.

....

Bin and Mei-mei did not easily accept life at the orphanage. The staff worker, Mei-ling, knew only that they had been turned in as abandoned children. Bin explained that his mother was looking for work and his father had been taken to the army. The orphanage was far from the shop, and he didn't know the address.

"I don't feel right about this," Mei-ling said to the director, Miss Hu, after getting the children to bed.

"There's nothing we can do about it," said Miss Hu. "The mother had left them to beg. We have to take them in."

"But what of the father?"

"If he's been conscripted, he won't be seen again. We'll have records here in case he comes. It's rough on the children, but they'll settle down in time. They seem like good kids."

"They are good kids. They've had good mothering. That's why I feel that there is something wrong."

For several days, Mei-ling devoted much time to the two children and to Dee-dee when he came. Mei-mei and Dee-dee had to get used to their real names, Gwei-hwa and Pung, because there were too many children who could answer to Little Sister or Little Brother. Mei-ling brought them into group games and told them stories and even slept with them at night for a while. Slowly they responded, but there was a deep sorrow in them. They often said, "I wonder what Baba and Mama are doing."

When the policeman brought Dee-dee, Miss Hu questioned him. He said that the house was a filthy mess, and the mother incompetent and neglectful. He had seen no choice but to take the child. He gave the address where they had lived. Mei-ling, on her day off, went to the place and found no trace of Jin-lan.

....

Taking Jin-lan for a beggar, people put money into her hand. She slowly tore it to bits. A Buddha-hearted woman brought her a bowl of rice gruel. She poured it on the ground. Day after day she sat, growing thinner and dirtier. Her fingers became like dry sticks. Her eyes seemed to sink into their sockets.

One night she staggered across the road and fell on the ground in an open place. When day came, she lay in the sun. Passing children threw stones at her. Her head was bleeding. Flies swarmed around her. Jin-lan was still lost in her fog.

As her body lay inert, she became aware of a light and a presence. "Mother!" she cried in joyous recognition.

Two men came with a wooden stretcher and carried her body to the potter's field where, with no box to confine it, it quickly grew up into morning glories and wild iris.

....

Fung Jung-ho's excitement grew as the pack train approached Kuanglo. He enjoyed driving the stocky little ponies with the big, red pompons on their heads. He liked the jingling bells of the lead pony and the sudden quickening of the pace when the animals sensed that they were near a resting place. The thick, white felt cloak he wore was comfortable, providing shade by day and a bed by night. His mind was full of questions. How could he find his family? They could not have kept up the rent on the shop. Where could they have gone?

As soon as the pack train reached its destination, the head driver took back the felt cloak and hat and paid Fung for his work. With the money tucked in his belt, he hastened to the shop. There was a new family there, makers of bean milk. They knew nothing about the former tenants.

Fung knocked at the next house. The neighbor woman greeted him, "How have you come back?"

"It wasn't easy. Where are my wife and children?"

"I don't know. The police took the children away. She ran after them and never came back here."

"You don't know where they were taken?"

"No, but I've heard of an orphanage outside the city."

"Have you heard nothing of my wife?"

"Nothing."

Inquiring around, Fung heard of a madwoman who had died because her children were taken from her. Could it have been Jin-lan? He would have to put off any further search for her until he found the children.

Finding where the orphanage was, he started the long walk, knowing he couldn't get there before night. No matter. He could sleep anywhere. As darkness fell he left the path, curled up behind a rock, and went to sleep. His nightmares had come true. Even if he found the children, would the orphanage release them to a homeless man with no job? The compulsion was still on him. He must find them somehow.

In the night a policeman shook him. "Identity papers?"

"I left them at home."

"No papers, the case is clear. You go to the army."

He was led away at gunpoint to where other strays were being rounded up. They were loaded into a truck, and the whole story began again.

....

One day, Connie Soong went to visit Mei-ling at the orphanage. She was startled when three children ran to her shouting, "Auntie Soong!" She recognized the Fung children.

"Why are you here?" she asked.

Bin explained, "Baba was taken to the army, and Mama couldn't take care of us, so we were brought here."

Deeply perturbed, Connie questioned Bin and Mei-ling. With what meager information she could get, she told the story to Gordon.

"I'll find out all I can," he said. "I liked that family."

He was able to uncover most of the story, including the fact that Fung had returned and talked to the neighbor. Then a blank. It was probable that he had been conscripted again, but there was no way to trace him.

A man at recruiting headquarters explained, "We are required to produce a certain quota of men for the army. We pay press gangs to bring them in. It has to be done."

"Isn't there a law against taking an only son, or the sole supporter of a family?"

"Of course there are laws, but they are impossible to enforce. Wouldn't every man find some ground for exemption? The army must have men."

"Where would this man have been taken?"

"To any of several training camps. There is no record."

Gordon had to give up. When he reported his findings to Connie, they shared real grief and frustration.

"Maybe we could adopt the children," said Connie.

"I don't think so," said Gordon thoughtfully. "My pay alone would be scanty for such a family. Unless you gave up your job to stay with them, we'd have to leave them in the care of servants. They're probably better off where they are. You say they have become fond of Mei-ling. They should not be uprooted again. We can keep in touch with them."

And so it was left.

....

Fung Jung-ho let the sun warm his bare body as he searched the seams of his ragged cotton uniform for lice. Suitable days for this task were rare. Itching seemed a normal condition. The little creatures were companions of a sort. Remembering that the blood in them was his own, he crushed them one after another and dropped them in a neat pile on the ground.

Fung was a soldier now, veteran of many a hard, hungry march and an occasional battle. He was always in unfamiliar parts of the country, where his speech would make him conspicuous if he tried to desert. This also made it difficult to enlist the cooperation of the local people. Life consisted mostly of sitting around, waiting for some rash move of the enemy which might call for action. The Japanese were firmly in control of many cities, but seldom ventured out of them. The war seemed to be going nowhere.

Fung hated the dwarf devils with all the passion of his own

disrupted life and his rage at what he had seen of burned villages and wanton destruction. He also hated his own leaders, who had ordered the burning of Hanfu and the ruthless conscription of men like himself. Had he been in command, he thought, there would have been more action. He felt that they often missed chances to harass the enemy. But he was not in command. He and his fellows could only wait for orders. They didn't even care much, as they were usually dull with hunger. Sometimes they got their pay and sometimes they didn't. When they did, it wasn't enough to buy anything. It looked like a lot, but the prices of things were so high that money was useless. Their meals were coarse rice or millet or tough, unleavened wheat cakes, badly cooked, sometimes with some vegetables, and occasionally a taste of meat or egg.

He looked at his body, lean and hard, and remembered how it used to look when he did nothing but sew all day. He liked having strong muscles and knowing how to use them, but he still felt a sharp sorrow when he thought of his lost family. How were they now? Would he ever see them again? It seemed wasteful for a good tailor to be sitting in the sun, picking lice and waiting for a call to go and kill people.

"*Mei yo ban fa,*" he murmured, "There's no help for it." If he must be a soldier he'd be a good one.

He was still searching his pants when the order came: "Prepare to move at dusk." With a sigh, he put his clothes on, checked and packed his equipment, and cleaned the gun he shared with another man. They had been two weeks in this northern place. He didn't know where it was, but he hoped the new move would take him back to where his feet wouldn't always be cold.

Leaving in the evening would mean a night march. As soon as his things were in order he lay down for a nap, waking only when called for the evening meal. He had just finished eating when the order came to move out, and to maintain silence on the road.

Monotonous hours passed. Then they took positions among rocks above a narrow path, and waited.

"The enemy will pass below us," said their officer. "They will either be Japanese or puppet troops. Either way, we are not to let them pass this point. Do not take prisoners. Kill them all. Don't worry if you hear them speaking Chinese. Puppets are traitors who are working for the Japanese, and deserve the same treatment."

As usual, there were not enough guns to go around, but each man had three hand grenades. It was one of these that defeated them.

Someone hurled a grenade at the first group to enter the pass, thus alerting those behind to the ambush. The enemy, being on familiar ground, scattered up the hill and fell on Fung's unit from above. Fung had no time to respond when a man leaped down on him. He expected to be killed, but instead was disarmed and held under guard.

"We are the Balu," his captor said. "We don't fight our own people. We only fight the dwarf devils."

Fung had heard of the Balu, the notorious Eighth Route Army. They were Communists, and his officers said they were even worse than the Japanese, that they killed without mercy, and that they were trying to destroy civilization. It seemed strange that they did not kill him at once, as he would have done if the situation were reversed.

When the action was over, Fung and his companions were led away, disarmed, into the hills. After climbing for most of the day, they came to a good-sized village in a remote valley. In a large room heated by a brick bed, they received generous bowls of millet porridge and a pile of quilts.

"Good night," said the guards. "Have a good sleep."

When Fung awoke, the man next to him was sitting up.

"Why do you suppose they didn't kill us?" he whispered.

"I can't imagine," said the other. "We'd have had to if the shoe were on the other foot. Our officers would kill us if we didn't. And if we could have kept them, we wouldn't have put them in any fancy guest room like this. I'm warm for the first time in weeks. I'm curious to see what comes next."

"So am I," said Fung. "I've never heard anything good about the Communists, but they don't seem so bad."

Other men began to stir, and soon the guard at the door called, "All out! The rice is ready."

The latrine, some distance from the house, was primitive but clean. The men quickly got ready to eat. It was already mid-morning, and they were ravenous. Breakfast consisted of a large bowl of millet porridge with bits of bean curd and cabbage in it. When that was gone a guide led them around the village and showed them how the people lived. The villagers and the soldiers seemed to be good friends, working and joking together. Most of the civilians were women and children, some busy spinning and weaving, others making cloth shoes or sewing padded clothing or quilts. Everyone, soldier or civilian, seemed well-fed and warmly dressed.

Fung compared the scene with what he had seen during his life in the army: ill-fed soldiers seizing food from half-starved, hostile villagers. It didn't make sense to him. His captors, by their own statement, were Communists, the most dreaded group in the country.

Back in their room, they were soon joined by two men dressed like the rest in plain, cotton-padded suits. Something in their manner showed that they represented authority.

"We are the political cadres," said one. "Have you been well treated?"

"Yes, sir."

"We don't say 'sir' here. Have you any questions?"

"Why didn't you kill us?"

"What good would it do to kill you? We are all Chinese. We all want to drive out the dwarf devils. We all hate those who rob and oppress the people, who take the last grain from a hungry village, who conscript men by force and force them to fight with empty stomachs and ragged clothing. They have told you lies about us."

The other man took over. "Who has treated you badly, the Balu or the Kuomintang?"

"The KMT."

"Who taxes the farmers so hard that they are starving?"

"The KMT."

"Who orders prisoners to be killed?"

"The KMT."

"Who orders villages to be burned and the people killed?"

"The KMT and the dwarf devils."

"Who snatched you from your homes and left your families without support?"

"The KMT."

"Who fails to pay you when it is due?"

"The KMT."

"Who has allowed the dwarf devils to take over half of China?"

"The KMT."

"Who always tells you the truth?"

"Not the KMT."

"Do you want to drive out the dwarf devils?"

"Yes."

"Let's look at the map."

They showed a map of China with Japanese-held territory in green, Kuomintang in blue, and Communist in red. The Northeast was clearly in Japanese hands, as were the main coastal and river cities and some other places. In most of North China, the Japanese held only cities and railroads, with the guerrillas hemming them in and controlling most of the countryside. The KMT still held most of South and Southwest China except for the coast. In the Northwest was the KMT blockade line, where the best of the KMT armies were stationed to cut off the infection of Communism from the rest of the country. North of that was Yenan, the Communist capital, and a solidly red area, from which large, red tentacles reached out all the way to the coast. In some areas red and blue were mixed, where the Communists and the KMT were fighting each other for control. Such an area was where they now were. The guerrilla group of the night before had been returning from a foray against a Japanese supply train, which they had blown up, capturing many weapons and much food.

"How long since you have attacked the dwarf devils?"

"A long time."

"And yet their supply lines are not far away. Would you like to attack them?"

"Yes."

"Does the KMT deserve your loyalty?"

"No."

"Would you like to join us? We'd welcome you. If not, you are free to return to your homes. Think it over."

Fung spoke up, "It's dangerous to return home. I escaped once and went home, and within a day I was picked up for having no papers, and sent to the army again."

"That's true," said the cadre. "That's the risk you take if you go.

It's for you to choose. If you stay with us it's not an easy life, but you'll receive the same food and clothing as the rest of us, and you'll help the people and fight the Japanese, and you can even learn to read.

"You may have the rest of the day to think about it. You may talk with the villagers and the soldiers, and with each other, and decide what you want to do. If you want to go, we'll give you food for the journey."

Fung and another man walked around the village, asking the people, "What do you think of the Balu?"

"We like them. They keep the landlords and the KMT away."

"We like them. They give us work in winter, and bring coal from the hills to keep us warm."

"We like them. We hope the KMT never comes back."

Fung tried another line, "How long has the Balu been here?"

"They first came two years ago. Then the KMT drove them out and after a few weeks they came again."

"What happened when the Balu came?"

"The first time we were very frightened, but we found that they were good to us. They brought us food and cotton, and helped us to set up cooperatives to make the things we needed. They taught us to work together. They didn't let the landlords and the KMT rob us. Some of our men and boys joined the Balu."

"What happened when the KMT came back.?"

"They took our crops, and killed everyone they thought might have helped the Balu. We would all have been killed if we hadn't hidden in the hills. Some were buried alive. Most of the houses were burned."

"What has become of your landlords?"

"Some were killed. Most ran away. They'd better not try to come back."

At the tailoring cooperative each of the captives was given a warm, padded suit to replace his thin, ragged uniform.

"We're not rich," said the head of the co-op, "but we have what we need, and everyone shares alike. You are now dressed the same as our leaders."

"I used to be a tailor," said Fung. "I had my own shop, but the Japanese bombed it and the KMT burned it."

"Maybe you can teach us," said the man politely. "We do our best, but our skill is very poor."

"I think you are doing very well. These garments are strongly made and serviceable."

Fung observed that the workers who needed warm hands in order to be able to do good work had coal fires or brick beds in their work rooms. The more active workers outside would sometimes come into a warm room for a while.

He saw soldiers carrying coal from a nearby mine in baskets slung from shoulder poles, to keep up the fires in the houses. Others were working in the cooperatives with the people. Some were building a house to replace one that the KMT had burned.

Late in the afternoon another meal was served: millet with cabbage boiled in it, a small, coarse wheat cake, and shreds of pickled turnip. After the meal, everyone watched a hilarious skit put on by a few comrades, showing the Japanese being put to rout by clever farmers. Then came a period of instruction in Marxist principles. There was some discussion of village problems. Then the cadres turned to the prisoners.

"Have you decided whether you want to join us? Remember that you must each decide in your own way. I will go into the next room, and you will come one by one and tell me your decision."

Fung's mind was in a whirl. Everything he had seen that day was the opposite of what he had been told about the Communists. Could the whole thing be just a sham? But had he any reason to believe that his old officers had told the truth? He had often known that they lied. Would he believe them rather than his own eyes?

He said to the cadre, "I want to stay."

Older Sister

Forever, she rides
in front of me
on the school bus,
a lime-green mohair

draped over pale
shoulders, her stiff
auburn flip bouncing
firmly. In the curved

mirror of the mahogany
dressing table, she teases,
rats, and sprays her hair
into submission. Year

after year, her class photos
reflect magazine-rack
knowledge of the properly
curving eyebrow,

the correct application
of blush to the cheek.
No sweaty back seats
on her conscience,

no cigarettes in her
drawers. Charlotte
wore bras that fit
and skirts that hugged

the knees. Charlotte
never used one more
chocolate chip
than the recipe required.

DEBRA MARQUART

....

How Bad News Comes

A telephone is ringing
like an emergency
in a room down the hall,
I think of the one
to whom bad news
is coming. At the market,
she's touching fruit,
or driving home,
strumming her fingers
on the steering wheel.
Humming with the radio
she thinks of her lover,
the one she's left
behind, or the one
she will see again,
remembering the soft heat
of his breath, the urgency
of his belly against hers.
This is the way life
insists on itself, his scent
still on her as she reaches
for the phone, happy
to catch it in mid-ring,
coming through
the door, her keys
still dangling in the lock.
Unclipping an earring
as she leans in to hear
the voice on the other end

saying, I've got some
bad news, feeling
in that long second
before the words come
the difference between
the way it was
and the way
it will be, that moment
before the groceries
fall to the floor.

ROGER MITCHELL

....

Whew

I read in a book that the Naskapi Eskimo once lived along the coast of Labrador. Maybe they still do, but a long time ago, and forever, they loved to tell stories. Only men told them, and only at night. As the people lay in their beds waiting for sleep, the story would begin. At regular intervals, the storyteller would pause, and the listeners would respond, as though pushing the story along, with a sound something like this: "Eh, eh." If you were standing off a little way in the snow listening, you would first hear a voice carrying a sack of words down a road and then stopping, as if to rest. Then a small group of voices, as if on cue, would come in like a chorus with "eh, eh." Good, they seem to be saying, tell us more.

The Naskapi had their big stories, their myths, but everyone preferred the little ones, the "tubaljimun," small tales of everyday life made up on the spot.

Crow said to Peanut, I want you for my bride. Peanut said, are you kidding? Your beak's too big. Anyway, I am two people. Crow said, well, fine, I'll have two brides, one for the day, one for the night.

By this time, the children are falling asleep. The little "eh, eh's" slip sideways from their mouths. They are no more than stray wind-brushes. The hut made of sticks and caribou hides and spruce boughs and fish bones begins to rise like a loaf of breathing with the smells of sleep and the small hairs across the tops of the toes and the big leggy dreams walking around on the night sky with no clothes on.

No one could have predicted it, but Peanut agreed. Crow, who was no fool, said, okay, come on, what is it, what do I have to do? Fly to the moon and bring me back a piece of it, she said.

And you know what?

What?

Crow left that day.

I can't believe it.

He still hasn't come back.

Too bad.

It's been ten years in fact, and Peanut, who, as you know, is known for her patience, and waited seven whole years, finally gave up and married Caribou. Caribou promised to stay on the ground.

Well, there it is.

I feel sorry for Crow, though. The moon *is* a long way out there.

Life is real, too.

He should be getting there about now. Whew, he says.

Eh, eh.

MICHAEL MOOS

....

Something in the Spring Mud

There must be something in the spring mud that wants to set us free
as we lunge blindly forward into the tangled forest.
A language I barely hear, just beyond the sound of the wind,
stirs the stray grass ends of an old nest.
It is not happiness itself that tastes so good,
but those seconds just before, with the full deep weight of loss
still around the neck and trailing over the shoulders,
like a shadow merging with the ground where we have just walked.
Not the full green rising translucent explosion of hepatica and
    bleeding hearts,
and the voices of warblers so long in reaching us,
but this gray time just before, the rain coming and going
in the still, bare branches.

Frame of Reference

Stones in the water do not know the suffering of stones in the sun.
—Haitian Proverb

I once believed those voices that said I was called by God. All other voices were as small winds sifting leaves, leaving trees unmoved.

I wore a habit made by my own hands with a silver needle and black thread. I could have worn skins or leaves. I could have worn sequins or ostrich plumes. I could have taken Marilyn Monroe as my patron saint.

No matter how small I made my sack of desire, it was always empty. There was no one to call my name except my mother, and she was far away, dreaming of my life and me in it.

Now I doubt everyone who is sure of God's voice. If Jesus was one of a kind, he had to have been the loneliest person in the world. In this, the saints-in-waiting imitated him.

....

Gestures to be Performed
from a Balcony

Here's the situation:
You are addressing your audience:
All you have to do is look down; then you'll see 'em.
There they are—thousands, zillions, in the square below.
You start to panic: why don't these people just stay home?
Why does this always happen to me?

Take a deep breath and follow these instructions:

If you are the President, do this very quickly:
Raise your arms above your head.
Here's how to do it:
Conjure up the image of a guy with an automatic.
He's saying, "Gimme everything you got!"
You also have to grin.
Grin like there's no tomorrow.
(The idea is to project eagerness, sincerity.)
A touch of the naive is always appreciated,
And if they think you're addled or merely slow
You can get them to agree to anything.

If you happen to be the Pope, do this:
Think about a bad pain. Really bad.
Maybe the hemorrhoids are acting up;
Maybe this is your first day out of traction
And you're getting muscle spasms.
Bend forward slightly at the waist
Just as if you're trying not to break the stitches.

Smile.
(Not too much; remember, you're Infallible.)
Keeping the arms close to the body,
Raise them slightly at the elbow,
Palms upward—got that?
Now, nod
(Don't forget the smiling).
Keep jogging your palms up and down.
Imagine, here,
That somebody has entered your office
In the Vatican,
Someone devout.
This person has respectfully deposited two cloth sacks
Into your palms.
You are hefting them up and down
Trying to determine the weight.
Okay, that should do it.

I'm sorry, but you'll have to get somebody else
To write your speeches.

....

Fribble

Last year at Deaf School
    I got pulled aside and spoken to
        because someone saw him kissing my hand.
Venu's dream: him and me over a strawberry fribble
    in a booth at Friendly's
        arms over each other's shoulders,
old soldiers in this old war.

After dinner and homework we wander the track
    the dorm parent says it's okay. We hold hands and run.
        Venu clutches his imperfect heart,
lifts his head, and laughs like a daredevil
    whose life expectancy is a broken line on a small brown hand.
        In my dreams he makes the sign, *please*

This year his teacher tells me our behavior is inappropriate.
    Bad do, she signs to Venu.
        Strawberry ice cream I love you, he signs,
from across the lunchroom, drinking his milk
    and humming along, alone at the detention table
        for pointing the wrong finger at his teacher who shrieks.

Venu, I'm married and I'm thirty-eight years old, I sign.
    He signs, *best sweetheart soon old.*
        Venu, our predicament is older than stone.

....

Amelia's House

When Amelia Earhart was seventeen and a junior at Central High School in St. Paul, she lived at 825 Fairmount Avenue. The house still looks like *then*. High and narrow. Three stories plus a turret capped in black. I often walk this neighborhood, a ramble of Victorian homes, kept, brought forward into the nineties, and by midday when I arrive, abandoned. Everyone's gone making money. Nobody there but me, an occasional cat, and sometimes a workman walking to or from his truck, tools in hand, hired to keep up appearances. *Who is this for?* Me, I guess, since I can walk for blocks hearing nothing but birds and the sound of my own breathing.

....

The backdoor is utilitarian. It has to do with the garden, the clothes-line, with throwing out water from the dishpan. It is a quarter of an hour's walk from my backdoor to this one, three-quarters of a century away. I stand here and it is as if I remember things I have no way of knowing: how this door opens into a kitchen where life was slow; the pitch and rhythm of walking the warp in that hardwood floor; a creak in the handle of the pump mounted over the sink; the measure of drawing that water. And when the sky shuts down on a dark green day with a deep root rain I remember the alley, not paved, with two deep ruts the width of a Model T Ford. Weeds grow between the ruts and I know the feeling of bumping along that wavering line in a car that smells of engine, oil, and heat, with bushes on either side, mostly lilac, not blooming but leaning in close, thick and heavily leaved.

....

There is another house. An earlier one. Amelia's childhood home in Atchison, Kansas. I think I will never get there, and forget about it.

But a year or two later, driving back from New Mexico, we flip a coin to determine the route home: Kansas or Nebraska? Kansas wins. I am staring out the window at the blue, blue sky when, suddenly, I remember Atchison. We look at a map and go. Amelia's Grandpa Otis was a judge in this railroad town. He built his home on a bluff overlooking the Missouri River. Amelia was born in a bedroom on the second floor. I stand at the foot of the bed in that room. There is a window, wide and deep, giving a view down the hill onto the river and beyond, as the state of Missouri stretches away on the other side. The child who grew up here *had room*. The place is alive with the natural marriage of imagination and possibility.

THERESA PAPPAS

The Meteora

Even this high up, in these dim
alcoves, where visions of hell
and heaven seep through the walls

Even up here, a monk
before me with a tray,
offering not food for the body
but simply the idea
of welcome: a small cube
that dusts my fingertips white,
a cool column of water

Even atop these looming rocks
marked by the desire to rise,
with ladders and nets, pulleys
and chiseled stairs

Even so, I hear the sheep bells
from those clustered flecks below,
clanking, not letting me forget
I'm still on earth

CAROL J. PIERMAN

....

Simply Huge

Scientists who are cloning cattle have discovered a curious
effect of their technique—large numbers of giant calves.
Chronicle of Higher Education

Though they remain in the uterus
a normal period of time,
the two thousand calves created by a new
cloning technique have grown
to an especially large size.

So large, they must be delivered
by Caesarean section.

Not what we intended, say scientists
trying to create precise copies
of big meat and milk producers.

By what operation of cellular logic
does the genetic material from a huge producer
become simply huge?

I am reminded that in a single day
the average cow belches
up to four hundred liters of methane,
contributing to global warming.

And the complex stomach
with its four divisions
holds thirty-five gallons of cud.

The *Almanac* warns, the udder is *not*
an upside-down milk bottle
waiting to be uncorked.

It is a gland that secretes milk
in response to hormones, triggered by
a calf's suckle or warm spray.

So much can come undone:
thunder can sour a herd's milk,
Mozart can make it sweeter.

The classics play softly in the dairy;
a syringe stands stud in the Dells.

....

Free Turkey—Ralphs Supermarket, November 16

Is this American, or what?
Spend a hundred bucks on groceries, get
a turkey free. It's perfect. It's the deal
we've all been waiting for—a free symbolic bird
to brighten Thanksgiving. You can't go wrong.
And so I go to Ralphs and buy a lot of food
the way I always do, except I never get this kind of present.
I'm excited: Even though we won't be cooking
on Thanksgiving, I can put the turkey in the freezer,
save it for a day we're really hungry. Not only
do I get the turkey, but I get to keep it for awhile,
savor my terrific shopping acumen, Ralphs generosity,
American promotion, loyalty to Mother Country and her
holidays. Twelve pounds of meat and bone: my just reward.

HOLLY PRADO

Cooking Ralphs Free Turkey, December 11

Lunch with someone loved.
Coffee: real espresso—
she and I are L.A. kids; we like it
tough and foreign in a cup that stains.
She's very ill; she's doing everything she can, is
taking charge. But I have dreamed

my plants are stolen, cat's found dead,
old car and driver's license gone, people
in my life for years just turn away.

Last night's new storm won't let us get home easily.
These flooded streets. The sky

a blot, with nothing I can quite
call "day" involved. I give my friend a book;
she gives us—Harry, me—a finely painted box,
its ocean life, its artichokes another dream:
She'd live next door so I can take her some
of anything I'm cooking, every dinnertime.

When I get home, I put the turkey in the oven,
a plump, young hen—bird sacrifice, that
gruesome truth about the lives we take to stay
alive. Our own: let go, the wisdom says. Give up
control. I've heard it, haven't you? A million times—

sacrifice what's precious. My generation, now,
is winter. I can't romanticize the weather as
my private enemy or angel. I only know year's end
will strip off every feather, leave me just the way it wants me—
a woman who's unarmed. The one
who drinks that stain the coffee leaves behind.

....

The Smell of Green

A pool at night; there is moonlight and a tree with sprawling branches towering over the pool. It is completely still; the moon shines through the tree's branches and is reflected on dark water. The scent of forest growth and pine needles permeates the cool night air.

Light catches the breaking of a bubble at the water's surface—a soft "plop" as the membrane breaks and air is joined to air. I can see the bottom of the pool—a sandy bottom, slightly lighter than the dark water, except where the moon is reflected and it is bright and breaking. More bubbles rise in succession from the bottom. I can see them faintly through the water, one after another, bubbles disintegrating into air; one form turning into another; one form becoming, in a state of *becoming,* another. I see the space between the two forms. The movement of the constant becoming. Bubbles rise. Thoughts rise. Bubbles rise and, with the breaking of the membrane, become pure air; thoughts rise and become . . . what? Energy. Particles. Atoms. Molecules. Protoplasm.

....

Among all the photos passed on to me after she died, I have found only one of my mother when she was pregnant with me. She is seated in my father's easy chair, her feet up, reading a book. She wears a brown maternity dress with a lace collar, and her hair is combed back, rolled into a long coil at the nape of her neck. When I saw this picture for the first time, I imagined myself resting beneath that roundness and a wave of pleasure and grief swept over me. That lump was *me,* was me becoming! It was a strange joy, a recognition of sorts, that passed through me, seeing myself as a part of my mother's body, inside her, unseen, but so obviously present.

I had developed well beyond the three prior fetuses that had miscarried, where each succeeding loss had become for her a grief of deepening despair over whether she would ever bear a child. As I was growing up, I loved to hear the story of my birth. In the countless retellings, I heard how her doctor had allowed her labor to continue forty-eight hours. She knew that she could die in this effort and demanded glasses of orange juice between contractions, so determined she was to hold me in her arms. Finally, they swabbed her abdomen and drew a scalpel in that clean, sure line.

But here in the photograph was this miracle, this roundness that was me, floating in salty humors of unshed tears for no more miscarried babies.

....

A circle forming—like the moon, but with a face—maybe my mother's face looking down at me in the crib.

I think of certain primal images like this one. They bob up like logs long held in some underwater vegetative net, released by currents and waves that are in their turn ruled by elements in an even larger universe. While sensory perceptions from my first forming might pierce my memory most clearly in images such as the one above, I think that sight is not the first sense to function. Rather, sight follows sound, which is perhaps second only to touch's first very tentative unfolding.

With a sense of urgency, the billboard hovering over the freeway claims that a fetus's sense of touch is operational at ten weeks. Few, if any, of us remember that touch, that first awareness of warm fluid on our skin, skin newly installed with its network of hairlike nerves, still rudimentary in connectors and bereft of protective shafts. Nor do most of us remember the resistance of our mother's body to our kicks and thrusts as we exercised newly formed muscles in involuntary spasms. To remember the experience of touch, even the touch of water, at that stage might have been too strong a dose of reality, too jarring a contact on skin as young as that. I imagine it being like the touch of a finger on the exposed dermis of a third-degree burn. No, I don't remember the touch of the amniotic fluid that bathed me in its warm tides, though it seems I must experience its primordial calm in my persistent attraction to sitting and dreaming before large bodies of water.

I look at my hand, the left one as it holds the page where I sit and write, the confluence of motion below the surface of skin where muscle and sinew play out their dance among the branchings of blue veins. And that skin, that sack of receptors and transmitters, thickened until now with the moisture of youth, has begun to thin and become transparent again, as it once was in the womb; only now, it is slowly drying and becoming wrinkled from the increasing drought of age.

What has this to do with becomings, with the senses and with memory? Perhaps it is the drought that creates the thirst to know, to imagine, to remember, to record. To wonder what the breaking bubble becomes at this end of the continuum.

What could have been my first perception of sound I suspect had been transposed into a recurring dream in early childhood, until it appeared fewer and fewer times and finally disappeared entirely when I was about eight. In this dream, I was lying by the side of a railroad track and heard a train approaching from miles off. The vibration of its wheels resounded through the earth and became increasingly loud in a distant, rhythmic roar. The images of railroad track and me lying by it were vague. At most, they were images that, in the twilight of waking, I superimposed on the more vivid aural image of the dream itself. Inside the dream it was always dark; I saw nothing, only heard the rhythmic cadence coming as if from far away. And yet, at the same time the sound was all around me, so that where I was lying actually vibrated to its beat. I was a part of that vibration too, in some way I could not fathom; and that association brought a sense of both comfort and dread, of becoming, perhaps, and of ending. A strange ambivalence.

When I think about this dream now, I sometimes convince myself that it was the sound of my mother's heart beating against and vibrating the fluid that surrounded my own newly-formed heart. Other times, the presence of both comfort and dread suggests the feeling of contractions, my mother's interminable crampings before her belly was split open finally, and I was lifted like an offering from the only world I knew. Perhaps I didn't want to leave the womb, was afraid, discomfited by the increasing pressure to leave and burst into . . . what? That great Unknown, which I now know would be bright with harsh lights, vast, noisy, and, compared to the warm bath where I was coming from, shockingly cold.

So was the non-touch of the amniotic fluid the first non-sense to develop? *Was* my proclivity for dreaming before water a kind of unconscious memory of a *pre*-sense that just happened to take up residence in my soul instead of my skin? And was sound the first remembered sense to develop? Unremembered touch, then remembered sound, and finally, remembered touch. In that order?

Because now the scene had shifted, and I began to know, to literally taste this bright, vast universe outside the womb. Everything went into my mouth, and this time the raw nerves were ready, sheathed and protected by three new layers of skin. This time the bath was in a bathinette my parents used for both me and, later, my younger brother. Made of white rubber sewn into a deep pouch, it was supported along its upper rim by a wooden frame that folded up like a lawn chair into a compact and flat package that could be stored away when not in use.

I loved my baths, judging from photographs my father took every weekend of his growing family and of the growing house he built by the eastern shore of White Bear Lake in the village of Mahtomedi, nine miles from St. Paul. We lived in the basement of the uncompleted house, and ate food cooked on an old tabletop gas stove. The refrigerator stood on four sturdy legs in one corner of the cement room. To brighten the atmosphere, my father had installed yellow print linoleum over the cold cement floor. As I sat in the warm suds, splashing and singing, the dark oval hole my lips formed in the photograph framed two new bottom teeth. My mother had been decapitated by the viewfinder, and was all arms and torso, a checkered house dress with plump appendages, standing back from the bathinette so the camera could home in on the main subject. Later, she wrapped a towel around me, and its rough nap deepened a pink glow the warm water had stimulated in my skin. Then my mother's hands went to work rubbing in fragrant cocoa butter until my eyelids drooped, and I was placed in a soft flannel bunting and put down in the crib.

This may not all be true. I don't actually remember the touch of the water, the towel, the smoothing on of the cocoa butter. I reconstruct it all from things my mother told me, and from my imagination, stimulated by photographs of my one-year-old self. In the process, I make the discovery that memory is as much creation as revelation.

In the realm of sight, though, there has been little need for imagining, because for years, going back to early childhood, I was able to call up images of very large globes of various colors. In my memory, the globes were close to me, shiny and reflective with a variety of bright hues. I was bathed this time, not in water, but in colored light. My eyes went from one large globe to another. At some point in my remembering, I realized that I must have been lying beneath the decorated tree of my first Christmas. Later, at age four or five, I remembered and asked my mother what had happened to the big colored balls we used to have on the tree, the ones as big as bowling balls (having accompanied an aunt and uncle the day before to a bowling alley, I had adequate experience for comparison). She didn't know what I was talking about. It was later, as a teenager, that the image and sense of pleasure it brought reminded me that, to an eight-month-old infant, Christmas balls hanging above her head and illuminated by their reflections off the colored lights would indeed loom large as bowling balls.

And then one recent Christmas, feeling fragile and smarting a little from the buffetings of middle age, I walked through a crowded department store gilded with decorations of the season. While absently fingering a fine woolen scarf on display, my eye was caught by something. Tucked up with the fake evergreens nesting on cornices and under archways were red and green glass globes, large as bowling balls; and as I stopped to gaze at them, I caught myself thinking, *yes, they were like that.*

It had been thirty-five years since I'd last thought of that fleeting image of the colored globes. But at this precise moment, the memory returned clean and complete as if it were just happening; as if my past existed within me and could be called up, complete and unchanged; as if I were again that teenager daydreaming, that eight-year-old questioning my mother, my experience validated at last.

....

One night we were returning home after having had Sunday dinner at my grandmother's in St. Paul. At the table, my parents had a bad argument, and the evening quickly deteriorated into a chaos of harsh words and even harsher emotions. The dinner ruined, we prepared to leave. But my grandmother intervened, weeping and pulling me by my arm in one direction toward her, protectively, not wanting me to go with my feuding parents, while at the same time my mother pulled me in the opposite direction out the door. I was frightened and whimpering, bewildered by the ferociousness of my parents' helpless rage, the anguish of my usually cheerful grandmother and the distinct impression I had of being fought over as if I were a prize, *of nearly being torn in half.*

Going home, I sat in the back of the maroon Ford. On Dale Street near the Baptist Church, we stopped at a light. I glanced at the car beside us, also stopped. I was young enough that I could just see out the car window. I thought about the people in the other vehicle; where had they been, where were they going? For the first time in my life I looked at other people and recognized that they had lives completely unique from my own. Though I couldn't articulate it then, I somehow understood that that other child had a different destination, different thoughts, different house, different toys—perhaps a totally different experience of the world than I had. Parked at the stoplight, my parents silent in the front seat, I was alone in the back, when the life of this child in the other car was set in relief against the background of my own. If my life was composed of such events as those that had transpired moments earlier, what were the events in the lives of the people in the next car? I was surprised and momentarily awestruck by this sudden perception of the separateness between myself and other individuals.

....

One cold winter day when I arrived home from second grade, my mother met me at the kitchen door with a surprise.

I heard their cries first from the top of the basement stairs—sharp yelps and high-pitched mews, like kittens. Lady, our Irish Setter, had delivered her pups—twelve in all—in the wooden box my father had made for her and placed near the furnace. The pups roiled around, blind, seeking the life-sustaining teats. The air hung heavy with the odor of birth and mother's milk and the damp, ever-present odor of mildew.

The pups' velvet fur felt warm and soft and new. I climbed into the box with them. Lady watched me, but didn't protest. I lay down next to her, my head on her flank, nose into her fur, eyeball to eyeball with the squirming puppies, absorbing their odor, their mystery, their miracle.

One of them waddled over and licked my hand. Unlike all the others, his chest was marked by a white blaze. Because of this marking, I could easily pick him out from the other eleven. I went every day to play with the puppies, but spent most of my time with this one. I gave him a name: Red Rufus, and when the time came to sell them, I insisted on keeping him. But we already had two dogs, and Rufus's mother was a fine bird dog, protested my parents, who were hunters. They regretted their decision when Rufus turned out to be not only gun-shy, but resistant to any kind of obedience training as well—just a Bozo goofus clown dog who never quite grew up.

With ears pricked forward and brow furrowed, Rufus spent long summer days cruising the shallows near our dock, occasionally lunging into the water and coming up with a squirming minnow. He'd fish until the lake froze over in November, and then he was out again in early March, peering through the spring-thinned ice for glimpses of his prey. He turned out to be an affection addict, who unabashedly and unequivocally demanded his due by plopping a big paw onto my father's newspaper, my mother's latest paperback mystery, or my current volume of Nancy Drew. When my brother and I took the rowboat out on the lake, Rufus ran along the shore, barking, devastating the peace of the neighborhood, and then swam out after us when we refused to obey his apparent orders to return where we could be safe and he could keep an eye on us. I feared he would tire and drown, but his big, devoted heart held out to the end.

The years passed; I became a teenager and got my driver's license. Then one night I opened the kitchen door in answer to his yelping summons and found him collapsed on the sidewalk. He had dragged himself three blocks from the highway, where he had been hit by a car. We took him to the vet's office, and the next day, I drove back again to see how he was. Dr. Marsh said the dog was old and probably wouldn't recover from the badly dislocated hind leg and serious internal injuries he'd sustained. The vet advised putting him to sleep. I signed the paper.

"May I see him?" I asked. "I'd like to say good-bye."

"Won't that just make you feel worse?" he asked. "You might cry and have trouble driving home."

I agreed that this might not be a good thing and left. In the late 1950s, it was not yet a virtue to cry over a loss. That kind of freedom would begin to come in the next decade.

....

I loved Sundays best of all—Sunday mornings in the summer, the lake still in the early hush before the neighbors along the shore started mowing their lawns or revving up their outboards. I'd dress in shorts and a T-shirt and head down to the lake to sit on the dock, legs dangling, watching the sunnies nibble my toes. The hum of a distant train droned from somewhere inland from the far shore and this was the only sound, except for birdsong, that broke the morning quiet.

Later, while a pot of Norwegian egg coffee simmered on the stove, my mother kneaded dough for cinnamon buns, set it to rise, and opened a can of kippers. Our Sunday breakfasts differed markedly from the ubiquitous bowl of oatmeal that on weekdays sent us off to school or office. But even then, the oatmeal was special, my mother's pride. Simmering all night in a double boiler on the back burner, it emerged lumpless and satiny, flavored with brown sugar and real cream. We ate in the dining room, my father absorbed in the morning newspaper, my mother shuttling food and empty dishes back and forth. But on Sundays, with time to relax, she joined us at the table.

Whether it was Sunday, Saturday, or a weekday, in the summer I was in the lake all day. For two years, from June through August, my best friend Ellen and I, along with the other neighborhood kids, commandeered the Werthheimer's diving board to practice swan dives and jack knifes. I have a memory fragment of myself, out of breath, dog paddling from where I have just come up from a deep dive to the wooden ladder nailed to the edge of the dock. I climb the ladder and stand panting and dripping, my nostrils burning from the lake. I can see the hot dock boards steaming from water left by previous divers. Skinny and flat chested in our sagging swimsuits, we are eight or nine years old, the age when our two permanent incisors seem way too big for our faces. I wait for my next turn on the board, talking breathlessly with Ellen about the merits of our last dives, my arms around myself, shivering and shifting my weight from one foot to the other.

....

It smelled green. The greenness and damp of thick layers of pine needles on the forest floor. Green, but not yet musty. And it once was green, a deep forest hue of shadowy glens near a rushing stream. But as the years wore on and the tent strained against its pegs in wind and rain, the sun seared its canvas fibers, and it lost its elasticity. It sagged and in some places let in drops of rain where stone-pricked holes had begun to fray larger, but which were still too small to notice and to patch. Over the years, the rich, deep color of its new time faded with age and wear to a mottled olive drab, which caused it to blend even more effectively into the underbrush, catching patches of sun dappling through the leaves of tall birches in perfect camouflage. The tent smelled of this drab green too, a worn smell, verging on musty, but still with the unmistakable tincture of the forest.

My father had purchased it so that he and the Indian, Francis, would have shelter during the long weekends when they drove the three hundred miles up to the North Shore to the property he had bought with his father in the late 1930s. I imagine the two men for days working their way through the thick underbrush, clearing the land for a narrow road, the hack of their machetes sounding the alarm that some bigger animal was taking over this five acres of forest. Then they went in with handsaws, felling trees. But not just any trees. That beautiful tall spruce, or this promising young hardwood had to stay; and that silent grove of birch could not be disturbed, would have to be circumvented. The road that emerged from all this care and hard work meandered like a tangle of yarn, barely wide enough for the old Ford to lumber through. Its headlights at night startled the mice scuttling in the underbrush and then shot skyward to light the stars as the car labored slowly up and down and around the route that led to the campsite.

At the end of each workday, I can see the men frying lake trout or herring in the aluminum fry pan that nested together with plates, cutlery, coffeepot, and saucepan into a compact, space-saving kit.

The aluminum cooking gear smelled like the tent because of the canvas bag it all fit tightly into—like the tent, but with a slight metallic tinge. When the pots clattered against themselves, they sounded out with a hollow thickness, like the side of a saucepan when one stirs cocoa about to boil.

Arnold Anderson, our next-door neighbor back home and my friend Ellen's father, came up to lend a hand when he could. He brewed the strong camp coffee, while Francis sat in silence, turning potatoes roasting in the coals at the edge of the campfire. As the embers died, they talked, the cocky Scots-Irishman with a head full of dreams he was just beginning to realize, the quiet Norwegian back from the war, and the Ojibway Indian, also a veteran, found in an alcoholic stupor in the gutter outside the Union Gospel Mission in St. Paul, and offered a job.

The road was eventually completed and graveled, and my parents decided to buy a second-hand house trailer, about sixteen feet long. One of the first of its kind, it was an oblong wooden box with wheels and painted brown with a tan rim up near the roof where two screened vents stuck up like periscopes. Four windows let in light and fresh air, and a sink, Coleman stove, and tiny icebox comprised the kitchen. It slept four not very comfortably, and I remember times my paternal grandparents joined us, so we must have doubled up somehow.

The trailer smelled too, not of green, but of wood and varnish, as if it had swelled up in an enormous déjà vu the minute it entered the woods of our property. The trailer was fitted with a fine copper screen door, in a wooden frame, that opened and closed with the twist of a delicate latch we had to grasp with the tips of our fingers, as if everything but the people were miniaturized in this scaled-down mobile dwelling. I loved watching for the golden copper strands of the door's screen to catch the morning sun in its delirium of radiance.

While my grandmother picked blueberries, my grandfather sat in the sun and read until lunchtime. Then, after a nap, he'd change into a rumpled white summer suit and my grandmother into a more formal "afternoon dress," and we'd all climb into the Ford and pay a visit to Cascade Falls, or to Grand Marais to shop. One weekend we even ventured over the Canadian border into the town of Fort William and brought back yards of tartan wool, Scottish mints, and English tea. At various points along the way, we stopped to take snapshots posed in front of the falls, or against the backdrop of the lake's horizon. We used my grandparents' old bellows camera, bound in scuffed leather.

In the summers of 1948 and 1949, polio caroused through the Midwest's households and seemed to settle with particular malevolence in the hot, muggy confines of its cities. It victimized children in particular, and to escape this scourge we spent two entire summers up North, my mother, brother, and I alone during the week and joined by my father on weekends.

One Friday night in 1949, he arrived very late. At first I didn't recognize him as I woke from sleep. His face was swollen around a three-inch gash just above his right eye. A purple bruise darkened his cheekbone. He lifted his pants leg, revealing the gauze and adhesive bandage wrapped around his right knee, saying something about the ignition key. Daddy has had an accident, my mother told my brother and me, and we should go back to sleep, that he was fine, that it was nothing, nothing at all.

I learned later that my father had been driving down Seventh Street in St. Paul, on his way home, when something between his two ears began to buzz loudly, and the car in front of him suddenly became two cars, then three, and the honking and buzzing doubled, tripled as the steering wheel snapped out of his hands, which had begun to jerk uncontrollably. The car came to an abrupt halt, sputtering into the mailbox just short of the corner of Seventh and Robert. He was twitching uncontrollably and moaning as two men pulled him out. A crowd gathered, a call was made for an ambulance, a handkerchief clamped in his teeth.

My father had just suffered his first seizure. The doctors initially diagnosed epilepsy. It wasn't until a year later that they cut into that curly head full of dreams and found the tumor. He came home thin, hairless, looking ten years older. He'd lost his speech and had to learn to speak again like a two year old. He cried easily.

It was a year after his surgery before we brought out the faded old tent from its storage place, hitched up the new silver trailer and returned to our deep green and sun-spattered glen in the north woods.

For me, the smell of canvas triggers memories of past security, mnemonic endorphins that soothe the pain, but fail to heal me of the chaos my father's illness inspired in each of our lives.

These old family photographs point the way inward to the path that memory charts and where I sense lie hidden the seeds of healing. The file devoted to pictures of my father is fat, and his sad smile is scattered also among those files dedicated to each of the others. His legacy begins to emerge as something noble and courageous, even at the same time that it has been devastating to those who loved him. Each of us accommodated this disaster into our lives in different ways. In searching for my father, I begin to find everyone else too—and not least of all, myself, becoming still.

ROCHELLE RATNER

November Poem

This morning all the hunters
sat at breakfast
in their green jungle suits
with here and there
something red

it's that time again
when grown men
paint their faces black
and stalk in pairs through woods
that don't belong to them

For the next month
they leave cars by the road
and disguise themselves

while I make a note
not to take that trail
behind my house—
it can wait a month

meanwhile this time is filled
with lugging boxes,
maybe 150 cartons of books
in which I hid for years
that I'll store in the attic here

taking half a box at a time
up the narrow ladder,
refusing all help

and I think of large men
lugging those deer through woods
back to their cars—
a man here says the easiest way
is to drape it over your shoulders,
then he says be careful.

JOHN REINHARD

....

Some Places out West

They celebrate the testicle
festival in this almost
town locked in place between
Missoula and Helena.

I saw my grandfathers' testicles,
Grandpa Andy's and Grandpa Ed's.
Both men in the hospital
and a few months short of dying
let the eel emerge one more time
from the gnarly sea grass.
This is where you come from, Son.
This is where you're going, Son.

Grandpa Ed's right nut was swelled up
big as casaba. "Elephant's Eye"
my Grandma Ruth called it while Ed
kept ringing the night nurse
to run away with him to Paris, France,
though he'd need a new pair of pants first.

My own testicles remind me of little church bells.
In fact, I used to ring them every day
including Sunday. They have their own rope
and if you pulled it right
they'd peal out "How Great Thou Art"
in spirited tones.

My friend Buck, the fisherman, is moving
to Japan where he's heard
that if you nestle your testicles just right
on the blue stream, set them like
figs in the honey vat, Zen trout
will rise and explain how
one creek remains a universe as long
as you allow the sky
and ocean to keep
passing through.

Sharing the quick nights
in her mother and father's bed,
my baby daughter thinks testicles
are kickballs you boot in your sleep
when dreams go bad.
I won't tell her different.
You never know. One day
well into the next century
she may find herself in Montana
where a boy will be aching
toward manhood. One dreamy kick
and it will be understood,
the life and death he already carries
between his legs, those bells
with their music of mourning
and the heavy weight of their delight.

....

Instructional Technologies

When, in the middle of his lecture, Professor Butler suddenly staggered forward, clawing madly at his chest, then collapsed across an empty desk before dropping face-first to the floor, we all thought he was faking it.

In fact, a few students applauded.

We waited ten seconds or so for Professor Butler to stand up and resume his lecture, but then someone noticed blood pooling beneath his face, a poppy-red bloom on the white tile, and a few women in the front row lifted their feet and started screaming. I thought maybe he'd really tricked us this time, that he had somehow slipped a capsule of food coloring into his mouth to make his collapse more realistic. But then we noticed the darkening of his pants, the spread of urine on the floor, and we figured even Professor Butler wouldn't have gone *that* far to make us pay attention in his class.

When the paramedics arrived, they rolled Dr. Butler to his back, his great belly rising like an empty beer barrel in a pool of water. His bulbous nose had been flattened to one side, and blood had clotted in his silver mustache, which was tinged a brownish yellow from all the cigarettes he'd smoked in his life. One of his front teeth, broken in half, remained on the floor. It looked like a peppermint Chiclet.

They wheeled Professor Butler out of the classroom and loaded him into a waiting ambulance, and even then I thought perhaps he'd really fooled us all, that maybe he'd planned the whole, elaborate scheme. I wondered about that up until the following Wednesday when a substitute teacher and fly-fisherman named Professor Paine arrived with Dr. Butler's lecture notes and changed the course of my life.

....

By that summer, I had decided I didn't want to become a teacher, but I was going through with it anyway. I'd been in college six years already, and when I tried to tell my father I was thinking about changing majors again, he popped his cork. He said, "William, when you're halfway over Niagara Falls bare-assed in a barrel, don't you think it's a bit too late to change your mind?" Vintage Dad. It *wasn't* too late, of course, but I was so close to getting out of college with a degree in *something*, I decided to stay in the barrel.

Instructional Technologies was required for all students seeking K-12 teaching certification. It was one of the last college courses I needed to finish my English Education major. The course met on Wednesday nights in the eight-week summer session from six to nine o'clock, and covered various technologies of instruction, such as how to use the chalkboard, overhead projectors, copy and ditto machines, VCRs, eight millimeter movie projectors, and so forth. Frankly, it was a bullshit course. An easy A if you could just manage to stay awake, which was a challenge sometimes.

When he was still alive, Professor Butler did his best to keep us interested. He had taught Instructional Technologies for centuries, and he brought to it the zeal of a Pentecostal preacher, pacing and coughing and gesticulating as he lectured: "Thumbtacks give you a nice, clean look, but once they're in it's like trying to draw the sword from the stone to get them back out again! It's like pulling spikes with your fingernails! Push pins with florescent plastic caps are the wave of the future. And they're easy to see if you drop them. In my early career as a teacher, the bottom of my shoes were so full of tacks I sounded like a tap-dancer when I walked down the halls. Clickety, clickety, clickety, I sounded like a dog without his toenails trimmed!"

When this enthusiasm failed to capture our attention, Professor Butler turned to melodrama. Occasionally, he'd break into song, bellowing a few off-key lines from *Oklahoma!* or *Les Misérables.* Sometimes he would drop to the floor and crawl around between the rows of desks, dragging his left leg. "I think I've had a stroke!" he would say. "But don't call an ambulance yet! We have a lesson plan to finish!" Most often, however, he'd feign a heart attack, clutching his chest with both hands, holding his breath until his face flushed red and his eyes bulged, and falling forward over an empty desk to the floor.

But he wouldn't be doing that anymore.

"He yelled 'wolf' once too often, man," Matt Gombie, one of the students in class, said, "and it came back to bite him in the ass."

....

The subject on the syllabus of that first class period without Dr. Butler was entitled, "Chalk Talk: Using the Chalkboard Effectively." Professor Paine, a tall, balding, tired-looking man in his fifties, with puffs of curly hair above his ears and a mustache that grew completely over his mouth, read in a soft monotone from Dr. Butler's notes:

"Never lean against a chalkboard wearing a dark shirt or coat. . . . To avoid the annoying screech new chalk sometimes makes on a clean chalkboard, soften the chalk by holding the tip in your mouth for a few seconds or lick it occasionally while you write. . . . Clean erasers by tumbling them for twenty minutes at home in your clothes dryer, on the cool cycle. Remember to remove other clothing before doing so." From time to time, he'd pause to shake his head at the material, then drink from a can of Jolt that rested on a table beside the lectern. He wore a rumpled shirt and tie and blue jeans, and when he unbuttoned his sport coat, we discovered that his tie was shaped like a fish hanging by its tail. A brown trout, it turned out. "Genus *Salmo trutta*," Professor Paine noted, enthusiastically, when someone inquired. "The native trout of Europe. First stocked in North America in 1883. A *majestic* fish! One of God's finer inspirations."

An hour into the class, two students in the back row had fallen asleep. Matt Gombie had drawn a naked girl on his desk in pencil, with breasts the size of melons, and smiling faces where the nipples should have been. Professor Paine suddenly stopped lecturing. He looked distraught.

"Dr. Butler was a good man," he said. "He *believed* in this course." Professor Paine shuffled the lecture notes and returned them to the file. "I, on the other hand, do not, even though it has fallen to me, as the associate dean of the College of Education, to finish teaching it. I cannot bear to read another word of this. Dr. Butler, rest his soul, has three hours of lecture notes here on how to use the chalkboard. Three hours! One wouldn't think that would be possible, but there it is. I read you the first hour. We've all suffered quite enough." He tapped the edge of the file on the lectern and sighed. "Class dismissed."

....

Fifteen minutes into the following week's class, Professor Paine had not yet arrived. While most of us sat quietly pondering our uncertain futures, other students debated how long we were obliged to wait for tardy professors before leaving. They'd nearly reached a consensus of fifteen minutes when Professor Paine walked through the door, trailed by his eleven-year-old son, a skinny boy he introduced as Peter ("Peter Paine?" someone whispered, to earn a burst of laughter), who wore green rubber fishing waders that came to the top of his thighs. The freckle-faced boy spent ten minutes clomping around in his waders, explaining how to show a movie on the VCR and how to pre-program it to record television shows. He said he had taped every episode of Babe Winkleman's "Good Fishing" on Saturday mornings at his mother's house. While Peter taught the class, Professor Paine sat on the table in front of the room, reading *Field & Stream*. He wore faded blue jeans, a blue T-shirt, and a fishing vest, the kind with a small cloud of fleece over one pocket.

"That's it," Professor Paine said, when the boy finished explaining things to us. "That's enough, Peter. Thank you." He looked at us. "Who *doesn't* understand how to program a VCR? Anyone? Anyone besides me, that is?"

No hands went up.

"Well!" he said. "There you have it. We're done." He looked up at the clock. It was not yet six-thirty. "We still have some time left. The Hex hatch is starting over on the White River. Late tonight, trophy brown trout will be out there slurping mayflies the size of hummingbirds. Peter and I are going night fishing. Anyone care to join us?"

No one moved. Matt Gombie raised his hand.

"Yes?" Professor Paine asked.

"You're asking us if we want to go fishing with you?"

"That's correct."

We all looked around at one another.

Kyle Prentice leaned over and whispered, "This guy's crazier than Butler."

I smiled and nodded. This was true, but I *liked* Professor Paine.

He was a hot spark in a room full of gasoline cans. He had an aura about him of unrealized potential, something I recognized in myself.

"You?" he asked, pointing to me. "You nodded. You want to go fishing?"

"Me?" I stammered. "Not tonight. No."

"Why not?"

"Well," I said, embarrassed, "I don't fish."

Kyle Prentice laughed.

"What's your name?" Professor Paine inquired.

"Bill," I said. "Bill Knight."

"Mr. Knight," Professor Paine said, "you live in central Wisconsin, surrounded by some of the finest brown trout streams in the Midwest, and you don't fish?"

"No," I said. "I don't." This was the truth. I had never fished in my life. My father didn't fish. *His* father didn't fish. I came from a line of non-fishermen whose sole purpose in life was to make money, who were good at it, and who rejected any activity that distracted them from that end. Like Dr. Butler, my grandfather had died working, while sitting in his leather chair at the bank that he owned. My father sat in that chair now. I was next in line. I felt like a veal calf in a chute at a processing plant.

Professor Paine shook his head sadly and left. His son followed him out of the room, the sound of his thumping waders fading in the distance down the hallway.

"Cool!" said Matt Gombie, who popped out of his desk. "Time to party, dudes!" he said, and left the room. The rest of us milled around awkwardly, pondering what to make of our good fortune.

"This is ridiculous," Sherry Warner said. "We're paying good money for this class, and he's not even teaching it." There's always some dizzy capitalist in every class who believes that educations are purchased like pork belly futures. "If this happens again," she added, "I'm calling the dean."

"He *is* the dean," Kyle Prentice said.

"No, he's not," Sherry said, "he's the associate dean. The dean of education is Dr. Gladdens. I know him. He plays golf with my dad."

"Man, don't call Dr. Glad Bag," said Kyle. "Just let it be. You learned how to work a VCR, didn't you? What's the problem?"

"The problem," Sherry said, "is that I paid for three hours and I only got fifteen minutes."

"Hey, the shit's on sale!" Kyle said. "Enjoy it!"

....

Professor Paine was in class waiting for us when we arrived the following week at six o'clock. He sat eating a Big Mac and reading *Fly Rod & Reel magazine.* He wore another of his fish ties, this one a rainbow trout, "Genus *Oncorhynchus mykiss,*" he'd written on the board. "A native. Migratory species are known as *steelhead.* A *glorious* fish!" The chairs were arranged in a circle around a table that held a ditto machine. Next to it was a large, white Canon photocopier and a smaller machine used to make ditto masters.

When we were all there, Professor Paine started class.

"Someone show us all how to make a photocopy. Here," he said. A nickel was squeezed between his fingers. Sherry Warner raised her hand. She took the nickel from Professor Paine, dropped it into the copy machine, and stopped.

"What should I copy?" she asked.

"Anything," Professor Paine answered.

Sherry looked troubled.

"Here," Professor Paine said, pulling his billfold from his back pocket. He opened it and handed her a twenty-dollar bill. "Copy this."

"Money?" she said. "That's illegal."

"Take a walk on the wild side," Professor Paine said.

Sherry froze.

"Just stick it on there and push the damn button," Matt Gombie yelled. "The man wants to go fishing."

Professor Paine stood up and looked at Matt. "What's your name, young man?"

"Me?" Matt said. "Matt Gombie."

"Mr. Gombie," the professor said, nodding. "Are you by any chance a trout fisherman?"

Matt Gombie shook his head no. The professor shrugged and sat back down. "Go ahead," he said to Sherry, "copy away."

Sherry Warner pushed the button. The machine hummed, the light flashed, and a piece of white paper kicked out, a dark copy of the twenty dollar bill in the middle.

"Very good," Professor Paine said.

"My name's Sherry Warner."

"Very good, Ms. Warner," the professor said, taking the photocopy from her hand. "Counterfeiting is a crime. You could be charged with a felony. How does that feel?"

"You *told* me to do it!"

The class laughed.

Professor Paine smiled at her. "How about the ditto machine, now? Can you finish the job?"

"What do you mean?"

"Here," he said, holding the photocopy out to her. "There's the ditto machine. Make us two copies, or so. Double or triple our money."

Sherry refused, so Professor Paine selected another woman sitting in the front row, a pretty, recently divorced older woman named Angela Childs. She looked to be about forty years old. On the nights she couldn't get a babysitter, she brought her two daughters, ages eight and ten, to class with her.

Angela made a tissue paper master on the Thermo Fax transparency machine, then hooked it to the ditto machine and quickly ran off four or five purple copies of the twenty dollar bill. When she finished, she sat back down at her desk.

"Well, there we go," said Professor Paine. "The photocopier and the ditto machine. The best friends of teachers and the poor. I guess we're done. Any questions?"

Sherry Warner raised her hand. "Professor Paine," she said, "we're paying for this class and I for one resent being short-changed like this."

"Short-changed?" he said. "Whatever do you mean? We made a hundred dollars here tonight!"

We all laughed, but Sherry ignored him.

"Your infantile jokes and your lack of effort are really unprofessional," Sherry said.

"I take it you're the student who called Dean Gladdens last week to complain about my teaching."

Sherry said, "You gave me no choice."

"Well," Professor Paine said, "your passion for learning is commendable. Misguided, but commendable."

Matt Gombie raised his hand. "Professor Paine," Matt said, "just so you know, the brevity thing, it's cool. Don't think Miss Manners here is expressing majority opinion."

"Well, now," the professor said, "she does have a point, though, doesn't she? While it's true that I will be retiring in the next few years, I could still put forth a little effort."

"Not necessary," Matt said. "Really. Things are cool the way they are."

"How about a bit of a lecture," Professor Paine said, "for old times' sake? Nothing too elaborate. Then next week I promise I'll put together something worthwhile for the remaining four weeks of this summer term. We might as well learn something useful as long as we're all together, right? Ms. Warner, does that sound satisfactory?"

Sherry nodded. Matt exhaled loudly and slouched in his desk. Professor Paine stood and walked to a spot behind the lectern.

"You're all studying to be teachers," he began. "Few things in life are more gratifying or pleasurable than teaching." He paused. "Well, hell, let's be honest. Sex is a lot better, at least when you're young. Even with my ex-wives, on the rare occasions it happened, it wasn't too bad. Then, of course, there's trout fishing, which is far better still. Let's just agree to forget the gratifying and pleasurable part, and cut right to the chase.

"The thing about teaching that nobody tells you is that people don't like teachers. When you become a teacher, everyone with so-called normal jobs is going to envy you because you can spend all summer fishing. And they're going to resent even the little bit of money you make because it's what keeps their property taxes so high. Conservative newspaper columnists are going to write every week that public school education in America is a failure, forgetting to mention along the way that the people who taught them to write were public school teachers. They're going to refer to the teachers' union with the same sneer they use when talking about communists. In a nutshell, then, people are going to want you to teach their children everything they need to know to succeed, they're going to criticize how you do it, and they're going to try to pay you as little as possible for doing it. But that's America. Get used to it."

He paused to smile. "Any questions so far?" No one said anything.

We all looked around the room at one another, as if deciding whether we should take notes or not.

"Now, my life, as you might have guessed by now, is in the toilet. Just as many of yours will be, someday. There's no avoiding it, really. It's the odds. Some lives are destined for happiness, and some lives end up in the toilet. Mine's one of the latter. I don't know how it happened. One day I woke up to discover I'd gone from being a boy to being a man, and frankly, I liked being a boy better. It was a more soulful time. Less bullshit to wade through. The best thing manhood's got going for it is mortality. When you're young, you can't even imagine dying, but when you're older, unless you're balls deep in a river in the middle of an insect hatch, death doesn't seem so terrible."

Sherry Warner raised her hand.

"Professor Paine," she said, "this has nothing to do with what you're supposed to be teaching us."

"On the contrary, Ms. Warner," he said, "this has *everything* to do with it. In fact, this will be the subject of class for the rest of the semester: Life. I will prepare you for life. And to make it interesting, I'll tell you what. If you don't like what you learn, I'll give you your money back. What did you all pay, one hundred and twelve dollars per credit for this course, to learn what any eleven year old could teach you in an hour or two? How to use chalkboards and photocopy machines and VCRs? Shame on you!"

He was shouting and wandering back and forth like a crazy man. His tie flopped around against his chest like a fish, which, of course, is what it was.

"Teaching is not about how to write on the chalkboard or how to show a movie on the VCR!" he said. "Teaching is about passion! It is about pouring water on the human soul and watching it bloom! Your job as a teacher is not to make fancy bulletin boards or to write without squeaking the goddamn chalk but to liberate! To help your students build a self worthy of its humanity! Give them a fish and they'll have a fish fry; *teach* them to fish, and goddamn it, they'll have something to live for!"

Matt Gombie leaned over to me and whispered, "I don't understand this shit, do you?"

"It's better than learning how to lick chalk," I said.

"Good point, dude," Matt said. In truth, I found in Professor Paine a kindred soul. My life was spiraling down the toilet, too.

"Well," Professor Paine said, pausing to catch his breath. "There you have it. We'll start next week. I want everyone to come to class with a swimsuit and a towel. We'll meet at six o'clock at the Aquatic Center."

"At the pool?" Angela said. "What for?"

Professor Paine smiled. "To learn about life," he said. "We'll start with insects."

....

One rarely sees college professors outside of the classroom, and then never when they're nearly naked. (Granted, some professors are occasionally seen naked by students, but they tend not to remain professors very long.) Professor Paine's skin looked like that of a raw chicken drumstick except for his neck and his arms, which were sun-tanned. A thick, pinkish scar ran down the center of his chest, and it looked like a nightcrawler stretched from his throat to six inches or so beneath his sternum.

"Quadruple bypass," he said, when he noticed me staring. "A souvenir from my third marriage." He held a one-gallon plastic ice cream bucket in his hands, with holes punched in the lid, and he wore baggy blue swimming trunks that made his legs look like sticks. Behind him was a plastic basket with scuba masks piled inside of it. "Gather over here, please," he said, as students in swimming suits wandered in. Only about twelve of us showed up, the others apparently deciding to drop the course and take it another time, when someone sane was teaching it. Four of the remaining students were women, including Sherry Warner, who wore a red, one-piece swimsuit, and rubber flip-flops on her feet. She had her brown hair pinned up off of her neck, and she wore mother-of-pearl toenail polish. Seeing her in a swimsuit gave me urges. I was glad the water in the pool was cold.

"Thank you all for coming," he said. "In the next four weeks, I'm going to do two things. I'm going to teach you how to teach. And I'm going to teach you how to fly-fish for trout. Both of these skills will be indispensable in your search to live a full and satisfying life."

We all nodded and looked around at one another. No one objected, not even Sherry Warner. We stood in the chlorinated air in our swimsuits, arms crossed over our chests. The water in the pool was still and clear.

"Let's get in carefully on the shallow end." We did as we were told, one after another jumping in and standing in waist-deep water, with Professor Paine in front of us. He held his plastic bucket under one arm, with the basket of scuba masks partly submerged in the water in front of him. "Now, ninety percent of the food trout eat lives underwater. The remaining ten percent of the time, they feed on the surface. Dry fly fishing targets that ten percent. I'm going to teach you to become dry fly fishermen and women. It's as sublime an act as the creation of the world."

He held his plastic bucket in front of him. "To fish soulfully," he said, "you must first become entomologists. You must be able to identify and match, by size and color, thousands of insects. I will teach you the first six. Learning the rest—along with the nymphs, wet flies, streamers, and terrestrials trout will sometimes eat—will take the remainder of your life, but it will be worth it. Far better than sitting in a La-Z-Boy in front of the tube, waiting to die." He pulled the cover from the bucket and tapped it, and hundreds of insects with clear, papery wings flew out and swirled around our heads. "Peter and I spent hours collecting these last night," he said. "I hope you enjoy them." A few of the bugs headed for the lights on the ceiling. The others stayed near the water. One landed on my lower lip and hung there, like a scar.

Two of the women and one of the men—Matt Gombie—started waving their arms around their heads and hurried for the ladder to leave the pool.

"This is bullshit, man," Matt said, as he pulled himself from the water. "Bugs! I hate bugs!" He stood on the side of the pool and pointed to Professor Paine, who looked at him calmly. "You're nuts, man!" Matt yelled. "Deranged. Wacko. I can't believe they let you teach here!"

When this disturbance ended, we watched quietly as the insects Professor Paine had released—various mayflies, mostly, and a few assorted others—hovered over the surface of the pool. Sometimes they would settle delicately on the water, then fly up and hover for awhile before landing again. Professor Paine handed each of us a scuba mask, and put one on himself.

"Now, the thing to remember is that we don't see what trout see. To tie flies that accurately match living organisms, we must get beneath the surface to see and think like a trout. That is the secret to all things—we must seek to see the world from angles previously unattempted. On an actual river, these flies would be emerging from the stream bottom, shedding the husks that covered them in the nymphal stage, and taking flight when they reached the surface. That is what we call a 'hatch.' They live as flies for maybe three days, tops. In the air, they mate and the female lays eggs, which land in the water and sink to the bottom, starting the whole process over again. Once they mate, they die, and drop to the water, spent. All of this sends trout into a feeding frenzy that is a wonder to behold. The only difference between mayflies and human beings, as far as I'm concerned, is that most of us never get into the air at all." He motioned to us. "Put on your masks and take a look. Make sure you hold your breath."

To tell the truth, I spent more time looking at Sherry Warner underwater than I did looking at the flies Professor Paine had released. Her wet swimsuit clung to her body in a most generous manner, and tiny silver bubbles collected in the small hairs on her arms and legs. You couldn't see much of Professor Paine's flies; only their legs and parts of their abdomens actually touched the water. The remaining parts of their bodies, and their wings, glimmered just above the surface, like a reflection on a pane of glass. Beneath the water, there was a clean line to everything, a softness and a slowness that relaxed me, a sense of perfect quiet.

We swam around for about forty-five minutes this way, sometimes pausing above the surface to catch our breath and to listen to Professor Paine lecture. He talked about light refraction and sight cones and line drag, and occasionally he discussed, with great reverence, insect hatches he'd witnessed on rivers named the Au Sable, the Beaverkill, the Blackfoot, and the Bois Brule. Eventually, two more students got out of the pool and headed home. Professor Paine ignored them.

When we had showered and dressed again, Professor Paine led us to our classroom, where we sat in our desks as he distributed small fly-tying kits to each of us—there were just seven students left, four women and three men—our wet hair still smelling of chlorine, our faces still marked by red lines where the scuba masks had pressed against the skin. Inside these fly-tying kits were assorted spools of thread, a bobbin, tweezers, tiny fishing hooks, small cellophane bags of fur and feathers, scissors, tiny tubes of head cement, and assorted small hardware. A small vise was also included, along with a magnifying glass mounted on a pivoting rod, which could be lowered over the tip of the vise, where the hook would be secured. I could see my fingerprints through this magnifying glass, unexplored territory, little whorls of ridges like the elevation markings on a topographic map. Professor Paine passed out photocopied instructions and photographs that explained how to tie six dry flies: an Adams, a March Brown, a Hexagenia mayfly, an Elk Hair Caddis, a Royal Coachman, and a Trico.

Professor Paine took us through the process of tying an Elk Hair Caddis that first night. "An elk's hair is hollow," he said, "and filled with air. It's as if God intended it should be used to make dry flies. But really, you can tie flies with anything. Human hair, even, will do in a pinch for some things. There's a German shepherd in my neighborhood that wanders loose, and sometimes I coax him close and buzz a bit of hair from his back—great stuff for wet flies. One of my ex-wives has a calico cat with hair like marabou—Checkers, she calls him. I tie a great leech with that stuff, a Checkers Leech, I call it. My ex thinks her cat loses patches of hair because it has problems with stress."

The first time through, Sherry tied the most impressive Elk Hair Caddis, each hair and feather in place. Mine looked like a glob of feathers left over after a cat eats a bird. I could not get the palmered hackle to stand up properly. When Professor Paine saw it, he smiled and shook his head. "Try again," he said to me. "And don't get discouraged. We're imitating God's perfection here. It's good to be humbled; it makes the world a grander place."

It took me four more attempts to tie a fly that looked remotely like the picture on the instructions. Our homework was to tie the remaining five flies before class the following week. Professor Paine wrote his telephone number and address on the chalkboard, and told us to feel free to call him for help if we needed it. He also encouraged us to trade telephone numbers, and urged us to contact one another for help. I traded numbers with Sherry Warner. I called her four times the first night. The fifth time, she said, "Why don't you just come to my room and I'll show you."

I went. Her fingers were long and slender. Her hair smelled like apricots. She sat cross-legged in a chair at her desk in blue jeans and a T-shirt, and I stood behind her, watching, breathing her in. The flies she tied were lovely. She tied two extra Hexagenias, cut the barbs off of the hooks, and pushed them through her pierced ears to wear as earrings.

....

In the classroom the next week, Professor Paine inspected the flies of the three students who remained in the class, Sherry Warner, myself, and Angela Childs. He did not seem at all bothered by the high attrition rate, and commented nonchalantly that eleven students had requested their money back and that he'd paid them, as promised.

Sherry's flies were beautiful. Even the twin hairs that protruded from the tail of her Trico—a fly about the size of a fruit fly—were tied exactly as they should have been. Professor Paine complimented the work that Angela and I did as well, but it was obvious we had more work to do.

In the remaining time that class period, which lasted to nearly midnight, Professor Paine introduced us to all of the equipment a fly-fisherman or -woman would need on the river. He showed us all of his own equipment—his neoprene waders, his Orvis graphite flyrod, his fishing vest filled with fly boxes and other necessities, his split willow creel, his cherry-handled landing net. He taught us to tie knots in tippet material as fine as Sherry Warner's hair. He also showed us home videos he took of his son pulling in beautiful brook trout in the early morning on a small meadow stream, and large, angry-looking brown trout caught at night on the White River. As I watched, sitting there in the dark, I felt as I did as a boy on Saturday mornings in springtime after my father left for work, when the newly-green world waited for me to dirty my knees in its glorious mud.

We met once more at the Aquatic Center in our swimsuits, where Professor Paine taught us fly-casting. Each of us received an hour-long lesson while the other two watched from the side of the pool and answered questions.

"The rhythm of proper fly-casting is like the rhythm of a heart-beat at rest," Dr. Paine said. "If you are in love, so much the better. Your heart will beat more strongly, and your casting will reflect your love. Your right arm and wrist are the metronome, but your heart sets the tempo." He demonstrated as he spoke. "You lift the line from the water, move the rod backward to one o'clock, wait for the line to load, then move forward to eleven o'clock again, and release." He did. The line floated in a perfect, tight loop, uncoiling to set the fly softly on the surface of the pool, between the diving boards.

Angela went first, and Professor Paine stood closely on her left side, reaching around her, guiding her right arm with his hand on her elbow. They laughed when she began her forward cast too quickly, snapping the line behind her like a bullwhip. But after a half-hour or so, he was standing six feet away from her, and Angela was casting confidently. All this time, I sat next to Sherry Warner at poolside, my left knee just brushing against her leg.

"Sherry and William!" Professor Paine would shout to us occa-sionally. "Tell me the proper size variations of an Elk Hair Caddis."

"Size twelve to size eighteen," we said, in unison, "with size sixteen preferred."

"Very good. What about a Trico?"

"Size twenty to twenty-four."

"Excellent. And what is the Latin name for the Hex mayfly we've tied?"

"*Hexagenia limbata*," we answered.

"Nicely done!" Professor Paine said. "And what is the preferred casting motion to prevent over-casting?"

"From eleven o'clock to one o'clock," Sherry said.

"Good," Professor Paine said. "Come in here and show me. William, you may come in as well. You can see better from in here." I could not tell if he meant I could better see Sherry Warner or her casting motion. Perhaps both. Then he smiled at Angela. "You cast wonderfully, my dear," he said to her. "There are few things so lovely or graceful as a beautiful woman with an expensive flyrod in her hand, using it well."

At the end of class that evening, nearly midnight, Professor Paine announced that our final exams would be held the following weekend, if that was possible for everyone. We would meet at his house on Friday morning, ride together to Gander Mountain to purchase the necessary equipment, then head north some three hundred miles to the Bois Brule River in northern Wisconsin for two days to fish for trout. The Brule River, he said, was *worthy* water, the kind of stream John might have chosen in which to baptize Jesus (assuming, of course, a hatch was not taking place, in which case the baptism would have had to wait awhile). Bald eagles soared over the Brule, he said, and the flesh of brook trout pulled from its waters was as orange as fresh tangerines.

I had to borrow money from my father to purchase my fishing equipment. I told him my Instructional Technologies class had turned out to be interesting after all, and that I needed money for class supplies. He readily passed along his MasterCard, pleased I had discovered a passion for my college education.

That weekend, the four of us drove north in Professor Paine's Ford Explorer, and we camped along the Brule River in a large dome tent set up on a bed of soft, rust-colored pine needles. The air smelled like cedar and fresh water, and the river was the most beautiful thing I'd ever seen. Professor Paine spent most of his time with Angela, which was fine with Sherry Warner and me. We went off by ourselves upstream, through several slow, languorous pools, and downstream of a small rapids we found some brook trout that rose to our Elk Hair Caddis flies as fast as we tossed them. Sherry taught me to set the hook by lifting my rod quickly, but gently, on the rise. I had never held any living thing in my hand that was as beautiful as a brook trout.

Sherry Warner and I spent a lot of time together that weekend. We caught fish, cleaned them, and ate them fried in butter over an open fire. That first evening, to our great fortune, we witnessed a short hatch of Hexagenia mayflies—*Hexagenia limbata*—huge, thick-bodied mayflies that fluttered in our flashlight beams, rising from the water into the open air like little witches riding brooms.

We stood in the flowing river in the dark, tossing our Hex patterns wherever we heard brown trout slurping or splashing on the surface, mosquitoes swarming our heads, and Sherry and I each caught and released two or three browns, the largest over twenty inches. Professor Paine and Angela sat on a rock on the shoreline holding citronella candles, laughing and clapping each time we hooked a fish and each time we missed one. He and Angela went back to the tent early, and Sherry Warner and I kept casting under the moon, pausing, sometimes, just to listen to the sound of everything.

....

I got an A in Instructional Technologies that semester. So did Angela Childs and Sherry Warner. But the story doesn't end there. Just as the fall semester was about to begin—I had switched majors again, and for awhile had hopes of becoming an ichthyologist—I learned that Professor Paine had been excused from his teaching post. Near the end of the summer, Matt Gombie had filed a grievance against him for unprofessional conduct, and the Faculty Senate, spurred into action after learning that Angela Childs had moved in with him, found him guilty and pressed forward with expulsion hearings. Dean Gladdens testified that Professor Paine sometimes spent only fifteen minutes of a three-hour course actually teaching it. Someone else reported that he'd once allowed his eleven-year-old son to substitute teach for him, and that he sometimes got his kicks by secretly shaving patches of body hair from dogs and cats. To avoid expulsion, and the loss of benefits that would bring, Professor Paine took an early retirement and moved with Angela, her children, and his son to Helena, Montana, to be near the finest inland trout waters in North America.

I never heard from him again.

A year later, Sherry Warner and I got married. Some people are surprised when they hear that part of the story. And most people believe that our story must end like a TV movie-of-the-week: that inspired by Professor Paine, Sherry and I must have gone on to become award-winning teachers, who show our students how to look beneath the surface of things. I always nod at that point and tell them they're half right, that Sherry is a gifted high school teacher.

More importantly, I tell them, she can tie dry flies that look so alive they seem to move and breathe as they dance over rushing freestone rivers and float down tranquil meadow streams. She is an artist with feathers and hair and thread, and I show her work whenever I can at the finest river-galleries in the world, populated by the most discriminating of buyers.

And me, well, I never did become a teacher. I never even graduated from college. But thanks to Professor Paine, I found my calling.

I became a trout fisherman.

....

Someone Else

There is always someone else.
Besides Oswald. Behind Ray. Before me.
Someone made me. They told me to.
I didn't know any better.
Ain't saying I'm sorry.

I'll leave broken children behind.
Let the bitch fear men from now on.
Killing is easy
but the blood makes a mess.

Everything goes away if I turn around,
switch the TV off, leave town.
Never met your Mea Culpa.
I never touched her, Mister.
You got the wrong guy.

Could have been any one
of a hundred, you know.

....

Sonny's Stand

Dead drunk,
but still on his feet,
Sonny braces himself like a gunfighter,
a Miller can his .45.
Can't be knocked down
by anything short of hot lead
or a whisper.

Campfire smoke swirls around him
like street dust from passing horses.
Everyone but his grizzled gang
has run for cover and slammed their doors.

Any minute now, a face will show
around the corner of the fire
and square off, eye to eye.
"Darling," he'll say
and someone will scream.

MARY KAY RUMMEL

A New Zealand Elegy

Sometimes a boat just slips from its mooring.
Night falls, a vagrant magpie perches
    in the rata grove.
Wind buffets the air. Rain pummels the ground
Soaking footpaths. Mud sinks the town.
Sometimes the rain pours its heart out.
Sometimes a boat just slips from its mooring.

VERN RUTSALA

....

Geography

In fourth grade we played Geography
every Tuesday, Mrs. Eustace
turning her blank globe slowly,
then stopping and poking her
long pointer at countries
seen only in outline.
Our hands shot up like
salutes—"Me, me, Mrs.
Eustace, me"—and ticked
names off with nine-year-old
aplomb: The Belgian Congo, Ceylon,
French Indo-China—
names now like dusty attic
souvenirs. But her pointer
never found some places—
Bataan, where my young
uncle was taken prisoner,
Guadalcanal, where Mr. Eustace
lost his leg. And we couldn't
know what other names that
blind globe was dreaming of:
Tarawa, Saipan, Okinawa,
Bastogne, Anzio, Monte Cassino.
Omaha Beach waited—in of
all places France!—for my
best friend's father to die
on D-Day. The globe kept
secret even stranger
lessons: Belsen, Treblinka,

Auschwitz, Hiroshima, Nagasaki.
How could we know that Mrs.
Eustace's key to her blank globe
with all the right answers
would be rewritten by history
until now it's mostly wrong—
the blush of the British Empire's
pink faded as the cheek of an
English rose—and would look like
one of those ancient maps that said,
Beyond Here There Be Monsters.

VERN RUTSALA

....

Taking the Old Road

Yesterday we fell for it again,
letting ourselves be herded
along I-5—all traffic
a single-minded seventy, roadsides
like blinders, farmland and towns
turned into vague rumors. Today we
wanted no more of being told
there was only one way to go
but had to ask three times
for the old road—no one
seemed to remember. Their directions
took us into hills, along roads with
aliases and alibis and no true identities.
We had their meaning—anything off
the freeway is an illusion,
those roads and towns edited out
of memory, but finally an old man
killing time on a corner understood
and sent us free of cloverleaves
and ramps. The traffic thinned
and we drove into our own past,
through towns with real names—
Woodburn, Aurora, Canby. Suddenly
a local version of the world appeared—
people on sidewalks, schools, houses,
and our eyes filled as we slowed
to a human speed passing landmarks
like the Chuckhole Tavern, Antique
Buffaloes, and Flo's Beauty Salon

and Ferry. We knew again how interstates
were meant to drain wit away with
their simple numbers.
And for us the map came alive
and Main Streets bounced into view
like those remembered from childhood,
dreaming by in evening light with
those mysterious lives of strangers
hovering under streetlamps, people
we would never know. Freeways pound
travel to amnesia the way airports do—
duplicates of each other, history
carefully washed away, a method
for losing the past—those towns, those
farms we came from as if they were
guilty secrets. But for miles we were
back there traveling the old two-lanes
in ancient heavy cars, our parents
talking quietly in the front seat,
as we counted livestock in misty
pastures and wondered about the people
woolgathering behind those single lighted
windows in all the lonely farmhouses.

Issei, the Japanese Lady

She wears brown as a carapace, anonymous as
Her lady friends, fall and wintering,
Leaving colors to the summer girls, the young.
She sits beside her husband
In silent acceptance of the space
Allotted her, blending into woodwork,
Her hands and feet clasped tight
In schooled conformity. She has served
So many cups of tea, her back is round.
She smells of tea; her fingers, stained.
According to a code of pleasantries
She trades platitudes with other ladies.
They nod, they smile, they bow.
Soundlessly she moves in soft gestures
Like falling snow in windless gray
Without echo, amassing. Every fiber
In her would repel disharmony:
The slammed door, loud conversations, opinion.
The ins and outs of her are clean
As rain washed buds are pure.
Her life is scrubbing. Daughters she gathers
Around her as chrysanthemums. They alone
Know the woman behind the serenity,
The paper screen, the brown.

THOMAS R. SMITH

....

The Shed

For Helen Holmen

Today we celebrate Aunt
Helen's ninetieth birthday.
I step away from the party,
open the door to the green
storage shed, once
a favored though obvious
sanctuary in games of hide-
and-seek with cousins.
Inside, Uncle Husky's
canvas creel
hovers on its leather
strap from the rafter
like the shadow of
a wingèd soul.
And in the corner, after
all these years, nets
and a rod and reel . . .
Ah, Aunt Helen!
This is an Egyptian tomb
stocked with things
dear to Husky in life,
only the thin, cancer-
ravaged fisherman's
sarcophagus missing. I look
down at the slab floor
and recognize the crack
that fissures all human

attempts at permanence,
dismay of builders,
crossing corner-
to-corner where the ground
has shifted. In the house
they're roaring at stories
over ice cream and
cake. When the old gather
their project is to praise
fierce humors of the tribe,
to reinforce the collapsing
roof of life, to fix
the colors that fade.
Each anecdote defies
the doctor and undertaker,
calls another buried
face to the window.
Only solitude blesses
absence, the holy
peace of such places
as this shed already
ancient when we played
here at the beginning
of our world, even then
a storeroom for endings
we could never have guessed.

The Franklin Ave. Bridge

If I walk down to the river, on a near-freezing, near-thawing January day. If I walk close to sunset, with the river white and rigid at the edges, at the center black and flowing. If I walk through the hard and the slushy stuff, sometimes gripping, sometimes sliding. If I see three small boys coming home from school with their coats flapping open. If I nearly crash into one careening down a homemade toboggan run on his front lawn. If I cross the Franklin Ave. bridge, with the moon at my back like a premonition, the sky before me a pulsing, radiant orange. If I stop, transfixed by all that is passing, racing, or glowing. How will I know (if I love the light at this moment) who holds me (as much as the darkness that is to come) in the world's open palm?

Mars and Venus, after Botticelli

Does anyone wonder what they've been up to? He reclining, as relaxed as a baby and as carelessly naked, except for the cloth slung low on the groin—the right hand slack and open in the place of his sex. One knee raised, exposing a long white inner thigh, the throat equally girlish and abandoned. No need for helmet or lance; toys now for baby faun's play. She is at ease also. But half upright, calmly awake, and fully clothed. Her breasts accentuated by a braidlike band that defines sleeves and neckline, her hair both loose and plaited. His lips are parted; hers are closed. He is lost in sleep; she gazes toward something off-frame, pondering the inexplicable, next thing.

....

The Age of Protest

Father Stephen, the eldest member of the monastery, had just returned from an overnight confinement in the county jail. He'd been arrested and fined for disorderly conduct. The old monk had been demonstrating with other antiabortion activists for over a year, but a melee had never occurred outside the clinic until yesterday.

"What happened?" Abbot Jeremy asked.

"The enemy attacked us first."

"Well, let's be more precise. Father Stephen, what action of yours led to the arrest?"

"I hit a woman who was grabbing at my placard. Don't fret. I didn't hurt her. I know the clergy should be present at these demonstrations, but I'm never going back there."

"That's a wise decision, Father." Abbot Jeremy was relieved that he didn't have to argue with him. "Write to the legislators," he advised. "Beg them to change the law. But stay away from that abortion clinic."

"I was stripped naked in jail. Can you imagine that?"

"So was Father Brian for trespassing at the missile base."

"The women were stripped, too. Mrs. Callahan must have been very humiliated. She's so obese. Why did they do that? Did they think we had concealed weapons?"

"It's probably routine procedure."

"Then they gave me orange coveralls to wear. I don't want to go through that again."

"You won't have to if you'll avoid those demonstrations."

The reasons for protesting never seemed to diminish. Other monks had been involved in demonstrations of one kind or another within recent weeks. Father Eric, who taught biology in the monastery's high school, had been to Wyoming again this summer to protest the hunting of endangered fowl. Brother Antonio, the

Spanish teacher and a Cuban by birth, had joined protesters at a nearby cement plant when several Central American employees were put on a bus and hauled away for deportation. Father Roger had returned to the state capitol with fellow environmentalists who were protesting the construction of a nuclear waste dump.

Father Anselm, the prior, disapproved of Abbot Jeremy's leniency in tolerating such behavior. He'd repeatedly predicted, "Sooner or later, one of the protesters is going to find himself in serious trouble." The prior believed that the monks' participation in public demonstrations was scandalous.

St. Benedict's ancient Rule referred to the worst kind of monks as wanderers who sponged off other monasteries. Father Anselm said, "These protesters of ours are by far the worst kind of monks."

Although the abbot did not look upon every protest as having equal merit, he had never prevented any monk from being engaged in a cause. Father Roger's was surely commendable because the proposed site for the nuclear dumping ground was practically in the monastery's back yard. Father Stephen's couldn't be faulted. Preserving human life was a lot more imperative than Father Eric's interest in saving some bird Abbot Jeremy had never heard of. But Father Stephen's arrest had disturbed the abbot. "Whatever you do, stay out of jail," he'd been telling the monks ever since Father Brian had been sentenced to six months in a federal prison. Maybe the prior was right about protests. Perhaps they should cease before any more monks got into serious trouble. Father Stephen had been lucky. Father Brian still had two months in jail.

The prior, who had retrieved the senior monk this morning, had of course been upset by his arrest. "He may be committed to protecting the unborn, but the old fool needs protection himself. Why was he ever allowed there?"

Abbot Jeremy agreed that a ninety-one-year-old man shouldn't be taking such risks. "The situation at the clinic may become even more violent from now on. I'll talk to him."

Now Brother Reginald was in his office with a request. Abbot Jeremy told him, "No, Brother, I don't think you should participate in the parade next Sunday. I'm sorry."

"I won't do anything to embarrass the community."

"You've heard what happened to Father Stephen. I'm a bit reluctant to let anyone else protest so soon after this incident. To tell the truth, I'm having second thoughts about protests."

"The Pride Parade isn't a protest. It's a celebration of our sexuality."

"I let you attend the big rally in Washington, DC. Given the church's attitude, I wonder if that wasn't a mistake."

"I protest the church's homophobia."

"Brother Reginald, please go back into your closet. Or at least back to work."

....

After Brother Reginald returned to the carpenter shop, Abbot Jeremy asked the prior to come back to his office and discuss the matter of protests.

Two years ago, on the day of his election to the abbacy, the new superior had chosen his novitiate classmate as prior. Some of the monks said this was nepotism. They were the ones who knew what would be in store for them with Father Anselm as the abbot's right-hand man, a monk who would not be hesitant about enforcing monastery rules.

Father Anselm and Abbot Jeremy had always been on intimate terms. The prior had found his other novitiate classmate to be compatible enough, but their relationship was not the same as the one that had begun with Jeremy and had lasted all these years. Father Anselm had shared things with him that he'd never considered confiding to Justin. Being Jeremy's friend was one thing, while serving as his prior was another. Father Anselm was becoming more and more discouraged.

"Have you cooled down?" the abbot asked the prior.

"For the moment."

"There are so many people in secular society who are convinced that monasticism is irrelevant in our age. They accuse monks of being indifferent to the world's problems. That hasn't been the case here. Some of ours have earnestly dedicated themselves to works of peace and social justice."

"And attempted vandalism," the prior said, referring to Father Brian's felony. "Monks belong in a monastery. Not in the streets. Not behind bars."

"Frankly, I'm worried that could happen again."

"When they ask, tell them to stay home. I can't begin naming all the crazy causes you've let them espouse."

Abbot Jeremy confessed, "I really don't place Father Eric's cause in the realm of social justice."

"Why should Brother Antonio have gone to the cement plant? After all, those workers were illegal aliens."

"I've always tried respecting the consciences of my monks."

"Jeremy, you're a pushover and a bullshitter besides. They're allowed to do whatever they wish only because you want them to like you. Admit it."

"Naturally, I want them to like me. What abbot seeks to be despised by his monks? Maybe I've lacked wisdom, though, by sanctioning some of their protests."

"You have, undoubtedly."

"Protesting was going on before I became abbot. Surely, you must remember we had monks marching in Selma and picketing supermarkets with the United Farm Workers. And you certainly must recall Father Edmund's demonstrating against the war in Vietnam. We have a history of protest. Should I stop it now?"

"The time has come for you to put an end to all forms of protest. I find it difficult performing my duties as prior under such an indulgent abbot. How often do I have to tell you this?"

"Yes, Anselm, the prior needs the abbot's backing."

"I would appreciate all the help you can give me."

"You shall have it," Abbot Jeremy promised. "Things will be different from now on. I'll be more supportive."

Leaving the abbot's office, Father Anselm said, "Something has to be done about smoking in the monastery."

Abbot Jeremy stared at the ashtray on his desk for several minutes. Reaching into his habit pocket, he grasped the crushproof box of cigarettes. Anselm couldn't do this to them, could he? The abbot sensed that the next protest was about to take place right here in the monastery.

"But, Anselm, you used to smoke."

The prior had followed the abbot to his room at the end of evening recreation. "I was concerned about my smoking," Father Anselm said. "If you're truly interested in safeguarding your health, you'll stop, too."

"Was it easy?"

"Yes. I'd made up my mind to quit."

"Remember our stealing cigarettes during the novitiate?"

In those days, smoking was forbidden to novices. So were a lot of other things in 1954. They couldn't listen to the radio, read newspapers, or go anywhere—not even over to the high school for basketball games. Early in the novitiate year, the three novices devised a scheme for filching smokes from the novice master. Once a week, two of them would keep him in the classroom, asking questions about the material covered that day. The third novice would sneak into the novice master's room and remove a package of cigarettes from the carton on top of his file cabinet. Apparently, Father Vincent never counted and never caught on. "Sometimes you had scruples about our thievery," Abbot Jeremy recalled, "but you hung in there."

"I hadn't smoked before I came to the monastery," Father Anselm said. "You and Justin introduced me to that vice."

"We smoked more reasonably back then. A pack could last three people a whole week."

"Sometimes we had to bum cigarettes from Father Luke."

"He gave them to the high school boys, also."

"Only the seniors."

"Justin still smokes."

"Is it asking too much for the monks to refrain from smoking in the community room? I noticed poor Father Alberic, your card partner tonight, waving smoke from your cigarettes away from his face. Everyone knows he has asthma."

"I didn't see him doing that."

"Of course not. You and all the other smokers are so insensitive to the rest of us."

"Anselm! You've known me ever since we were novices. I've never been insensitive."

"I can think of an instance when we were novices."

Abbot Jeremy was startled. "What?"

"You laughed at Justin when we had our heads shaved on the morning of investiture. Without any hair on his head, his big ears were even more prominent. You called him Mickey Mouse."

"I was only joking. Remember, Anselm, the movies we got to see once a month when we were junior monks?"

"You're changing the subject."

"Father Gerard was so prudish. He purposely caused a break in the film when the mushy stuff appeared on the screen."

"Which reminds me," Father Anselm said, "I'd better put the kibosh on certain videos some of the monks are renting."

Now in their sixties, the abbot and prior often reminisced about how different monastic observance had been in their spent youth. The former ridiculed many customs of the past while the latter viewed them nostalgically. Abbot Jeremy kept talking about the old days, stalling the prior as long as he could, but Father Anselm eventually called him back to reality. "What shall we do about all the smoking in the monastery?"

"Are you and Father Alberic the only ones protesting?"

"There are others. This is a legitimate protest, for once."

"I'll put up a sign. You'll see that the rule is obeyed?"

"You know I will."

The following day, Abbot Jeremy posted a notice on the bulletin board: For the sake of charity, there will be no more smoking in the community room.

Abbot Jeremy's decree earned him gratitude from monks who'd never smoked. "We can breathe at recreation," many of them said. "You've lifted a burden from us."

Father Justin was furious. "Anselm has become a pain-in-the-ass. Why do you keep him on as prior? You should boot him out of that job."

"He said a lot of people were complaining."

"Hell! Anselm will want you to outlaw smoking in the rest of the monastery, including our rooms. I'm warning you."

"Justin, did you think I was being insensitive when I called you Mickey Mouse the day we entered the novitiate?"

"No. But you are being very insensitive now by denying smokers their rights."

....

"I went through three packs a day," Brother Ralph, the retired farm manager, told his abbot. "I even smoked in the barn. That was really bad." Brother Ralph lived in the infirmary with the other elderly monks and boasted of being the healthiest one there because he'd kicked the smoking habit twenty years ago. He didn't object to the new infirmary rule.

"Well, how is everyone else reacting to the ban on smoking up here in the infirmary?"

"Pretty pissed off, but they'll get over it."

The abbot had reluctantly yielded to laying down the law in the infirmary. "Those old fellows don't have many pleasures left in life as it is," he'd told the prior. He knew Father Dunstan and Brother Gabriel smoked pipes, but he couldn't recall many cigarette smokers among the seniors. Most of them preferred cigars. Even Father Stephen.

"Pretty pissed off," Brother Ralph repeated.

"Well, I suppose there are some monks of your generation who chew tobacco," Abbot Jeremy said.

"Not anymore. The prior told the infirmarian nix on that, too. Said they were spitting on the floor."

....

So far, the prior, with the abbot's consent, had succeeded in banning smoking in the lobby and in the various offices occupied by monks. His next move in the antismoking crusade was the prohibiting of monks from lighting up in the privacy of their cells.

Abbot Jeremy suggested, "How about having all the smokers live in one wing of the cloister?"

"No."

"What are we going to do in the wintertime if we can't smoke in our rooms? Go outdoors?"

"I suppose."

"We could go over to the school."

"The headmaster has decreed there will be no smoking in the faculty lounge or anywhere else in the building when school starts. I'm backing him up wholeheartedly."

"But Father Peter is a smoker. How could he decide that?"

"Haven't you noticed? He quit last month."

"A lot of them have quit, haven't they?" Abbot Jeremy had observed that a good number of the monks who used to smoke were now chewing gum, which he considered a nasty habit.

"Have you thought of wearing the patch?" Father Anselm asked. "I know of eight monks who are."

"Anselm, I don't want to give up smoking. I don't even give up smoking for Lent."

....

Soon it was all out of Abbot Jeremy's hands. He'd given the prior so much latitude that Father Anselm didn't regard it necessary to consult the monastery superior anymore. He made the guest house a smoke-free zone, all of the shops and the courtyard in the quadrangle. Monks couldn't even step outdoors to smoke within the monastic confines. The prior said they'd been making a mess in the courtyard, depositing butts in the fountain and scattering them in the grass. Smoking was prohibited in front of the church and in the doorways of the other buildings to which the public had access.

"We'll have to go out behind the barn, so to speak," Abbot Jeremy told Father Justin.

"You will. I'm quitting."

"Justin!"

"Smoking is an addiction like alcoholism. You've got to hit bottom. I've hit mine. I'm hacking all the time and I'm winded after walking up three flights of stairs."

"Well, suck throat lozenges and take the elevator."

"Get with it, Jeremy. We're all capitulating."

One positive result of the ban on smoking was the approval it had won Abbot Jeremy. St. Benedict said an abbot should be loved more than feared, and Abbot Jeremy perceived that an increasing number of monks genuinely loved him. Much to his surprise, former smokers extolled his concern for their welfare. He accepted their praise with only a tinge of guilt for not giving any credit to the prior and without admitting to them that he himself was still a smoker.

"Thanks to you," Father Roger told him, "we no longer have to suffer the consequences of secondhand smoke in the monastery. The environmental organization is considering us for its Clean Air Award this year."

"That would indeed be an honor," Abbot Jeremy said.

By winter, smoking was no longer permitted anywhere on the monastery's property. Even visitors were asked to refrain from smoking in their parked cars. Four students who had been caught smoking were told not to return to school after the Christmas holiday. The few remaining monastery smokers wanted a compromise of some kind, but it was apparent the abbot was incapable of negotiating with his prior. The prior had usurped abbatial authority. St. Benedict had cautioned against this in his Rule: "Some priors, thinking of themselves as second abbots, usurp tyrannical power and foster contention and discord in their communities."

....

Father Mark thought the smokers should split from the community and make a new foundation. He and two other monks were sneaking smokes in the windbreak over at the farm, cursing the abbot whose cowardice was to blame for this inconvenience. They'd had to put on parkas and trudge through snowdrifts to an area presumably safe from the prior's surveillance.

"We'll call the place Holy Smoke Monastery," Brother Sylvester said.

"No," Father Colman said. "Let's get rid of the abbot. It's obvious he can't function anymore."

"Isn't murder still a mortal sin?" Brother Sylvester asked.

"Cut the clowning. This is serious. We have legal recourse for removing an incompetent abbot."

"You guys are off the wall," Brother Sylvester said. "We don't have a valid motive for wanting to start another monastery or for sacking the abbot."

"Let's go back," Father Mark suggested. "I'm getting cold."

"Yep, I'm still smoking," Brother Reginald said on the day Abbot Jeremy dropped by the carpenter shop.

"Isn't it incredible how many of the monks have given up smoking?"

"Thanks to the prior's unrelenting incentive."

"I never thought he'd go to such extremes. But you know, to a man, every one tells me he's glad he stopped smoking."

"Father Sean told me his sense of smell has become more acute. It's made him realize some of the monks don't shower often enough."

"Do you suppose the prior will want to do something about that, as well?"

Brother Reginald laughed. "What brings you to the shop?"

"I'm hiking over to the rest area on the highway for a smoke. Where do you go when you crave a weed?"

"I get in the pickup and drive to town."

"Let's go now. I need to buy another carton of cigarettes at the discount store." Months ago, the prior had instructed the monastery procurator to cancel all tobacco orders.

Aside from his excellence as a craftsman, the abbot had never known much else about the carpenter who was one of the younger members of the community. Within the next few weeks, Abbot Jeremy and Brother Reginald developed a friendship as they drove the short distance to town and back. Sometimes they stopped at a café and had coffee in the smokers' section.

They'd become familiar enough for Abbot Jeremy to ask one morning in Emma's Eatery, "How long have you known you're gay?"

"Since high school."

Abbot Jeremy grinned. "I bet you wanted to take your boyfriend to the prom."

"I sure did, but he was straight."

"You aren't sore for having missed the parade last June?"

"Nah, they got along without me."

"Of course you must know there are a couple other monks your age who are like you." Father Bernard, the novice master, had informed him, "They tell you right away nowadays. They're very up-front."

Brother Reginald feigned shock. "Good heavens! Right when smoking has been suppressed, homosexuality is taking over the monastery."

Stubbing out his cigarette and lighting another, Abbot Jeremy said, "There's someone else. It just occurred to me that the smoking ban could easily be rescinded or made less stringent by threatening to out him."

Brother Reginald expressed an unwillingness to play this trump card. "Absolutely not," he said. "I oppose the blackmailing of closet cases. Gosh! Do you mean the prior?"

Abbot Jeremy was ashamed of himself. "It would be an insensitive act," he said, remembering Anselm's trepidation years ago when he'd revealed his secret. "We won't do that."

As the season of Lent was approaching, the young monk told his abbot, "I'm giving up cigarettes."

"Really? Why, Brother?"

"We're supposed to do penance in Lent, aren't we? Besides, these trips to town twice a day are taking up too much of my time. I'm falling behind with work in the carpenter shop."

"Some of the monks are fussing because I'm never in my office when they want to see me. Maybe we should go to town only once a day."

"I don't intend to resume smoking after Lent."

Abbot Jeremy likewise surrendered on Ash Wednesday. Smoking is becoming so unpopular that I might just as well give in now, he reasoned, instead of waiting for Congress to declare it a criminal offense everywhere throughout the land. I'm not going to risk being incarcerated. I won't protest.

....

Summer of '94

1.
My legs were sore from swimming

When I got up
Trish was already in the shower.
I had a moment to feel old,
That clap of a hand
On my shoulder

2.
We were reading the latest polls
In an out-of-town paper

The waitress refilled our coffees.
Are you voters? she asked

Yeah. I nodded.

As she bobbed away,
I realized
She'd actually said "boaters"

Trish looked up, why did you say that?

How would she know, I said.
But I was still thinking

Of an acquaintance
Who was running for governor

We were sitting outside
On a fashionable deck

Above a marshy estuary,
Swans and geese in the sun, boats of bass fishermen

Across the water
Reeds had been removed, the muck
Hauled up,
A marina jammed an entire Sunday morning

Pass the jelly, said Trish

3.
That evening we walked
Through the shopping district.
A harmless town.
Spell of the marsh and idling water,
Main Street curved,
Slipped over the bridge.
Occasional scent of the big lake
Dropping in and mingling.
The beach wasn't many miles
Away.

It's true, I said, I haven't seen him
In twenty-five years. He's pudgier
In the picture.
He's one of the gang, though
I used to sell dope to
A couple of times a week

MARK VINZ

....

Gifts

When his parents got old enough not to care much about holidays, they kept their artificial tree in the hall closet, decorated just the way they liked it—forever ready for Christmas, if they remembered to take it out. How strange for him to be home on a muggy July afternoon and discover it there, like a favorite uncle who's been away a long time and now stands grinning on the front steps, stamping the fresh snow from his boots, pockets of his overcoat stuffed with brightly-wrapped packages.

When he looks a little deeper into the closet, he discovers his mother's party dress shrouded in plastic, his dead grandmother's most treasured books, his father's felt fedora from the forties, even that old uncle's silver-headed walking stick. What else is in there, he can only imagine—his baseball cards, perhaps, his sister's hula hoop, stamp albums, electric train. . . . He'd like to look some more, but not now, not with his children clamoring to get out in the car, get away, get anywhere more interesting than their grandparents' house.

Late tonight, he's going to take that tree to the living room and plug it in and pile the presents around it. It's all right there in the closet, everything they've ever needed.

MARK VINZ

....

Manners

"Hey, mister man, fuck you!" two small children begin to call as I walk by their house on the far side of the street. They come to the sidewalk and then to the curb. "Fuck you, fuck you," they shout, hopping from one foot to the other—brother and sister, perhaps, not more than four or five years old. "Fuck you?" they cry expectantly— I can't help waving, and they wave back, then hesitate. "Fuck you very much," they call together, just before I disappear around the corner.

....

The Hammer

Here is an instrument as blunt
and hard-headed as its employer.
What has it done? It has forced the nail
waist deep into the wood,
while the nail has spoiled its pleasure
by bending. Now the hammer must
remove the nail with its huge teeth,
curved like goat horns.
The hammer must undo what is half-done
and begin again with a new, willing nail,
a nail that seems guileless as it says, "I do."

Crude work is in the hammer's very nature.
No one wonders where it is to be grasped
with the whole hand. It's clearly designed
to strike, to crack a brown-haired coconut
or a marrowbone. It's a fist, only harder.
The hammer's simple tongue is easily acquired:
a few elementary ejaculations
and one is fluent.

Deep in autumn I sometimes hear
a distant, solitary hammer
drumming on shingles or a two-by-four
while the falling leaves foreshadow
something whiter and more serious.
How soon our days end—
yet the manly hammer is the last to retire.
Its head grows cold, its eyesight poor.
Is that a nail, the shadow of a nail,
a thumbnail? We'll know in a moment.

Peaches

I have eaten peach after peach
without hesitation or apology, and each
was a disappointment. Outwardly
they looked ideal, smooth as a pony muzzle
or pool table felt, sunset colored,
and when I held them I sensed
either their heartbeats or my own.

I overbought, too, thinking how lovely
they looked together, a troupe of California peaches
visiting Minnesota in July, the only month
they'd find palatable. I wondered what exactly
I expected of them. Flavor, I suppose.

Or I thought the stone
might offer me I can't say what,
like tea leaves or a fortune cookie,
some hint of a changed life.
Still moist, still bearing a tassel of flesh,
the stone requests a sympathetic burial;
it believes that any amicable clay, even mine,
is suitable for resurrection.

SUZANNE OSTRO ZAVRIAN

....

Tumbleweeds

I

We're driving down a long highway that loops through California, and somewhere we pass a sign that says Thermal Spring Ahead. A little way on it's about four o'clock in the afternoon, that time of sad, rich light when the color is washed-out brick with long shadows stretching thin; we're going through the Mojave, dun and flat and scraggly with bits of bleached-out brush, when around a curve is a hole filled with water and in it three people are sitting, water up to their necks: a middle-aged, round-faced, snub-nosed lady; an old man with white hair and a skinny neck; and a lumpy thirty year old. They're sitting in that circle of water with wisps of steam rising up, just looking at each other. And all there is is the flat Mojave, the small, round water embedded in it like an old mirror, three heads, and a weathered hand-painted sign with an arrow saying Thermal Spring.

Lonesome, that's America, lonesome. Like hearing music you've never heard before—you don't know what it is or where it's from, but it has a sound to it of sweet, second-rate sadness. You may not know the composer, but you know right away it's stamped Made in America. It's stamped Lonesome Cowboy. It's stamped with every cliché in the book, which is probably a catalogue.

You can hear it on the jukebox in Hopper's diner; you can hear it in the train whistle crossing the continent, hooting along the banks of Sheeler's Rouge River, flattening the dusty weeds along miles of railroad tracks and in thousands of vacant lots, blowing the white skirts of Marsh's overweight girls with too much powder and mosquito bites on their legs, going down under the trestles as the train passes through.

When I was a kid I'd lie awake and hear the streetcar come clanging up through the Baltimore night. It made everything emptier and bigger, stretching into a space through which the streetcar clanged at

1:00 A.M. Sometimes I'd dream that a train was coming through the bedroom—child-size, it moved noiselessly across the room. In the first car, looking straight ahead like a tin soldier, was the conductor, and all the cars were empty and dark—the train never made a sound, just crossed my bedroom and disappeared out the other side. And the conductor never even acknowledged I was there.

You don't know who made the music, but you recognize that long, drawn-out whistle across the land.

America, where everybody's rootless, everybody's going someplace else or thinking wistfully about the people who already went someplace else and sent back a postcard saying, "It's going to be wonderful here! We're thinking of moving on." Restlessness comes with the territory, dissatisfaction's so much a part of things you don't even notice it, like weather. And the people who do stay put, who make themselves part of one place, while they're sleeping, baking pies, having company for dinner, waving flags, tying ribbons around the trees in front of the house so they don't wander off and disappear, the places themselves are moving, coming down around them, being bulldozed under their very feet, so they're out on the street with all their belongings while everyone else is racing into the future, a future so tacky it's coming apart before they even arrive.

Further on, where it's even flatter, if that's possible, we come upon a yellow sign standing high and skinny against the gray-beige earth, and on the sign are the words Caution Turtle Crossing. It pleases me; I like turtles. I feel an affinity to them—or maybe it's envy. Ponderous but light, they travel carrying everything with them, and when they feel threatened they pull themselves in and stay put, becoming part of the ground. I can't pull myself in. I have to pull myself together, and when I do, the seams usually come apart. I want to slow the car to a crawl and very, very slowly look left and then right—maybe an hour or so each way—to see if there are any turtles coming, but we just roar through and the sign becomes part of the past, clanking along with the rest of it like a bunch of tin cans tied to a dog's tail.

I think, We're driving through this flat, empty space looking for truth. Maybe where it's hot enough, empty enough, bare enough, what you don't need sloughs off, which is just about everything. And whatever's left after all the junk's gone is as good as true. Or as close to true as we'll ever get.

Once I drove up to Acoma Pueblo, straight up the mesa on that road like an arrow pointed at the sky. On top, the squat little houses and lanes were silent in the bleached-out heat. As I walked around the dusty streets, in front of one of the yellowish houses with its mica windows that looked like it had been excavated from time, I saw a card table covered with little clay animals. Next to it were two Indian women—an old one sitting, a young one standing. I walked over and looked. Then I picked up one of the animals and asked the young woman, "Is this a turtle?"

"No," she said. "It's clay."

II

When I was six years old, I was lying one night in my bed dreamily looking out over the roofs through the back bedroom window on a beautiful, still, moon-flooded night, slightly hazy like it gets. I closed my eyes for a second and when I opened them again there was God and his twin brother kicking a football around over the treetops. He—or they—was short and chubby, with a round face and a bald spot, and he was dressed in a football uniform, except he wasn't wearing a helmet. They looked pretty goofy—tame but goofy. It might have been awesome, but it was so boring I fell asleep. I was not yet of an age for revelation. Besides, it was Baltimore.

My mother came there from the mountains of West Virginia, where she seemed to have grown up hydroponically instead of nourished from the soil. Her parents were Orthodox Jews from Lithuania who'd ended up in a little Appalachian town because the great-uncles peddled cloth down the eastern seaboard and for some reason had landed there. They didn't put down much in the way of roots in that hardscrabble Protestant soil. And all my mother seemed to have taken from the land was a Protestant glaze that belied the Sabbath candles and the intoned prayers but that made her genteel, socially acceptable anywhere.

My father was from the Ukraine, where it was either emigrate or be drafted into the army for twenty-five years. His parents, in turn, were born someplace else—either Poland or Russia, depending on where the border was that day. When asked, my Aunt Sara said she didn't know the name of the village because it was too small to have a name. And by the time I asked again, everybody was dead. Not that it would have made much difference—nobody in that family ever volunteered any information or answered personal questions. They'd just look at you for a minute and then talk about something else.

Not only was there no place of origin, their name wasn't even theirs. Immigration had chopped off the last syllable, along with any character it might have had. Even the original name denoted nothing—it wasn't Jewish, it was Russian, very Russian. That is, if it wasn't Polish. When I married, not knowing any better, even the poor shreds of the original name were lost, subsumed forever in that of a stranger's from a completely different place.

What I have in the way of family inheritance are my maternal great-grandmother's brass Sabbath candlestick holders and four silver vodka glasses belonging to my paternal grandfather. I didn't even get the samovar—when the aunts moved, they gave it to the man next door. They were none of them very sentimental.

The vodka glasses have a little village scene engraved on them. A house, a couple of trees, a path . . . and I would think, if I had been born in that town in the Ukraine, I would have backtracked, looking for the trail that led back somewhere, someplace, through the fir trees and the wolf howl, with the silent "schuss, schuss" of the sledge runners on the snow, to where the little village waited, deep in snow, the smoke from the chimney blending with the white sky, and my grandmother would have baked fresh white rolls and there would be dishes of cherry jam to eat with the tea steaming on the samovar, and I, Susana Markovna Ostrovskaya, would be home.

III

Instead, I was growing up in Baltimore, with the snow piled high and white in winter on the roof outside the bedroom window, where my mother could scoop it up in a bowl and sprinkle it with sugar and vanilla to make me snow pudding. The snow stayed for weeks in my childhood, the snapping, biting cold keeping the street drifts frozen until early March, when the thaw would send rivers running through the gutters so that I could sail all sorts of things down the swift-running water that gurgled through the miniature canyons of ice.

My birthday was around then, too. It was my first experience with permanence. February 29, which arrived for my birthday and then disappeared for the next three years. I was born outside Time. When my birthday did happen—haphazardly, it seemed—it was with a snow-white cake ordered specially each year. White doves hovered over its glittering white icing, poised to dart down among the pink cream rosebuds to peck at the silver balls scattered over the sugar field. It was a grand cake! Each year my father went to the tiny bakery on the small, round place at the end of the street where the pavements were brick and the houses were small colonial buildings that glow in my memory. He would discuss it with Miss Mary, who was round-faced with gray hair pulled back in a tight bun, looking in her apron like all the plump dumpling ladies in my children's books. And she would send back for me little diamond- and crescent-shaped cakes iced in lemon frosting that were my delight.

But Miss Mary is long dead and the bakery vanished without a trace and the old houses are torn down and replaced by concrete bunkers, leaving cracks in my memory that can never be filled in again.

Baltimore, where in summer the thick, sweet smell of the Bay lay over the city so that you could tell the direction of the wind by its odor, and every grocery store had a hand-lettered sign that said Crab Cakes, 5¢. On Friday nights the dining room table was covered with newspaper, heaped with big pepper-coated hard crabs, bottles of cold beer, and wooden mallets—every ten minutes or so I'd dash for the bathroom to put my face upside-down under the faucet to cool my burning mouth. "Drink some cold beer," my father would advise his ten-year-old daughter—but then, he was Russian.

Baltimore, where in my childhood were the last vestiges of the summer peddlers, with their calls of "Ol' clothes, o-o-ol' clothes," "Rags and bo-o-ones," with the voice rising sharp on the last syllable, and "Cra-a-abs, fre-e-esh cra-a-abs!"

Baltimore, where the unseen Bay was the fulcrum of the city. Teenagers, we piled into cars and drove down to the tepid water to swim with the jellyfish during those stifling summer days. And all the time we played in that piss-warm water I was half-aware of a nagging discomfort, having registered the crude signs on our way to the water that said No Jews or Negroes. Or am I imagining the wording? For in the beautiful cool, green evenings of summer my father took us for drives into Greenspring Valley, and I remember a huge, tasteful billboard somewhere along the way that said Greenspring Valley: Caucasians Only. No, I guess the Bay people wouldn't have known how to spell "Caucasian." Jews and Negroes were about as many syllables as they could handle.

IV

So I migrated north. Years later, when I went back, I drove to my old street. It had been beautiful, its long, looping central sidewalk winding around huge, ugly stone urns filled with flowers, between bushes shining with bright red berries, around wrought-iron fountains that splashed happily through summer, and every week I skated the length of its Saturday street sparkling with sun as I looped the urns and sped down the incline and generally made its bliss mine.

The urns are gone, the fountains razed and the curving sidewalk erased so that now it runs straight as a die between two borders of yellowing cropped grass. There is no more street for flying down the imagination of morning.

So now I'm driving on a straight road east through the Mojave while the western edge of the continent is migrating north. In thirty million years California will be in Alaska, if it doesn't fall into the Pacific first. We seem to have been born with an innate nostalgia for place, but where is it?

Out here there are communities that have been a thousand years on the land. Is that how long it takes to put down roots? Part of it is probably how you treat the land, starting from knowing you own nothing, not even the earth you're buried in. America never learned that. We were always so sure the land was ours that we did what we wanted with it—pulled its wings off, straightened it, poisoned it, razed it, stripped it, cut it down, chopped it up, skinned it. And then threw it out back behind the house where nobody'd ever notice. And if they did, we'd just tell them somebody else did it.

We drive through clear air and abandoned towns: Mesa Verde, Casa Grande, whose real names are dust, deserted when the water ran out; Tombstone and Last Chance, built on gold and, like all lust, blown away on the wind. And under our road is an ancient sea bed with weathered signs that say Caucasians Only, No Indians Allowed.

We're heading toward Death Valley, the lowest, maybe least complicated point on the continent. No towns, no people, no water. Nothing but heat and colors; borax, sulfur, and salt; ochre canyons and the Panamints lavender against the heat. Sometimes a puff of hot wind, sometimes a bird crossing way up high. Then, just when you begin to think you're home free, you come on a hotel with its own landing strip and bright-green golf course and, since it's Easter, bumper-to-bumper Easter Sunrise traffic, everybody coming in for the Resurrection.

When I first came to the desert, for weeks it was dun, dry, desiccated; there was nothing but tumbleweeds and dust devils. The sandy soil blew, and day after day the sky ached with blue. Then one day it was gray. And it rained. Suddenly there was freshness, a soft haze, and then the most extraordinary smell, suffocating in its pungency. It was only later that I came to recognize it as piñon and juniper and sage and wild spinach and saltash and snakes and toads and god knows what else, but then I was new. I went outside and stood, sucking in breath after breath, trying to absorb the smell like a sponge before it was sucked up and gone. There were two old Indians standing outside a way off, talking, and I went over, still needing to name things, and asked, "What's that smell?" And one of them said, "Rain."

V

Did you know that in the deep Southwest there's a snake called the Speckled Racer? His scales are blue and yellow—when he moves fast, he's green.

Just think, "I'm going out and get me that blue and yellow snake that owes me five bucks."

"It was that lowdown blue and yellow snake that got me pregnant, Paw."

"We don't rent to no blue and yellow snakes."

That snake could run for president of the United States.

ELIZABETH ZELVIN

....

The Last Firefly

as the moon rises it circles
the apple tree lush since its pruning
drifts on the scent of stock and nasturtium
waking as the garden dreams
its bright golds and roses turned to pearl
the firefly neither reflects nor casts its light
it simply is   solitary

not as in my childhood I remember
dozens, hundreds winking in the night air
like theatergoers in a vast arena
lighting their candles to applaud
the great celestial concert of the spheres

in this country town the wetlands are in danger
oyster and scallop, heron and osprey at risk
the fishermen perform acts of civil disobedience
on the beach, defending their right to the striped bass
sightings of bluebirds are reported in the paper
and more than one great elm survived the blight
only to fall in the last big hurricane

but here in the silvery dark
the last firefly, obedient only
to its own impulse to be luminous
pricks the night with amber
singing with yellow light its clear small song

....

*The following two poems are excerpted from a
twenty-poem series called "The Red Cross Dog."*

Signals

I have heard that the dead
speak to the living; they may be
gone for years when out of nowhere
a voice says, "Bob, this is your mother
talking: Stop it." And he'll put down
the big wrench he had threatened
the little guy's head with and go home
to bed. We think the dead
have forgotten us and then they send
signals that they have not forgotten, that
they are right there beside us or in the corner
of the kitchen by my blue water bowl,
my full food bowl, something behind me
wagging like crazy, which could be my tail
but is not; I believe it is the tail of my
dead dad; he is saying in his own way,
"You know, you really deserve this good life."

Loss

Digging up the bones. Reburying them.
Digging up the bones to see if they're still there.
Reburying them. Digging up the bones
to lick them one more time—licking them white
one more time under the white moon.
Burying them. Digging them up, just
to smell them, sniff any trace
of life there. Reburying them. Digging them up
to relieve the itch of my desire to see them,
to inhale their fading odor of blood, to
polish their hollows with my tongue,
turning them into something else, something
only I will recognize now. Burying them
in a place where even I can't find them.

CONTRIBUTORS' NOTES

Stephen Ajay has published two books with New Rivers Press: *Abracadabra* and *The Whales Are Burning*. He has traveled widely in India and Nepal. His work has appeared in numerous literary journals. Originally from New York City, he teaches at the California College of Arts and Crafts in Oakland, California, where he is a professor of English.

Robert Alexander is the author of *White Pine Sucker River: Poems 1970–1990* (New Rivers, 1993) and co-editor, along with Mark Vinz and C. W. Truesdale, of *The Party Train: A Collection of North American Prose Poetry* (New Rivers, 1996). He lives in Madison, Wisconsin, and is working on a Civil War narrative about the battle of Five Forks.

Patricia Barone has published two books with New Rivers Press in the Minnesota Voices series: *The Wind* in 1987, and *Handmade Paper* in 1994. Her work has been anthologized in *American Voices: Webs of Diversity* (Prentice Hall, 1998); *Bless Me Father: Stories of Catholic Childhood* (Plume/Penguin, 1994); and *The Next Parish Over: A Collection of Irish-American Writing* (New Rivers Press, 1993).

Sigrid Bergie is the author of *Turning Out the Lights* (New Rivers Press, 1989), which was nominated for a Minnesota Book Award. She is the editor of *Where Laugh Touches Tears* (COMPAS anthology, 1991). She was a Loft Mentor winner in 1986. She teaches classes, workshops, and conferences to writers and teachers of all ages.

James Bertolino's seventh and eighth volumes of poetry, *First Credo* (1986) and *Snail River* (1995), were published by the QRL Award Series at Princeton University. Earlier books include *Precinct Kali & The Gertrude Spicer Story, New & Selected Poems,* and *Making Space for Our Living*. He lives on Guemes Island, Washington, and teaches at Willamette University in Salem, Oregon.

Ron Block is the author of *Dismal River: A Narrative Poem* (New Rivers, 1990) and *The Dirty Shame Hotel,* a collection of short stories published by New Rivers in 1998. Born in Gothenburg, Nebraska, he has lived in Lincoln, Kennebunkport, New Orleans, Syracuse, Minneapolis, Fargo, and Milwaukee, where he taught at Marquette University. He lives in North Platte, Nebraska, which more or less brings him full circle. His work has appeared in *Ploughshares, Prairie Schooner, North Dakota Quarterly, The Iowa Review,* and other magazines.

Madelyn Camrud is a native of North Dakota, born in Grand Forks and raised in rural Thompson. She has degrees in visual arts and creative writing from the University of North Dakota and is the author of *This House Is Filled with Cracks* (New Rivers Press, 1994). Her poems have appeared in such journals as *North Dakota Quarterly, Kalliope,* and the *Nebraska Review,* and in several anthologies.

Siv Cedering is the author of three novels, six books for children, and ten collections of poetry. Her work has appeared in more than one hundred anthologies and textbooks. Also an artist and illustrator, she has created poetry sculptures for a show in Bridgehampton, New York, and paintings for a museum in Seattle.

Sharon Chmielarz has had two books of poetry published by New Rivers Press: *Different Arrangements* and *But I Won't Go Out in a Boat*. From her manuscript about Maria Anna "Nannerl" Mozart she's had poems appear in *The Iowa Review, Prairie Schooner* and *The American Voice*.

Victor Contoski's books include nine books of poetry and translations of contemporary Polish poetry. He lives in Lawrence, Kansas, where he is a professor of English. He won the third US Postal Chess Championship.

Kathleen Coskran is the principal of Lake Country School in south Minneapolis. Her short fiction and essays have appeared in numerous publications and anthologies. Her collection of short stories, *The High Price of Everything*, published by New Rivers Press, won a Minnesota Book Award. She has also been the recipient of artist fellowships from the Bush Foundation and the National Endowment for the Arts.

Barbara Croft is the author of *Primary Colors and Other Stories*, a 1989 Minnesota Voices Project winner, published by New Rivers Press in 1991. With her husband, poet Norman Hane, she edits *Writer to Writer*, a literary journal that focuses on the craft of writing. Her fiction has appeared in *The Kenyon Review, Another Chicago Magazine*, and other publications. She is the 1998 winner of the Drue Heinz Literature Prize.

Barbara Crow is the author of *Coming Up for Light and Air*, which was published by New Rivers Press in 1995. "Journeys" and "Hemispheres" are from her collection, *Hemispheres*. Formerly a journalist and classical music programmer and announcer, Barbara works at the North Dakota Museum of Art. She lives in Grand Forks with husband Jay, whom she met in her homeland of New Zealand soon after his return from wintering-over in Antarctica. They were married in Japan and have four children.

Alan Davis, who teaches in the M.F.A. program at Moorhead State, is the author of *Rumors from the Lost World*, a collection of stories, and the editor of *American Fiction*, an annual anthology. He is the recipient of a Loft-McKnight Award of Distinction in Creative Prose, a Minnesota State Arts Board Fellowship, and a Fulbright-Hays grant to Indonesia. He has also received a Fulbright Fellowship to spend a year in Slovenia, where he taught creative writing and American literature at the University of Ljubljana.

Gary Eller grew up in North Dakota, worked as a pharmacist in Alaska, and graduated from the Iowa Writers Workshop in 1989. His literary honors include the 1993 River City Award, a Minnesota Voices Project award, a Pushcart Prize nomination, and an NEA fellowship. He's working on an Alaska novel, *Salt*, and on a memoir, *The Next Best Thing*. He teaches writing part-time at Iowa State University.

Heid E. Erdrich teaches at the University of St. Thomas in St. Paul, Minnesota. She is a member of the Turtle Mountain Band of Ojibway. She grew up in the flat landscape of the Red River Valley of North Dakota. Heid believes that deprivation hints at the divine. She alternately worries that her poems might shock her ancestors and wonders why they keep sending her these outrageous poems.

Susan Firer's third book, *The Lives of the Saints and Everything*, won the Cleveland State University Poetry Center Prize and the Posner Award. Her work has been published in many literary reviews and anthologies, including *The Best American Poetry 1992*, *The Iowa Review*, *Prairie Schooner*, and others. New Rivers Press published her first book in 1979.

Diane Glancy is Associate Professor at Macalester College in St. Paul. She is also the 1998 Eidlestein-Keller visiting writer at the University of Minnesota. Her novel *Flutie* was published by Moyer Bell in 1998. Her collection of essays, *The Cold-and-Hunger Dance*, was published by the University of Nebraska Press, also in 1998.

Ann Lundberg Grunke lives and works in St. Cloud. Her fiction has appeared in magazines, literary journals, and anthologies. Her short story collection, *Revealing the Unknown to a Pair of Lovers*, was published in 1995 by New Rivers Press as part of the Minnesota Voices Project and won the 1996 Minnesota Book Award for Short Fiction.

Penny Harter has published fifteen books of poems, five since 1994: *Shadow Play: Night Haiku; Stages and Views; Grandmother's Milk; Turtle Blessing;* and *Lizard Light: Poems from the Earth. Contemporary Authors Autobiography Series*, 1998, includes her autobiographical essay. She has won prizes from the New Jersey State Council on the Arts, the Geraldine R. Dodge Foundation, and the Poetry Society of America. She writes and teaches in Santa Fe, New Mexico. New Rivers published her *White Flowers in the Snow* in 1981.

Margaret Hasse is a poet, educator, and organizational consultant living in St. Paul, Minnesota. Her publications include *Stars Above, Stars Below* (New Rivers Press, 1984), and *In a Sheep's Eye, Darling* (Milkweed Editions, 1988). In 1993, she was awarded a National Endowment for the Arts Fellowship in poetry.

David Haynes is the author of five novels for adults and two books for children. His New Rivers Press books are *Right by My Side*, which was nominated for a Minnesota Book Award for best novel and also selected by the American Library Association as one of 1994's best books for young adults, and *Heathens*. These books were winners of the 1992 and 1995 Minnesota Voices Project, respectively. In 1996 he was selected by Granta magazine as one of the best young American novelists.

John Herschel lives in California.

Greg Hewett, a native of upstate New York, moved to Minnesota in 1989. His poetry has appeared in many journals, including *The Pacific Review, Poetry Motel,* and *The Little Magazine,* and his book, *To Collect the Flesh,* was published by New Rivers Press in 1996. Besides the Minnesota Voices Competition, he has won a Loft award for gay and lesbian writers. In addition, he has been a Fulbright Professor at the University of Oslo, Norway, and a Fulbright Scholar at the University of Copenhagen, Denmark. He has taught at Hamline University in St. Paul, Minnesota, and at the University of Wisconsin-River Falls. He teaches creative writing and literature at Carleton College in Northfield, Minnesota.

Judith Hougen received her B.A. from Bethel College and her M.F.A. in creative writing from the University of Montana. She is a past recipient of the Loft-McKnight Award and the Mentor Series Award. Her first collection of poetry, *The Second Thing I Remember,* was published as a Minnesota Voices Project selection. Her work has also appeared in numerous magazines and anthologies. She teaches English and writing at Northwestern College in Roseville, Minnesota.

Among Susu Jeffrey's poetry collections is a spoken word CD, *Mississippi Mother.* "It's the riskiest thing I've ever put out because it's not a book, but there are liner notes with a visual art component. I like to push the form. Beyond content and style, in the CD format you get to probe that emotional-vocal range. And four musicians collaborated, enriched, some of the poems."

Deborah Keenan is the author of five collections of poetry, including *Household Wounds* and *Happiness.* Keenan is a professor in two graduate programs at Hamline University and teaches at The Loft. She is the recipient of two Bush Foundation Fellowships, a National Endowment for the Arts Fellowship, and the Loft-McKnight Poet of Distinction Award.

Martha King's books include *Seventeen Walking Sticks* (Stop Press, 1997), which is a brief memoir and a cycle of poems responding to a set of drawings by Basil King. She edited the newsletter *Giants Play Well in the Drizzle* from 1983 to 1993 and is currently director of publications for the National MS Society.

Duke Klassen is a fifth generation native of Spring Hill, Minnesota. He received the 1992 Chelsea Award for Fiction and was a finalist in *Best American Short Stories* of 1994. His collection of short stories, *The Dance Hall at Spring Hill,* was published by New Rivers Press in 1996. He and his wife, LaDes Glanzer, are silversmiths in Minneapolis.

Nicholas Kolumban is a native of Hungary. He teaches ESL at Raritan Valley Community College in New Jersey. His poems and translations have appeared in *American Poetry Review, Antioch Review, Another Chicago Magazine, Chariton Review, Iowa Review, Poetry East,* and elsewhere. He has six books of poems to his credit, two of them translations. His book entitled *Surgery on My Soul* was published by Box Turtle Press in 1996.

When he is not working on his own writing, Ian Graham Leask is a literary consultant and artistic mentor. He is originally from London, England, and makes his home in Minneapolis because his children go to school there. He is the author of *The Wounded and Other Stories About Sons and Fathers,* published by New Rivers Press in 1992, and his work was selected for the previous New Rivers Press anthologies, *Stiller's Pond, Perimeter of Light,* and *Two Worlds Walking.*

Bea Exner Liu was born in Northfield, Minnesota, and graduated from Carleton College. From 1935 to 1945 she lived in China, where she worked as a teacher. A year before her death in 1997, she published her memoir, *Remembering China: 1935-1945,* with New Rivers Press.

Debra Marquart is an assistant professor of English at Iowa State University and the editor of *Flyway Literary Review*. Marquart's poetry collection, *Everything's a Verb*, was published by New Rivers Press in 1995. In 1996, Marquart released a spoken word CD of jazz poetry, *A Regular Dervish*, with her band, The Bone People. Her work has appeared in numerous literary journals, including *New Letters, River City, Zone 3, Cumberland Poetry Review, Kalliope, Witness, Threepenny Review*, and the *North Dakota Quarterly*.

Roger Mitchell is the author of six books of poetry, including *The Word for Everything* (BkMk, 1996) and *Braid* (The Figures, 1997). Awards for his poetry include The Midland Poetry Award for his first book, *Letters from Siberia and Other Poems* (New Rivers, 1971), a Borestone Mountain Award, two from the Arvon Foundation, one from PEN International, plus fellowships from the Indiana Arts Commission and the National Endowment for the Arts. He has also written a work of nonfiction, *Clear Pond: The Reconstruction of a Life*, which won the John Ben Snow Award at Syracuse University Press. He is the author, as well, of numerous reviews and essays and teaches at Indiana University in Bloomington.

Michael Moos has published three poetry collections: *Hawk Hover, Morning Windows*, and *A Long Way to See*. His work has also appeared in the poetry anthologies, *Minnesota Writes: Poetry* (Milkweed Editions), *Inheriting the Land: Contemporary Voices from the Midwest* (University of Minnesota Press), *From the Belly of the Shark* (Random House), and *Dog Music: A Poetry Anthology* (St. Martin's Press). He has been awarded a National Endowment for the Arts Fellowship, a Loft-McKnight Award in Poetry, a Minnesota State Arts Board Artist Assistance Grant, and has been a winner of the Minnesota Voices Project competition. He has an M.F.A. in Poetry from Columbia University. He lives in St. Paul, Minnesota, and teaches in the English Department at Breck School and The Loft.

Yvette Nelson grew up in Franklin, Minnesota, and graduated from the College of St. Catherine in 1964. Her book *We'll Come When It Rains* won the 1984 Minnesota Voices Project competition. She lives in Minneapolis and earns her keep as an editor and writer of educational materials. She is the author of a manuscript that focuses more on displacement than on the beauty and indifference of the anchoring land—the heart of her first collection.

Kathryn Nocerino is a poet, short story writer, and critic who lives in Noo Yawk. She has three books of poetry in print: *Wax Lips* and *Death of the Plankton Bar & Grill* (New Rivers Press), and *Candles in the Daytime* (Warthog Press). Two of her short stories appear in Penguin Books anthologies. Ms. N's literary career continues to be compromised by her unaccountable attachment to humor and a near-suicidal aversion to academic schmaltz.

Sheryl Noethe's first book, *The Descent of Heaven Over the Lake*, was published by New Rivers Press. Her second book is a teaching text entitled *Poetry Everywhere*. She has collaborated to produce a CD of her poetry set to music entitled *Jumbo Love Cycle*. She lives in Montana with her firefighter husband and two spaniels. Sheryl directs the Missoula Writing Collaborative, which places writers in classrooms. Winner of a 1990 National Endowment for the Arts award, she has also been awarded a McKnight Fellowship and the Hugo Prize for Poetry.

Monica Ochtrup is the author of two books of poetry, both winners in the Minnesota Voices Project competition. She has received a Loft-McKnight Award of Distinction in Poetry. An essay on her work was published by Dr. Dorothea Steiner, associate professor of American Studies at the University of Salzburg, Austria. Monica lives in St. Paul, Minnesota, where in the spring of 1998, she and her husband, Bob, also celebrate a thirtieth anniversary.

Theresa Pappas's first collection of poems, *Flash Paper,* was published by New Rivers Press. Her poems have appeared in *Sou'wester, Carolina Quarterly, Black Warrior Review, Kansas Quarterly,* and other journals. She has taught at Tufts University and Iowa State University and worked as a Visiting Artist in Iowa. She lives in Tuscaloosa, Alabama.

Carol J. Pierman, a poet and essayist, is author of *The Naturalized Citizen* (News Rivers Press) and *The Age of Krypton* (Carnegie Mellon University Press). A native of northwest Ohio, she teaches at the University of Alabama.

Holly Prado's seventh book, *Esperanza: Poems for Orpheus,* was published in 1998 by Cahuenga Press. Her first book was published by New Rivers Press in 1976, which encouraged her entire writing life. Her poetry and prose have appeared, in the meantime, in many national and international publications. She lives and works in Los Angeles, California.

Nancy Raeburn is a native of the Twin Cities. Her memoir, *Mykonos,* a 1990 Minnesota Voices Project winner published in 1992 by New Rivers Press, is an account of the ten years she lived and painted on a Greek island. She is a contributor to *Tanzania on Tuesday: Writing by American Women Abroad* (New Rivers Press, 1997). She is also a recipient of the Academy of American Poets College Prize and the Wendy Parrish Prize for Poetry from Macalester College in St. Paul, Minnesota.

New Rivers Press published Rochelle Ratner's first two poetry books: *A Birthday of Waters* and *False Trees.* Since then, she has published eleven more poetry books. Coffee House Press has published two novels, *Bobby's Girl* (1986) and *The Lion's Share* (1992). She is executive editor of *American Book Review,* on the Board of Directors of the National Book Critics Circle.

John Reinhard is the author of two collections of poems, *On the Road to Patsy Cline* and *Burning the Prairie,* both winners of the Minnesota Voices Project competition. He is the recipient of a 1998 Loft-McKnight Award of Distinction in Poetry. He lives in Minnesota with his wife, Chris, and their two children, Quinn Maclean and Matthew Mitchell.

Wisconsin writer Ron Rindo has published two collections of short stories with New Rivers Press, *Secrets Men Keep* (1995) and *Suburban Metaphysics and Other Stories* (1990), both Minnesota Voices Project winners. Each of these books also received Outstanding Achievement Recognition from the Wisconsin Library Association, an award given to the top ten books of the year by Wisconsin writers. He lives in Berlin, Wisconsin, with his wife, Ellen, and twin children, Claire and Tyler.

Gail Rixen is the author of *Pictures of Three Seasons* (New Rivers Press, 1991) and *Chicken Logic* (Sidewalks, 1997). She lives near Nebish, Minnesota, where she is known to farm, teach, write, or build on any given day.

Mary Kay Rummel's poetry book, *This Body She's Entered,* was a Minnesota Voices Project winner in 1988. She co-authored *Teachers' Reading/Teachers' Lives,* which was published by SUNY Press in 1997 and an anthology, *American Voices: Webs of Diversity,* published by Merrill in 1998. She teaches at the University of Minnesota in Duluth and lives in Fridley.

Of Vern Rutsala's nine books, *Laments* was published by New Rivers Press. His most recent collections—*Selected Poems* and *Little-Known Sports*—received the Oregon Book Award and the Juniper Prize, respectively. Other awards include a Guggenheim Fellowship, two NEA grants, two Carolyn Kizer Poetry Prizes, a Masters' Fellowship from the Oregon Arts Commission, and the Duncan Lawrie Prize from the Arvon Foundation. He teaches at Lewis and Clark College.

Jessica Kawasuna Saiki was born in Hilo, Hawaii, in 1928. She remembers the Pearl Harbor days of World War II as a Honolulu resident. After the war, she moved to Chicago and has been a mainlander to the present day—but the heart of her writing still lies in Hawaii. Her two short story collections are *Once, Lotus Garden* and *From the Lanai and Other Hawaii Stories.*

Thomas R. Smith has published three books of poetry: *Keeping the Star* (New Rivers Press), *Horse of Earth* (Holy Cow! Press), and *The Lost Music* (Bookpress). He has also edited a selection of the Canadian poet Alden Nowlan's work, *What Happened When He Went to the Store for Bread* (Nineties Press). He lives with his wife, the artist Krista Spieler, in River Falls, Wisconsin.

Madelon Sprengnether is a professor of English at the University of Minnesota, where she teaches critical and creative writing. She is the author of a book of poems, *The Normal Heart,* a book of personal essays, *Rivers, Stories, Houses, Dreams,* and co-editor of a collection of travel writing by women, *The House on Via Gombito.* She has received grants from the Bush Foundation, The Loft, and the National Endowment for the Arts. She also is the author of a manuscript of prose poems, *The Angel of Duluth,* and of a series of film-memoir essays, *Shadow Loves.*

Benet Tvedten is a Benedictine monk of Blue Cloud Abbey, Marvin, South Dakota. His novella *All Manner of Monks* received the Minnesota Voices Project Award in 1985. Besides writing fiction, he is the author of a commentary on the Rule of St. Benedict.

Robert VanderMolen lives and works as a house painter in Grand Rapids, Michigan, where he was born in 1947. He is the author of eight collections of poetry, including *Peaches* (Sky Press, 1998); and two chapbooks, *Of Pines* (Paradigm Press, 1989), and *Night Weather* (Northern Lights Press, 1991). He has had poems published in *Grand Street, Sulfur, Artful Dodge, House Organ, Epoch, Mudfish, Parnassus,* and *Fine Madness.* He earned his B.A. from Michigan State University in 1971, and his MFA from the University of Oregon in 1973. He received a National Endowment for the Arts Fellowship in 1995.

Mark Vinz has published two books of prose poems with New Rivers Press, *The Weird Kid* and *Late Night Calls,* and he co-edited *The Party Train: An Anthology of North American Prose Poetry.* He is the author of several published short stories and poems, including *Minnesota Gothic,* a collection of poetry and photographs in collaboration with Wayne Gudmundson. He teaches at Moorhead State University.

Connie Wanek, raised in New Mexico, now lives with her husband and two children in Duluth, Minnesota, where she works renovating old houses. Her first book, *Bonfire,* was published by New Rivers Press in 1997. Other publications include poems in *Poetry, The Virginia Quarterly Review, Poetry East, Country Journal, The Seattle Review,* and many others.

Suzanne Ostro Zavrian has published both poetry and prose in a number of literary magazines and anthologies. Her first book, *Demolition Zone,* was published by New Rivers Press; her second, *Dream of the Whale,* by Toothpaste Press. She lives in New York City.

Elizabeth Zelvin is a New York City psychotherapist who directs a treatment program for homeless substance abusers. New Rivers Press published her first poetry collection, *I Am the Daughter.* Ms. Zelvin co-edited, with S. L. A. Straussner, *Gender and Addictions: Men and Women in Treatment* (Jason Aronson), a main selection of the Psychotherapy Book Club. She observes fireflies on Long Island's East End.

Patricia Zontelli's poems, "Signals" and "Loss," are excerpted from a twenty-poem series called "The Red Cross Dog."